About the Author

Matthew Booth is a writer of historical crime fiction, as well as being a short story writer and radio scriptwriter. As an expert in crime and supernatural fiction, Matthew has provided a number of academic talks on such subjects as Sherlock Holmes, the works of Agatha Christie, crime fiction, Count Dracula, horror fiction, and the facts and theories concerning the crimes of Jack the Ripper. He is a member of the Crime Writers' Association and is the primary editor of its monthly magazine, *Red Herrings*. He lives with his wife in Manchester, England.

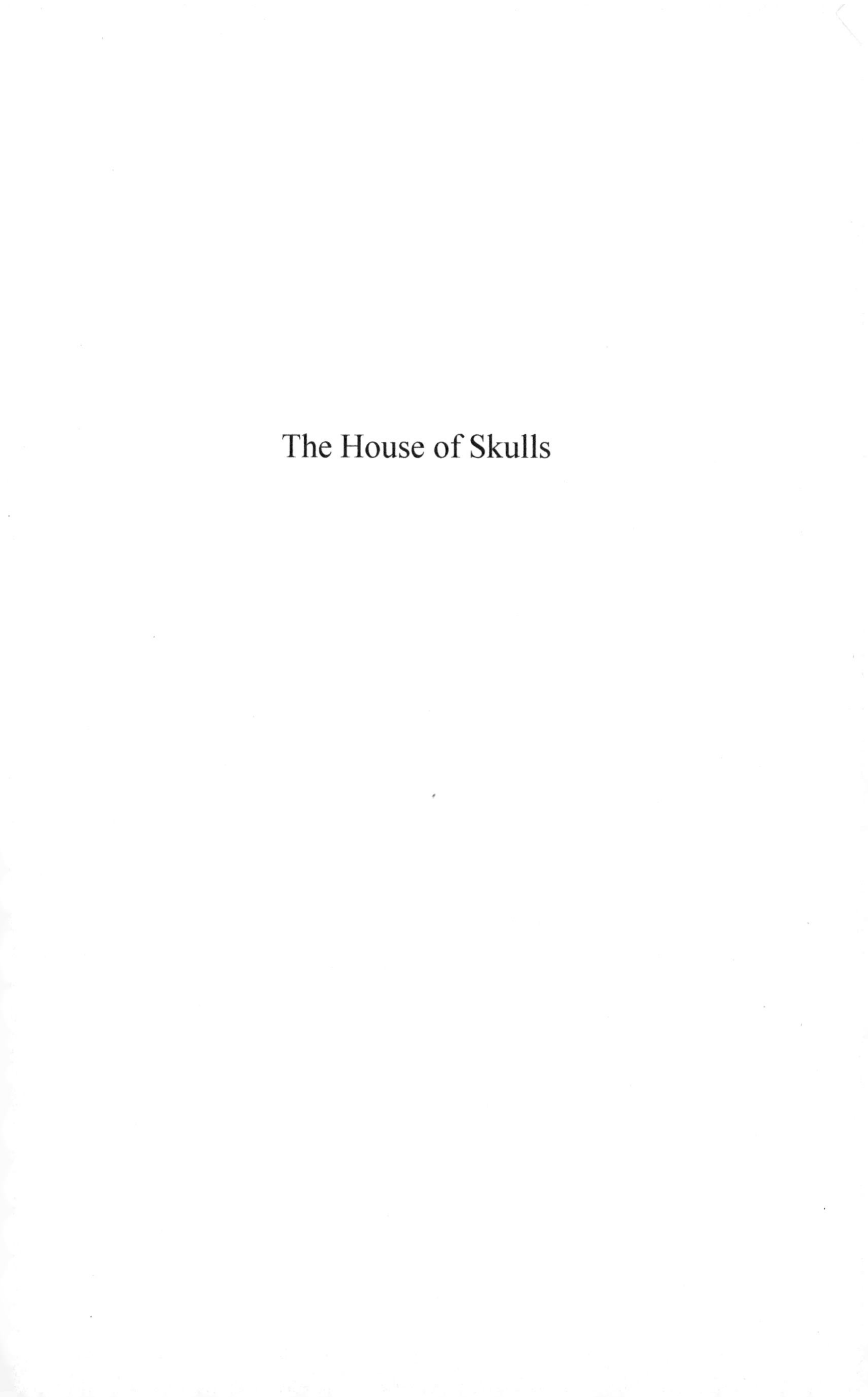

The House of Skulls

Matthew Booth

The House of Skulls

Pegasus

PEGASUS PAPERBACK

A CIP catalogue record for this title is
available from the British Library.

ISBN 978 1 80468 030 8

Pegasus is an imprint of
Pegasus Elliot Mackenzie Publishers Ltd.
www.pegasuspublishers.com

First Published in 2023

Pegasus
Sheraton House Castle Park
Cambridge England

Printed & Bound in Great Britain

To the Good Comrades,
With thanks for the years of friendship

CHAPTER ONE

There were two of them waiting for him.

They stepped out of the shadows of a shop entrance as he approached, their hats pulled down low over their eyes and the collars of their coats pulled tightly across the lower portions of their faces. There was no need: it was too dark on that lonely street of a damaged capital for him to recognize either of them and the night air wasn't cold enough to require much protection against it. He might not be able to see their faces, but he knew them for what they were and their purpose was clearly marked in their balanced stances and square shoulders. Until then, his senses had been numbed by the beer and whisky but now, they seemed so sharp that he might have cut himself on them. The darkness of the night sky seemed to intensify, as complete as the blackouts of the last few years, but without the usual sounds of engines and the whistles of falling bombs. Those noises were now recent memories, but the depth of silence which replaced them in this current blackness was just as terrifying and intimidating.

He thought about turning on his heels and running back to *The Hanged Man*, but it would do no good. Even if he made it, the doors would be shut. No sanctuary there. In any case, the two men wouldn't let him get more than a few feet away from them. He would feel their hands on his shoulders, or their feet across his ankles, or their knees in the back of his legs. He would be on the ground within seconds and he'd suffer for the attempt to flee. He was aware, suddenly, that his breathing had become shallow, as if his body was trying to get as many breaths into his lungs as possible, before the time came when there would be no more breaths at all. His upper lip began to itch, tickled by fear and sweat.

One of them, the bigger of the two, gripped him by the arm. The voice, thick with menace, was harsh and uncompromising. "You're wanted, kid."

The second man, shorter but no less dangerous, grunted confirmation of it. He placed his hands slowly into the pockets of his coat. Were his fingers closing around the butt of a gun, the handle of a knife, or a cudgel? Fear played easy tricks with a man's mind. They walked him a small distance down the street, flanking him on either side, the big man's hand still wrapped around his elbow. Any sudden movement would dislocate the joint or, worse, break the limb completely. They turned right into an alleyway, where a car was waiting, its round, hooded lamps blurred by the slowly gathering mist. They got him inside roughly, as if he was already dead meat, unfeeling and cold, worth neither their time nor consideration. They sat on either side of him on the back seat and he felt at last the unmistakable muzzle of a gun in his ribs. The engine was started, purring into life, and the car began to move. They drove in silence.

This was it, he thought. A few more hours and then nothing more. Only dark, unknown death. No more life, no more troubles, his existence nothing more than a series of someone else's memories. That final whisky would be the last drink he would ever have; the cold beef sandwich would be the last meal he would ever eat; and Jenny, with her blonde hair and blue eyes, would be the last girl he would ever touch. From now, he would only know pain and fear, until that final, forgiving feeling of nothingness and the hope that someone, somewhere, would miss him.

CHAPTER TWO

She had not made an appointment. When she had made that initial, tentative telephone call to him, he had said that an appointment wasn't necessary. She had taken him at his word; he knew more about these things than she did. She had never hired a private detective before and now, as she walked down the dull, anonymous corridor of the building whose address he had given to her, she wondered whether she would be better to turn back and go home. In that moment, she doubted that he could do anything to help her, that she was making a mistake, and she wondered how she had become so desperate as to approach a man like him. Her thoughts were scattered by the sound of her knuckles against the glass panel of the office door. She heard the assured command to enter, the voice authoritative, and she turned the handle of the door swiftly, so that any further doubts could have no time to manifest themselves in her fragile conscience.

"Mr Priest?" she asked. A foolish and unnecessary question, but he made no comment.

"Take a seat, Mrs Clayton," he said in reply, pointing to one of two chairs which were set on the opposite side of the desk to him.

Margaret Clayton closed the door gently and walked across the office. It was more spacious than she had expected, given the shabbiness of the external corridor. Two broad windows were in the far wall, behind the desk, with the same black lettering as was stencilled on the frosted panel of the door: *Alexander Priest: Private Investigations*. A set of filing cabinets were set to one side of them, on top of which was a selection of whisky bottles, some unopened and others half empty. Next to it was an old, wooden hatstand. There was a second, adjacent room, set off to the left of the main office, and she could see a small sink, a dirty towel on a rack, and various cups and glasses. There was an electric fan standing in one corner of the office, but she doubted it had been used recently. The recent weather had hardly required it. If she had expected any adornments on the walls, photographs or paintings, she was disappointed.

Margaret sat down opposite him. He wasn't handsome, not quite, but there was a confidence and a capability about his face which she found compelling. His features were dark, his expression serious and determined, which made the fairness of his blond hair seem all the more striking. His eyes were a cold, uncompromising shade of blue, and the lips were a thin line of confrontation under a nose which looked as though it had suffered a fair share of punishment in the past. The idea was reinforced by the single scar across his chin. Margaret had the impression that he was the sort of man some women would find captivating, but who they would never take home for tea. He took the cigarette from his lips and balanced it on the edge of a glass ashtray. Margaret Clayton declined his offer of one, smiling nervously at him.

"What can I do for you, Mrs Clayton?" he asked.

"It's my daughter," stammered Margaret. "I haven't seen her for six weeks."

He contemplated her for a moment, before pulling a foolscap pad towards him and taking a pencil from a mug on the corner of the desk. "What's her name?"

"Nancy."

She opened her handbag and her fingers scurried around inside it. She pulled out a photograph and handed it over to him. Priest saw the image of a good-looking girl smiling back at him. Early twenties, dressed in a floral, summer dress, pushing wind-swept hair out of her face. Around her slim neck, he could see a pendant and charm, maybe an angel, but he couldn't be sure. The girl shared her mother's dark hair, so black that he could convince himself that it had a deep, blue sheen to it. The girl's eyes were bright and unfettered and Priest suspected that, at one time, Margaret Clayton's own eyes would have glittered with the same sparkle; now, they were heavy with anxiety and fear. It was an expression Priest knew well. It was the look in the eye of every distraught parent he had come across whose child had vanished and it was always the same.

"How old is Nancy, Mrs Clayton?" Priest asked.

"Twenty-three."

Priest nodded. "Would I be right in saying that the police aren't interested in what's happened to her?"

She shifted in her seat, as if the question had offended her. He didn't seem too concerned if it had. "What makes you say that?"

He shrugged, handing the photograph back to her. "Most people come to someone like me when they've run out of options. Your instinct would have been to call the police, not come to a private detective. For you to even be here, the police must have proved to be a dead end for you. Besides," he added, his voice lowering, "if I know the police, they'll say that a girl Nancy's age has every right to disappear and there's nothing any copper could do about it. Am I right?"

She nodded, but the tears which had begun to fall had been enough of an answer. She took out a handkerchief from beneath the cuff of her jacket and dabbed at her eyes. Priest remained silent. She would speak again when she needed to and no words from him would be useful now.

"They seemed to expect me to leave it at that," she said, eventually. "As if I could just sit at home and wait for Nancy to come back, without doing something positive to find her. I found your name in the directory," she said, as if it was somehow necessary for him to know it.

"You must have passed over a dozen other names before you got to mine."

Her pale cheeks flushed a little. "My father was called Alexander, too. Alex."

"That's what people call me, when they're not calling me something worse." He gave her a brief smile. "Tell me about Nancy."

He leaned back in the leather chair and stretched out his legs, clasping his fingers together behind his head. He seemed to have forgotten about the cigarette in the glass ashtray, the smoke now curling its way to the ceiling, as the cigarette slowly burned away its existence. As she gathered her thoughts, Margaret found herself transfixed by the trail of smoke, as though its gentle upward flight had a kind of hypnotic hold over her. Priest said nothing. He just waited, untroubled by the silence which stretched out between them.

"There's just Nancy and me," Margaret said at last. "My husband died in the war. He was shot down off the coast of Norway." For a moment, her expression became distracted by the memory. Her eyes flickered as her mind returned to the present. "What service were you in, Mr Priest?"

She hadn't meant to pry, the question occurring to her innocently and without malice, but the manner in which his glare darkened and his jaw clenched showed that she had intruded into his privacy. She began to stammer an apology, but he dismissed it. When he spoke, his words were polite, but the voice was packed with ice. "Please go on, Mrs Clayton."

"Nancy and I have always been close," said Margaret, not wishing to prolong the sudden discomfort. "We were not so much mother and daughter, as sisters. Friends, even. There was nothing we couldn't talk to each other about. I never once thought anything could come between us."

"Not even a man?"

She looked up at him. "Why do you say that?"

He shrugged. "Men often come between a girl and her parents."

"I don't want you to get the wrong idea about Nancy, Mr Priest. I suspect you see all kinds of people in your line of work and I suppose not all of them, men or women, are particularly nice people."

"I've met a lot of people, Mrs Clayton," said Priest. "Not all of them would curdle milk."

If Margaret had any reply to offer, she kept it to herself. "Nancy has had brief love affairs, of course, but none of them have been what you might call serious. I had hopes that she might walk out with a young man called Gordon Parish for longer than she did, but it never happened. He was a very polite boy, with beautiful manners. My husband had been friends with Gordon's father. He would have approved of Nancy and Gordon getting married. I was never in any doubt about that."

"But Nancy wasn't interested in marrying Gordon?" He watched Margaret shake her head. "You can't force her to marry anybody."

"Of course not." Her eyes drifted back to the cigarette. She pointed to it. "Do you think I could have one of those?"

Priest reached inside the pocket of the jacket which was hanging on the back of his chair. He took out the crumpled packet of cigarettes and a box of matches. He lit one for her. She inhaled, her creased brows and narrowed eyes suggesting that it was not a fully formed habit or, perhaps, a long-forgotten one. Priest made no comment. He knew that stress, anxiety, and fear could manifest itself in ways no quack could predict.

"Recently, I've had the feeling that Nancy and I were drifting apart," she continued, the smoke shrouding her face as best it could. Perhaps that was why she had requested a cigarette, to provide some semblance of camouflage, either against his probing eye or this unfamiliar, sordid exposing of her private pain.

"In what sort of way?" Priest stubbed out the forgotten cigarette in the ashtray and lit a fresh one.

"It's difficult to explain to a stranger." She rose from her seat and began to pace the office, as if movement might help to formulate the words to express her thoughts. "She had become distant, almost hostile. Nancy used to confide in me, Mr Priest. She would tell me about her work, about her friends, about anything which was troubling her. And if I could tell something was on her mind, I was always able to ask her about it. I'm not saying that it didn't sometimes need coaxing out of her, but it would come in the end. But recently..."

Priest waited for the sentence to finish, but it never did, not beyond the small gasp of breath and the faint whimper from the back of her throat. He inhaled deeply on his own cigarette. "Where did she work?"

Margaret seemed grateful for the change of subject and the resumed control over her voice reflected it. "She is a secretary to a solicitor. Do you know the firm of Quayle, Hopkins & Stowell?"

"Doesn't sound familiar."

"She's been there a little over a year. She enjoys the work, finds it interesting, and she likes Mr Quayle. It's his work she does, in the main."

"What do they do there?"

Margaret smiled shyly and shook her head. "I'm afraid I don't really know. Buying and selling property, I think. The legal side of it, that is."

Priest nodded aimlessly, flicking the ash of his cigarette into the ashtray. "What about friends?"

"She has friends, of course. More a case of a few close friends, rather than a large group of them. Quality, not quantity. I have asked them if they know anything about what might have happened, but they say not."

"Can any of them explain your daughter's change in attitude?"

"They all told me that they couldn't think of anything which might be troubling Nancy."

"Not even to hazard a guess?"

"No."

"Do you believe them?"

She seemed horrified by the question. "Of course. Why would I not believe them? They're all good girls."

Priest sighed gently and leaned back in his chair. "Tell me about the last time you saw Nancy."

Margaret stubbed out the cigarette. "It was like any other day. I had no reason to think anything was going to happen. I had prepared breakfast, as I usually did, but she didn't want it. That was one of the things which had changed. We used to share all our meals." There was a small, sad pause. "Not any more. For the past few months, I've eaten alone. Not that I mind. Not really."

The lie, so obvious and yet so understandable, was followed by a pause made of lead. Priest leaned forward in his seat. "Go on."

Margaret inhaled deeply before exhaling loudly. "She kissed me goodbye, said she might be late that evening, and left for work. She didn't come home. I haven't seen her since."

Priest allowed her a moment of quiet, to gather her thoughts. "And this was six weeks ago?"

"A little over."

"Did you at least check with Quayle, Hopkins & Stowell that she turned up to work that day?"

Margaret nodded sharply. "She had."

Priest smiled, neither insolently nor warmly, just a strange twist of his lips. "Did Nancy often work late in the evenings?"

"Not often, but sometimes. She would always ring to say she was leaving the office, though, so that I would know when to expect her home."

"And she stopped doing that?" He watched her nod. "Something else which had changed in your relationship."

Another nod. "That, not eating together, not telling me about her day, going out in the evening more regularly, locking herself away in her bedroom."

Priest pursed his lips. "I don't want to upset you, Mrs Clayton, but don't you think there's only one likely explanation for all this?"

Margaret, defiant, refused to admit anything. "If Nancy had met someone, why should she feel she had to keep him a secret?"

Priest suspected Margaret Clayton could think of a handful of reasons, including the one which was foremost in his own mind: parental disapproval. As an answer to a problem, though, it seemed only to open floodgates to a wave of further questions.

Margaret had begun to sob silently once more. Priest, suddenly conscious of his own awkwardness in her company, pulled his handkerchief out of his pocket and passed it over. "I'm sorry, it's all I've got."

She didn't seem to mind. She sobbed a word of gratitude and dabbed her eyes. She took a moment to compose herself and he allowed her to have it. Smiling gently, and with no small amount of embarrassment, she handed the handkerchief back to him and fixed her glare on his eyes. "Will you help me, Mr Priest?"

In reply, Priest rose from his desk and pulled on his jacket. He took his hat from the wooden stand beside the filing cabinets, ignoring the allure of the bottles of whisky, and escorted Margaret Clayton to the office door. They stepped out into the outer corridor and Priest closed the door behind them, the snap of the lock sealing their contract better than any signature on a dotted line.

CHAPTER THREE

The house was small, but respectable. The furnishings were plain and functional, but not to the extent that their overriding impression was one of poverty. The wooden dining table and chairs were simple, without any ostentation, the small settee and its single matching armchair comfortable but practical, and the hems of the plain curtains were slightly frayed. The ornaments on the homely fireplace were inexpensive but no less charming for it and the family photographs scattered amongst them suggested a closeness and happiness which did not need money to improve it. Whatever money Margaret Clayton's husband had earned in his work, and whatever funds she now ran the house with after his death, it was not plentiful, but the family home was nevertheless rich in integrity. Priest could empathise: truly honest work never made anything more than a few shillings. If it did, perhaps his suit wouldn't be at least a year past its best.

Nancy Clayton's bedroom, like the rest of the house, was simple, but honest. The bed was set against the wall behind the door, its blankets neatly folded, and a small, stuffed bear propped against the pillows. Priest wasn't sure which he thought was more pathetic: the pristine bed, waiting for its weary occupant to return to its well-prepared comfort, or the torn ears and missing bead of the bear's eye. Priest could not help thinking that neither would be of any use to anyone now, except as a cruel reminder of kinder times. He turned away from the bed and stepped further into the room. A small dressing table was under the window and a simple set of drawers and matching wardrobe were placed in the alcove of the far wall. Priest walked to the window and pushed aside the net curtains. The room looked out over the back yard, the shared privy in the far corner, next to the gate which served as protection from intruders, with a small greenhouse, long unattended, and a modest, wooden outhouse in the opposite corner.

Priest turned away from the window and let his eyes drift across the room. He was conscious of Margaret watching him, as if expecting him to speak at any moment, daring to hope that he might have the answers and solution to her pain. He avoided matching her gaze. He had no answers to give.

"It's a very neat room." Just something to say.

"Nancy was always particular in her habits," Margaret replied, her smile emphasising her pride. She looked around the room, finally coming to rest on the bed. Her thoughts must have instantly echoed Priest's own, because the pride evaporated into that particularly cruel blend of fear and sadness with which he was only too familiar.

Priest walked slowly towards her, his hands in his pockets. "Would you mind waiting for me downstairs, please, Mrs Clayton?" She began to stammer a protest, but he held up his hand to stop her. "I won't be long and I promise I won't disturb anything."

He walked her to the door and she stepped out onto the landing. She looked back at him, perhaps for some reassurance, but his face remained impassive. With a gentle nod of her head, she made her way to the stairs. Priest watched until she disappeared from view and then closed the door behind her. He told himself that he had dismissed her in order to protect her, that it was nothing to do with any embarrassment at having to deal with a grieving, heartbroken woman. But he told himself a lot of things and he didn't believe anywhere close to half of them.

He examined the room efficiently, but at his own pace. He opened the wardrobe gently, taking in the blouses, cardigans, and skirts. They were fashionable but not extravagant, no more were the summer frocks and evening dresses which were set to one side of the wardrobe space. The shoes on the base of the cabinet weren't new but they were well maintained and Priest suspected that some of them were used both for day and evening wear. Nevertheless, there was at least one new, unused pair, because he could see an unopened box tucked away in the corner of the wardrobe, partly hidden by the long hems of the evening gowns and summer skirts, waiting perhaps for an older pair finally to give way. Another example of the frugality so prevalent in the family circumstances, in part forced on them by the war but perhaps something which had always been part of their lives.

Priest turned away from the wardrobe and sat down carefully at the dressing table. He looked at himself in the mirror, not liking the grim twist of his mouth and barely recognising the eyes which glared back at him. He wondered how often Nancy Clayton had looked into the same glass and had similar feelings about the reflection which stared back at her. Her mother might not want to admit it, but Priest's instincts told him that a man was involved somewhere in the girl's disappearance, if not the actual cause of it. Priest found himself now thinking about how often Nancy had sat there, thinking about the man she felt compelled to keep a secret. Had he made these small but cosy walls of her bedroom seem suffocating and oppressive? Had his appearance in Nancy's life promised something more alluring than the poor honesty of the family home? Suddenly, remembering the wide smile and happiness of the photo which Margaret had shown him, Priest felt overwhelmingly depressed.

He pulled at the dresser's drawers. They contained nothing of any particular interest: various vanity cases, hairbrushes, discarded pens and scraps of paper, which he found contained attempts at poetry and various doodles. He was no expert, but he doubted either were of any artistic value. Carefully, he pulled each drawer out completely, looking for keys taped to the underside or the back. Nothing. He pushed them all back into place and leaned back in the chair. Looking at the surface of the desk, there was still less to interest him. A musical box, containing a small, mechanical ballerina, but which had no secrets to tell; a small jewellery box, filled with rudimentary necklaces, rings, and bracelets, as well as an incongruously attractive, and in Priest's judgment, comparatively expensive locket. He prised it open; inside was a photograph of a baby, presumably Nancy herself, and an inscription, *To Nancy, With love on your 21st birthday, Mum and Dad.* He placed it gently where he had found it, ignoring any feeling of being an invader into a private happiness.

He rose from the dressing table and walked back towards the bed. Gently, so as not to disturb its neatness, he sat down on it. There was a slight squeak from the metal springs under the mattress. A small chest of drawers, a younger brother of the one beside the wardrobe, was placed beside the bed. A lamp, a water carafe and glass, and a paperback detective novel were neatly arranged on the top. None of that interested Priest. Pulling open the drawers, he found a collection of similar novels, each with a title as ludicrous as the last. Nancy clearly had some interest in crime, even if it was only the fictional kind. Priest hoped her involvement had stopped there.

Smiling coldly to himself, he pushed the drawer shut. None of the others held anything of interest to him.

It had been a waste of time. He had expected to find something to give him a starting point, but there had been nothing. He walked slowly back towards the door.

"Damn it," he hissed.

Something, instinct or premonition, made him look back into the room, as if he felt it was not done with him. He walked back to the wardrobe and pulled open the doors, this time with more determination, as if to leave the room in no doubt as to who was in charge of the situation. Kneeling down, he pushed aside the dresses and pulled out the shoe box which he had seen earlier, but disregarded. He sat back down on the bed, ignoring its neatness now, and put the box down beside him, pulling off the lid and casting it aside.

The box did not contain shoes.

There were old napkins from restaurants and cocktails bars, various matchbooks from similar places, and stationary from at least three hotels. More than ever, Priest was conscious of the presence of a secret lover in the background, the items in the box trophies and mementos of assignations, drinks and dinners with him, and various other *rendezvous*, each kept by Nancy out of some instinctive sentimentality. Priest looked at the names of the restaurants, bars, and hotels, all of which were both too expensive and exclusive to be likely haunts of Nancy Clayton. He thought again of the frugality of her life, of the modesty of her bedroom and the family home, none of which chimed in tune with the social life she seemed to have been leading. The man, whoever he was, seemed more clearly defined in Priest's mind than ever.

But there was something else. A matchbook, one of many, its background black, contrasting with the brilliant white of the image of a cocktail glass, garnished with a pearl in place of an olive, and a crescent moon shining above it. The lettering was in that same intense colour of silver, spelling out the name of the club, *The Midnight Pearl*. It meant nothing to him, not in that moment, so he tossed the matchbook back into the box with the others.

As he did so, his eyes fell then on the bundle of photographs, held together tightly by a rubber band. It was lying in the corner of the box, but

Priest suspected it should have held pride of place. He picked it up and pulled the band away from it. Slowly, his breath frozen in his lungs, he looked through the pictures which spread out in front of him. They were mainly of Nancy, laughing and smiling, yet almost unrecognisable from the girl in the photo Margaret Clayton had shown him. In these images, there was little trace of the obvious shyness and timidity, barely even a trace of her youth. Surrounded by cocktail glasses and men in dinner jackets, in a dress far more extravagant and alluring than anything hanging in that dull, wooden wardrobe, Nancy seemed like an alternate version of herself. A cigarette in her gloved hands, expensive pearls around her slim neck, and her hair styled like something from the American silver screen, she seemed as far away from this small bedroom in the East End terraced house as a newly formed butterfly from a cold winter's day.

Priest continued to look through the photographs. Not all of them showed Nancy: some were general snatches of time, with no discernible central subject, preferring to show groups of people dancing, drinking, and in conversation. They were not professional images, but there was an atmosphere to them, so that Priest seemed able to smell the cigarette smoke, taste the cold ice of the cocktails, and hear the brass notes of the band in the background. In several of them, he could see the same tall-stemmed glass, and its pearl and crescent moon decoration, stencilled on the walls above the curved leather settees which fitted snugly into the purpose-built alcoves of the room. His eyes flickered back to the small black matchbook which sported the same image. Whatever and wherever it was, at some point, and on more than one occasion, Nancy Clayton had drunk and danced the nights away in *The Midnight Pearl*.

He looked back through them all, looking for any other detail which might be of some use to him. It was on his third examination that he saw two things which he had overlooked previously. One made no immediate sense to him; the second turned his blood to water.

The first was a man's arm resting on the table at one of the alcove settees. His face was just out of shot, turned to his right as if in conversation with someone beside him. To his left, her arms linked around his elbow, sat Nancy. She was staring at the camera, smiling broadly, her head almost resting on the man's left shoulder. In her face, Priest could see what he could only interpret as a loving pride. She didn't seem to care that he wasn't reciprocating, that his attention was elsewhere, with only the back of his head facing her. A cigarette burned between the fingers of his hand, the sleeve of his tuxedo slightly pulled up his forearm, revealing the cuffs of his dress shirt, held together by a curious link, carved into the shape of what looked like an ancient Egyptian scarab. Even with the lack of quality of the print, Priest could sense that they were expensive. Idly, Priest thought to himself that *The Midnight Pearl* must be an exclusive club, if dinner suits and ball gowns were the required attire.

The second thing he noticed after careful study of the photographs was a face he recognised. It was in the background of several of the pictures, as if it was only ever caught by accident, the man never designed to be the focus of attention. But no matter how far into the shadows he thought he was, Priest knew it was Harry Wolfe. The slim, vicious features, the dark eyes, and the cruel mouth were unmistakable. Priest knew that if Harry Wolfe was in *The Midnight Pearl*, Jack Raeburn wasn't far away. It was a foregone conclusion, as natural as night following day, and it meant that two of the most dangerous men in the city were in the same club where Nancy Clayton was drinking cocktails and holding on to a man whose face was hidden, either by accident or design.

Suddenly, looking at the pictures sickened him. He collected them together and put the rubber band back around them. He picked up the matchbook with the club emblem on it and put it under the taut protection of the band. The entire package he put in his inside pocket. He wasn't sure why, in that moment, but he knew that the photographs, whatever they meant, were safer in his possession than Margaret Clayton's. The less she knew the better, just until he was sure of a few things.

Priest looked back at the whole contents of the shoe box. The napkins, the notepads, the other matchbooks: in themselves, they were innocuous, but Priest could not help thinking that they were dangerous when put together. He gathered up the contents of the box, wrapped them all in one of the larger napkins, and tucked them into his inside pocket. He put the lid back on the now empty shoe box and placed it back in the wardrobe. He closed the doors once more and walked swiftly out of the room.

CHAPTER FOUR

In daylight, *The Midnight Pearl* was unimpressive. Priest could imagine what it would be like when the lights were at their brightest and the music at its loudest, but the evening was a long way off and now the place was little more than an old, lifeless structure nestling between others of its kind, waiting to come to life. The sign above the door was anaemic without the fluorescent vibrancy of its twilight glory; the emblem of the club, stencilled on the frosted glass of the windows, seemed dejected and lonely without the energy of the night crowds who were its purpose. In the late autumn sun, there was nothing to suggest that the club was anything other than one of many places in London still grateful to be standing after the roaring malice of war.

Priest stood near Bond Street underground station, staring at the entrance to the club, a short distance from Oxford Street. The wreckage of the Blitz was still visible all around him; buildings wrenched in two, the streets still filled with debris and the aftermath of carnage. Priest had read somewhere about the total number of deaths caused by the Luftwaffe. He had no real evidence of the accuracy of the figures quoted, but he could believe them. They were eye-watering, but he still wondered if they were high enough. He could remember the propaganda messages, declaring that "London Could Take It", and he could recall the insistent belief of the capital that it was true. Now, with the devastation over, the ruins of the city, echoed in any of the major cities of the country, seemed to shout out the opposite. All he could see around him was desolation and decay. London, and England as a whole, had not been able to take it; not as assuredly as they would have had people believe, and certainly, not without a price.

Priest spat onto the pavement and lit a cigarette, trying to rid his mouth of the bitter taste of pessimism. He concentrated his attention on *The Midnight Pearl*, on its double-fronted entrance and the awning which covered it. He tried to imagine Nancy Clayton walking through the doors, the man with the scarab cufflinks by her side, her heart filled with happiness and her mind unaware of any possibility of danger. But that danger was not far behind her, not if Jack Raeburn owned the club. There would be records of ownership of *The Midnight Pearl*, details of the registration of title deeds, and bank transactions, a trail of papers and signatures which even a man like Raeburn could not dodge. But Priest didn't need any of them to be sure. The photo of Wolfe was enough to convince Priest that Raeburn owned or had stakes in the club. He didn't need any other proof.

A movement across the street brought his vision back into focus. A car had pulled up outside the club and two men had climbed out of it. One, Priest did not recognise. Tall, with shoulders like a suspension bridge and a face which told dark, unpleasant stories. The other, much shorter but no less dangerous, was Harry Wolfe himself. Priest recognised the outline of the man, small, dapper, his steps short and mincing, although nobody would ever comment on it more than once. Even from this distance, Priest could see the downward turn of the thin lips and narrowed eyes, always searching for a threat or an attack. The tall man stood to attention, waiting for Wolfe to make his way around the car and to the double-fronted entrance of the club. But Wolfe was motionless, sniffing the air for any scent of trouble. He straightened his tie and pulled the black leather gloves tighter over his thin fingers, as if the business with the tie had shaken them loose.

Priest ran across the street, avoiding a bus and several cars and ignoring their horns of protest. By the time he reached the car, Wolfe had moved to the doors of the club and had pulled one of them open. The tall man, now conscious of Priest's approach, stood between him and Wolfe. Priest looked him in the eye and held his gaze. If the taller man was impressed, his ugly face didn't realise it.

"Too early to open for business, surely, Wolfe," said Priest, still not looking any further than the pockmarked cheeks of the bodyguard.

Wolfe smiled, so thinly that it might have been a snarl. "You're welcome any time, Mr Priest."

"I can't dance."

Wolfe shrugged. "Plenty of other entertainment here."

Priest didn't doubt it. He began to reach into his inside pocket, but the tall man threw out an arm and his fingers closed around Priest's wrist. It hurt, the grip strong and uncompromising, but Priest didn't show it. He looked over to Wolfe. "Tell him he's too eager. It's broad daylight, after all."

Wolfe was by the taller man's side now, his furtive, dark eyes glaring at Priest. He patted the man's forearm, presumably because he couldn't reach the shoulders. The grip loosened and the arm went back to the man's side. Priest watched the blunt fingers curl into a fist.

"Let's all take it a little slower, shall we?" said Wolfe.

"I just want to show you a photograph," said Priest. He moved his hand out of his inside pocket with the speed and dynamic of a snail. He found the photograph of Nancy sitting in the alcove seat, her arms wrapped around the unidentified man. He held it up in front of Wolfe. "Recognise her?"

Wolfe peered at the girl's face, almost too theatrically to be convincing. "No."

Priest nodded towards the club. "It was taken here."

"A lot of people enjoy themselves here," smiled Wolfe.

"Look at the man she's latched onto. Know those scarab cufflinks?"

Wolfe didn't look anywhere other than in Priest's face. "No."

Priest smiled. He put the photograph back in its place and returned it to his pocket. "Does Jack own this place, Wolfe?"

"Whether he does or doesn't makes no difference to you, Mr Priest. *The Midnight Pearl* is a popular venue, a place for people to forget their troubles. Times like these, Mr Priest, everyone needs a release. People have suffered a lot over the past few years. Time to get back on our feet."

"And this place helps people do that?"

"Music, songs, dances, drinks. Who doesn't love it, Mr Priest?"

"And plenty of other entertainment besides?"

Wolfe looked disappointed. "Come in one night, see for yourself. Who knows? You might even learn to enjoy life yourself. Put the war behind you."

Priest scowled. "Some of us need more than a dance to do that, Wolfe."

"It wouldn't do for us all to be the same."

There was nothing to be said in reply to that. "I suppose this place is expensive. Only for the privileged few, right?" Wolfe made no comment, so Priest continued. "You see, the girl in the photograph wasn't rich. I'm wondering how she could afford to come here."

"People come here with guests," sneered Wolfe. "Didn't you say something about a man being with her?"

"That's right." Priest shrugged. "I just wondered if you might know whose guest she was."

Wolfe smiled back at him, a sly, wicked laugh escaping from his lips. "We're both busy men, Mr Priest. You'll excuse me, I'm sure."

Priest watched Wolfe walk back towards the club and pull open one of the doors. He looked back at Priest, his expression as blank as a new page, and stepped inside, the door swinging shut behind him. The tall man still loomed over Priest, his stare hard and his mouth twisted by nastiness. Priest raised his hat in salute and walked away. As he crossed Oxford Street once more, he looked back towards the club. The tall man hadn't moved. He was still staring in Priest's direction, and Priest was willing to bet, his hands were still balled into fists.

CHAPTER FIVE

The offices of Quayle, Hopkins & Stowell were located off the Strand. They were imposing rather than extravagant, with the kind of anonymous façade which suggested that they might at one time have been government buildings. The Royal Arms were carved into the stonework which formed the arched entrance to the premises and the large oak doors beneath them suggested both formality and efficiency. The other occupants of the building were similarly professional: accountancy firms, architects, stockbrokers. The old man who was posted at the front desk pointed the way to the Otis lift, telling Priest that the offices he wanted were on the fourth floor. There was another one of him waiting by the lift. He ushered Priest inside, stepped in with him, and closed the heavy metal grille on themselves.

Priest made his way down a carpeted corridor, lined on either side with glass-panelled doors. He came at last to a pair of doors, beside which was a brass plaque bearing the name Quayle, Hopkins & Stowell. He pushed one of them open and stepped inside. He found himself facing an attractive but cool blonde, whose features were as feline as her tidiness. She smiled at him, but it was professional only. Priest handed her a business card, which she took as if it might infect her with something unpleasant.

"I telephoned ahead," Priest explained. "I have an appointment with Mr Quayle."

"Yes, I took the call," the woman declared, as if he was an idiot for not realising it. "This way, please."

He followed her past two rows of typists, their fingers dancing over the clattering keys of the machines, like manic crickets he had heard once in an American twilight. A couple of the girls watched him as he passed, but he ignored them. There was nothing in them for him. The blonde stopped outside a door and knocked once. She smiled at him and she opened the door. He didn't return it. There was nothing in her for him either.

"Mr Priest, as arranged, sir," she said into the room, before standing aside and allowing Priest to step inside.

The man seated behind the desk rose to greet him. Priest accepted the outstretched hand first and then the offer of one of the seats set out for visitors. The blonde offered him coffee, but he refused.

"I'd hate to be a problem for you," he said. She simply smiled, just as professionally as before, and left the room.

The man had sat down once more. "I'm Leonard Quayle, Mr Priest."

He was not as impressive as his offices. He wasn't much above average height, his features handsome without being striking. His hair was dark, slightly mottled with grey, and scraped back from a broad forehead, beneath which a pair of dark eyes gazed out through the lenses of rimless, steel spectacles. His grey suit was expensive, but he didn't wear it with sufficient style to justify its cost. He was dapper, almost prim, but there was very little elegance about the neatness. Priest had the idea of a man who earned good money and thought he ought to spend it to prove the fact.

"I don't suppose I can pretend not to know why you're here, Mr Priest," he said.

Priest smiled and lit a cigarette, Quayle refusing one. "I wouldn't think so, Mr Quayle."

"It's about Nancy, of course."

"She's been your secretary for a little over a year, yes?"

"Around that. I would have to check her file to be certain."

"Any complaints about her work?"

"None."

Priest caught the hesitation in Quayle's tone of voice. "Sure about that?"

Quayle leaned back in his chair. "Look, Mr Priest, I appreciate you have a job to do, but I have told the police all I know."

"But I'm not the police."

Quayle smiled. "I don't know what else I can tell you."

"You haven't told me anything yet."

"Am I under any obligation to do so?"

Priest exhaled smoke. "None, that I can see. But I don't see any reason why you wouldn't want to speak to me either. It makes me wonder."

"About what?"

"About what you're afraid of me finding out."

The smile turned into a laugh as fake as the receptionist's shade of blonde. "I'm not afraid of anything. What should I be afraid of?"

Priest shrugged. "Did Nancy have a boyfriend that you knew of?"

Quayle picked up a pen and began to turn it over in his fingers. "I had a suspicion about that."

"Care to elaborate?"

"I told the police."

Priest snorted. "Don't be childish, Mr Quayle. We both know you've got something to say, so best to just say it. You having suspicions is one thing, but me having them is something else."

"Is that supposed to have any specific meaning?" Quayle bristled, but Priest remained impassive.

"Take it however you like."

"I don't like your manners, Mr Priest."

"I don't like tailor-made grey suits, Mr Quayle, but we all have to get along."

Quayle considered him for a moment, taking in the impassive insolence, the scar on the chin, and the cold glare of the blue eyes. He smiled and laughed gently to himself. He removed his spectacles and began to polish them with the red handkerchief which he pulled from his top pocket. Priest watched him absently.

"Forgive me, Mr Priest," said Quayle. "You must understand that it's not every day that a private detective comes into my office to interrogate me. Perhaps I can be permitted some degree of caution?"

Priest spread his hands, as if in conciliation. "I just want to know about Nancy, Mr Quayle."

"She was a good worker. Eager, efficient, polite."

"Popular with the other girls in the office?"

Quayle shrugged. "I assume so. I never heard of any unpleasantness. As my secretary, she would not have had much to do with the general typists, of course."

"Was she your personal secretary?"

"Yes. That is to say, she only did work for me. Each of the partners here has their own secretary. The typists outside are for the other staff. I shall have to find a replacement, I suppose."

Priest smiled. "Unless we find Nancy."

Quayle bowed his head. "Of course, yes."

"In the meantime, who's doing your work?"

Quayle made a vague gesture to signify the outside office. "One of the girls. Hardly ideal, but the Devil is driving."

Priest said nothing for a moment. He lit another cigarette, Quayle again refusing one. "Why do you think Nancy's work had started to suffer?"

Quayle glared at him. "I'm not sure I understand."

"Earlier, when you were marching all over me, I got the impression that Nancy's work wasn't up to it. But you've just said she was efficient. I wondered about the confusion."

Quayle bared his teeth and his fingers got to work again on the pen. "I don't want to give you the wrong idea."

"Let me worry about getting the wrong idea."

Quayle inhaled deeply, placing the pen carefully down on the blotter of his desk. "It wasn't that Nancy was incompetent. Quite the opposite. If she had been, I would have taken the mistakes she made for granted. It was the fact that she was so good at what she did that the mistakes seemed so stark."

"What sort of mistakes?"

"Little things, so little that I feel foolish for mentioning them. Putting the wrong date on letters, spelling errors, missing out paragraphs of dictation. Careless mistakes, really, but they seemed all the stranger because Nancy was usually so meticulous."

"Any idea of the reason for them?" Priest waited for a more substantial reply than the meagre shrug of the shoulders. "The boyfriend you wondered about, let's say. Might there be something in that?"

"I'm not prone to gossip, Mr Priest."

"But sometimes you just can't help overhearing, right?" Priest smiled slyly.

Quayle removed his spectacles and polished them again. Priest had doubted they needed cleaning the first time; now, he was sure of it. "Didn't the war teach us that walls have ears?"

"Amongst other things," said Priest, grimly. "Any idea who this man might have been?"

"No. The romances of my staff are no concern of mine. As long as their work is done and done correctly…" He let the sentence finish itself with silence.

"How long ago did you notice the change in her work?"

"A few weeks ago, perhaps."

"Did you question her about it?"

Quayle nodded. "I had some words with her. She promised me that everything was all right and that she would be more careful."

"Did you believe her? About everything being all right?"

The spectacles were replaced carefully. "I had no reason not to."

Priest was silent for a moment. He finished the cigarette and stubbed it out. He rose from his chair and walked around the office, his hands in his pockets and his head lowered. The carpet was a deep crimson colour and it reminded Priest of blood. He turned his attention away from it and looked at the framed certificates which were placed strategically on the walls. They were testament to Quayle's qualifications, his legal authority to practise law, and confirmation of various awards which had been bestowed on him. A man highly respected by his profession, thought Priest, and perhaps a man who liked to be reminded of it. He was struck suddenly by the lack of any other, more private personality to the office. The framed certificates and the leather-bound volumes of legal texts on the shelves against the opposite wall were declarations of his professional dedication, but there was nothing to give any clue about the man behind them.

"You a married man, Mr Quayle?" he asked.

Quayle seemed momentarily taken aback by the question. "Yes, as a matter of fact."

"How long?"

"Twelve years." Quayle narrowed his eyes. "I'm sorry, is this of any relevance to you?"

"I'm just curious about people." Priest smiled, glibly. "Habit."

He turned his gaze back to the frames on the wall. There were photographs of Quayle in dinner suits, brandishing various awards, sipping champagne, and accepting honours. Many of the faces Priest did not know, but their appearances and obvious affluence spoke of their probable importance. But some of the faces were familiar. Priest recognised politicians, mostly minor but some more senior, and people whom he took to be businessmen and dignitaries. For the first time, he began to wonder how connected and influential Leonard Quayle might be and how deceiving his natural diffidence in appearance and manner was.

As his eyes glanced over the photographs, they began to see the same face occurring on multiple occasions. It was handsome, as dynamic as Quayle was reserved, the dark hair swept back from a high, intelligent brow, which, unlike Quayle's style, emphasised his features rather than detracted from them. His smile was broad, the laughter lines around his cheeks deep but impressive, and the eyes flashed with a calm, self-assurance. He was perhaps the same age as Quayle, but he wore the years with confidence, so that he seemed several years younger. Priest had seen faces in the cinema which might have paled by comparison, and almost immediately, he felt a sense of loathing fester inside him.

"I know this man, don't I?" he said, pointing to the photographs.

Quayle came to his side and followed his gaze. "Thomas Marriott."

"The financier?"

"He began as a banker, yes. He has a number of business concerns now."

"Such as?"

Quayle laughed gently. "I cannot say."

"Oh?"

"Mr Marriott is not only an old friend," said Quayle in mock confidentiality, "but a client. As I am sure you can appreciate in your own line of business, Mr Priest, a client is entitled to confidentiality." Quayle made a show of consulting his watch. "Is there anything else you need, Mr Priest? I'm rather busy, you see."

Priest held up a hand in a negligible gesture of apology. "I'll go, thank you, Mr Quayle. Can I leave one of these with you? Just in case anything occurs to you which might help." He had taken out his battered, leather wallet, and from inside it, he took one of the business cards he carried, which gave only his name, profession, and telephone exchange. He didn't want Quayle surprising him in the office with an unscheduled visit, so the address was kept private for now.

Quayle took the card and placed it on his desk in a manner which suggested it might not last the rest of the day. Priest smiled crookedly and nodded his head in thanks. He placed his hat on the back of his head and tapped the brim in a farewell salute. He pulled open the office door, paused, and turned back at looked across at the solicitor.

"Did Nancy ever mention somewhere called *The Midnight Pearl*?" he asked.

"Not that I recall," was the answer Quayle gave, but it was only said after his eyes had widened behind the lenses of his spectacles and his smiling lips had straightened out and parted gently. The whole shift of expression was swift, so quick as to be almost imperceptible, but Priest had noticed it. To him, it had seemed to take place so slowly that every crease of the mouth and every fleck of spittle on the parting lips was magnified. His benign and helpful expression was replaced as quickly as it had vanished, but Priest could not forget the shift in demeanour.

Once outside, Priest lit another cigarette and looked up at the windows of the building. He saw Quayle at once looking down on him, the receiver of the telephone on his desk placed to his ear. As their eyes locked across the distance between them, Quayle let go of the Venetian blinds which covered the windows and stepped out of view. It had taken Priest no more than five minutes to get outside, meaning that Quayle had telephoned somebody and as soon as possible after Priest had mentioned *The Midnight Pearl*. None of it might mean anything, of course, and Priest might be running with the fairies, but he doubted it.

Suddenly, he was desperate for the pubs to open and the anticipated taste of a decent beer overpowered him. He crossed the street and looked back again at the offices of Quayle, Hopkins & Stowell. There was no sign in the window of Quayle now and Priest assumed that the phone call, whoever it had been with and whatever it had been about, had ended.

It was as he turned away from the building that Priest saw him. A small, ill-kempt man, standing on a distant street corner, staring directly at him. He was too far away to recognise, but Priest could see that his hands were thrust into the pockets of what seemed to be a tattered raincoat and an equally shabby hat was perched ungainly on his head. It seemed to be a size too small. He was smoking furiously and his stance made it obvious that he was watching Priest. For a moment, they stared at each other, neither of them quite sure who was supposed to move next. Finally, the stranger flicked his cigarette expertly into the gutter. He crossed the street, as if he had lost all interest in Priest and had business elsewhere, which suited Priest just fine. He had his own business and it was no less important than anyone else's. He had walked only a few feet before he glanced back over his shoulder. He couldn't see the little man any more and the whole incident duly passed from his mind.

But if Alex Priest had looked over his shoulder a second time, he would have seen the stranger walking in the same direction as him, but down the opposite side of the street. And he would have seen that those shrewd eyes were fixed closely on Priest's retreating back.

CHAPTER SIX

Priest drank a pint of beer and ate one half of an uninspiring tongue sandwich in a pub on Bow Street. *The Runners' Retreat* was a place he knew well. It was somewhere he could be assured of a quiet drink without interruption and without the cold glances of bankers and businessmen, who thought he was too coarse to be permitted entry to other places in London's West End. Priest knew that his suit was not well-enough cut, that his tie was not from an old school, that the cuffs of his overcoat were frayed and one of the buttons missing from the front, and he knew that his hat had lost much of its colour and shape over the years. He knew, too, that he might not seem respectable enough for some of the people who drank in these places. His expression was too abrupt, his eyes too confrontational, and his attitude too grim. Those places could keep themselves to themselves, he thought; here, he was just another paying customer and his shillings and pence were as good as anybody's and probably more honest.

He walked out of the pub, waving a brief farewell to the man behind the bar, and crossed the street to a telephone box. He pulled open the door and lifted the receiver. Within a few seconds, he had been connected to Quayle's offices. The professional and clipped tones of the cool blonde froze in his ear.

"Is Mr Quayle available, please?" asked Priest, his voice lifted slightly.

"I'm afraid he's left the office for the day."

Priest smiled. The phone call he had witnessed had presumably ended with an urgent need for a personal meeting. "Do you know where he's gone?"

"No."

"Could you get a message to him?"

"I'm sure I could try." Then, after a moment's thought: "May I ask who is calling?"

Priest blew gently down the receiver, causing a small hurricane on the other end of the line, and hung up. Stepping out of the box, he walked slowly back into *The Runners' Retreat*. The man behind the bar was talking now to a new customer, a tall, thin man dressed in black. His age was uncertain, but the whiteness of his impressive, extravagant beard and his wild, unruly hair suggested he was nearer to sixty than fifty. His clothes were not shabby, but they were far from new and the remnants of chalk and ink were evident both on the sleeves of the coat and the hands which poked out from beneath them. There was the smell of old books about him, the aura of a lecture hall, and Priest remembered that he'd been told once that the man was an academic, a historian, and an expert in ancient religions and the occult. To Priest, the man looked crazy enough to be an expert in all that. Priest could never remember the man's name, but he had an idea that he was German. Maybe that was reason enough to keep forgetting it. Priest smiled at his prejudices, petty and otherwise.

As he approached, the barman raised an eyebrow. "Back so soon, Mr Priest?"

"Some days drive you to drink, Billy." He spilled some coins onto the bar. "How about we see how far that lot takes us?"

Billy smiled and scooped up the coins. "You're the boss, Mr Priest, but it's still early."

"I've got a watch, Billy," said Priest, "but I haven't got a drink."

He watched whilst the pint of beer was pulled from the cask with an easy dexterity. His eyes drifted automatically to the bottles of whisky which glittered against the mirrored background of the bar. Billy was right, after a fashion. It was too early for that sort of indulgence. A beer or two wouldn't hurt, but those dark bottles and their promises were a different matter. Billy placed the glass of bitter, the colour of varnished oak, in front of Priest and bowed his head, as if in some acknowledgment of his duty being concluded.

"Ever heard of a man called Leonard Quayle, Billy?" asked Priest, wiping some excess foam from the side of the glass. The young man gave it a moment's thought only, before shaking his head. Priest drank some of the beer. "What about Thomas Marriott?"

More thought, but for longer this time, and with a flicker of distant recognition in Billy's light grey eyes. "Rings a bell. Can't seem to place it."

The old academic spoke, but it was as much to the foam of his beer than to either Priest or Billy. The accent was soft, but perceptibly German. "Phoenix."

Billy clicked his fingers and nodded, as he began to polish a glass. "Right you are, Herr Hoffmanstahl."

Hoffmanstahl. As soon as he heard it, Priest made a mental note to pin it to the wall of his memory, never to be forgotten again. "Phoenix?"

Hoffmanstahl nodded. "Of course."

Priest smiled, as if he knew a joke was being played but he was the only one who didn't get it. "You're saying it as if I should know what it means."

Billy stopped working on the glass and placed it on the rack above his head, flicking the wet cloth onto his shoulder with the sort of flourish only bartenders can manage. "Phoenix Developments. You must have heard of it."

"Pretend I've been hibernating," said Priest.

Billy grinned and walked away to the other end of the bar. Priest watched him sort through some discarded newspapers, neatly folded in a stack, and pull one out. He flicked through the pages, and eventually, stopped. He folded the paper open at the relevant page and walked back towards Priest. He slid the paper across the bar at him and pointed at the article. "Phoenix."

Priest looked down at the newspaper. He saw Marriott at once, the familiar grin looming out of several photographs set against various backgrounds: sitting behind a large desk, his hands clasped in front of him, ready for business; shaking hands with a government minister outside the Palace of Westminster; standing beside the shattered remains of a bombed building, his face now grim with concern, suitably saddened by the devastation which surrounded him. The article itself seemed to be more of an interview with him, setting out, as far as Priest could understand it, a plan to rebuild the city, what Marriott said was his clear view towards a better future after the war. Priest sneered: if that was Marriott's purpose, it hadn't taken much thought to come up with the name of the project to execute it.

Priest read some of the interview, Marriott's own words: 'We won the war and I thank God we did, but it is useless to say it was not at a price. Our cities and towns have suffered immeasurably from Hitler's campaign of terror. Look at any one of the major cities in the country and you will see for yourself. We achieved victory, but at what cost? Peace has cost us our resilience. I don't just mean in ruined buildings, but in people's lives. England is bombed, bitter, and bankrupt and we must look to change that. We must start to rebuild, to forge a better, cleaner, brighter future. We have lived through enough fear, pain, and darkness. For our own sake, our children's, and the country's as a whole, we must start to get back on our feet. TGM Investments are committed to that process.'

Priest had to drain his beer. He pushed the paper away and gestured to Billy. No words were needed. When the fresh drink had been pulled, Priest gestured to the discarded paper. "So, what's his plan?"

"Have you not read the article, Herr Priest?" Hoffmanstahl asked.

"Never was much of a reader."

"A shame, but not, perhaps, a surprise." Hoffmanstahl turned on his stool. "It's about pulling the country back to its feet."

"Off its arse, more like," contributed Billy.

Hoffmanstahl ignored him. "The principal feature of the project, its backbone, if you will, seems to be property development. Building new accommodation, houses, flats, that sort of thing. In the process, it offers employment and gives people somewhere to live. Every country needs rebuilding after war."

"Perhaps some people should stop causing them," said Priest.

Hoffmanstahl glared at him. "You think because I am a German that I must condone my country's conflicts with yours?"

"I think every man picks a side."

The old academic nodded. "True enough. And I picked my side after the Somme. I came over here almost three decades ago, Herr Priest. I do not recognise my place of birth any more. A man's home is not where he came into the world, but where he feels he belongs. You are still young, but you will learn it."

"You stood against your own?"

Hoffmanstahl nodded. "I was one of the king's loyal enemy aliens. I served this country as well as you did. Not with guns or grenades, but with brains. Translating documents, offering military insights from history. A country should learn from its mistakes. The old wheel turns and the same spokes come up. We must never dismiss them."

Priest said nothing. He was not about to think about the old man's words, but he was conscious, perhaps for the first time, that war like everything else, was more complex than he had given credit for. A change of subject was indicated. "So, Phoenix. All this foot-kissing and back-slapping in the press is just for a property deal?"

Hoffmanstahl held up a warning finger. "This man, Marriott, has plans. Housing, hospitals, schools, businesses — to get them all working once more. Dispel the memory of the war. Invest to reinvest."

"His words or yours, Hoffmanstahl?"

The academic shrugged and wiped foam off his vast beard. "You sound as if you don't agree with what he's trying to do."

Priest shrugged. "I'm just wary of Greeks bearing gifts."

"He isn't from Greece," said Billy, without irony.

Priest sipped some of the beer and thought about everything for a moment. They were nothing other than idle thoughts, none of them distinct, all of them without conclusions. It was as if a chorus of voices were suddenly whispering in his head, with no particular voice rising in supremacy above the others. Finally, with a decisive moment, he pushed himself off the barstool and asked Billy to watch his drink.

"Don't let anyone charm you into giving it to them for free," he said.

He went back outside and ran across the street to the phone box. There was a man inside now, deep in conversation, and Priest began to drum his fingers on one of the glass panels of the door. The man turned round and mouthed a crude command. Priest's fingers carried on drumming; the man carried on talking. At last, sneering back at Priest, he ended his call and pulled open the door. He brushed heavily past Priest as he stepped out of the box.

"Ever heard of good manners, old man?" he spat.

"Complain to the papers," said Priest, closing the door behind him.

He flicked open the telephone directory. He found the telephone number for TGM Investments without breaking a sweat. He was connected with no less difficulty and a gentle purr of a woman's voice seemed to kiss his ear gently. It was a pleasant contrast to Leonard Quayle's blonde queen of cold.

"TGM Investments, may I help?"

Priest lifted his voice again. "Would it be possible to speak to Mr Thomas Marriott, please?"

"I'm afraid Mr Marriott is unavailable today."

Priest was already flicking back through the directory. There were many Marriotts but only two with matching first initials. One had an address in St John's Wood, the other in Belgravia. "That's a nuisance. Do you happen to know if I will catch him at home?"

"I'm afraid I couldn't say, sir."

Priest put a smile into his voice. "I'll try the St John's Wood residence."

"St John's…?"

The confused tone of the reply and the hesitant pause before it told him everything he wanted. He terminated the call. Taking a pencil and notebook from his coat pocket, he licked the tip, and made a hurried note of the Belgravia address. He smiled to himself, kicked open the door of the telephone box, and sauntered back to *The Runners' Retreat.* Billy had kept watch over what remained of his drink and Priest finished it in silence, smiling to himself. He would have ordered another, but once he had bought Hoffmanstahl a drink in return for his information, the small collection of coins had given all they could offer.

"Look after yourselves, gentlemen," he said. He lit a cigarette and walked outside.

CHAPTER SEVEN

The house was in Eaton Place. It seemed ironic to Priest that Marriott, a man seeking to reverse the devastation of the war, should live in the Belgravia area, one of the lightest hit areas of the conflict, both in terms of casualties and damage. The V1s and V2s had done their work well enough, leaving significant scars across the area, but the more densely populated areas to the east of the city had suffered more than this relatively small square of privilege. What damage there had been, and remained, had been concentrated largely on Eaton Square, around the corner, which had suffered no fewer than nine direct hits from the bombs. It had always been Priest's theory that this particular concentration of devastation had been a mistake and that nearby Victoria Station had been the intended and far more strategic target.

The row of houses on either side of the street were largely identical, joined in regular terraces of classical design. Each was set back from the pavements, accessible only by individual series of steps which led to black front doors, topped with glass panels and framed by portico designed pillars. There was a balcony above the pillars, behind which were three windows, each replicated on the ascending four floors of the properties. Below him, protected from the street traffic by a series of black, iron railings, Priest could see similar windows which, he presumed, looked into the cellars. He suspected those cellars, and even the attics high above him, were larger and more prestigious than his office. He breathed deeply, but all he could smell on the late afternoon air were the usual traces of traffic and industry. There was no distinctive smell of money, but there was no doubt that it was swirling all around him.

He checked his notebook for the address he had written down from the phone directory and walked up the small stairway to the front door. He knocked, feeling as if his hand merely touching the paint of the door had in some way besmirched it. He waited a little over a minute for a response. He would not have been surprised if a butler, or at least a maid, had answered the call, but if he was expecting it, he was to be proved wrong.

"Can I help you?"

She was silhouetted against the inside lighting of the house, but he had an instinctive impression of beauty. He could tell from the halo of light around her head that she was blonde, and from the cut and style of the hair, he sensed that she was expensive. She was dressed in a plaid two-piece, one hand resting on the elegant outline of her hips and the other holding a glass of something which might have been water, but probably wasn't. One of the long, impressive legs was stretched out towards him, the other balancing her weight with ease. As she stepped forward into the light, he was struck at once by her natural beauty, which the lipstick and rouge complimented rather than exaggerated. Her eyebrows were naturally arched, her lips pursed in a perpetual invitation of a kiss, and the jade green of her eyes glittered with a feline allure. Priest tensed, his natural anxiety in the wake of beauty coiling inside him like a snake. He held his breath, and almost unconsciously, he felt his hands curl into defensive fists.

"Can I help you?" she asked again.

"I'm looking for Thomas Marriott."

"He's not at home. He shouldn't be too long if you would like to wait." She stepped aside to allow him to enter. "I'm Evelyn Marriott, Thomas' wife."

He handed her one of the business cards. "Alex Priest."

She was staring at the card. "A private detective?"

"That's right."

She ran the tip of her tongue along her bottom lip. "Come in, Mr Priest."

He smiled swiftly and stepped into the hall. She was at once conscious of the sweet smell of alcohol. "Would you like a drink?"

He pointed to the glass. "What are you having?"

"Gin."

His lip curled slightly. "Whisky, if you have it."

She walked past him and into the living room. She could sense him behind her and she heard him quietly clear his throat. She poured the whisky into a crystal tumbler. "Ice?"

"A single cube."

She handed him the drink. His eyes were on her and she found herself transfixed by their depth of blue. There was something cold about them, as there was about the thin snarl of the lips. He had taken off his hat and the fair hair beneath it was slightly unsettled. He looked as if he could do some damage if he wanted to and the scar on his chin suggested that he might have had to prove it at some point; but any impression of toughness was somehow undercut by a clear vulnerability behind those impressive eyes. His clothes were nothing impressive and she was unable to shake off the idea that he might have been forced at some point to sleep in them. She found herself wondering what it would be like to see him in a bespoke suit, a dinner jacket, tennis attire, anything approaching her husband's sophistication. Somehow, she doubted the effect would be successful. Besides, she thought that if he were dressed any differently, she might not feel the overwhelming urge to kiss him.

"I didn't know private detectives existed in real life," she said.

"We're a necessary evil."

She laughed. Priest tried to ignore how much he liked the sound. "You seem on edge, Mr Priest."

He shook his head. "Not at all, Mrs Marriott."

"Call me Evelyn. May I call you Alex?"

"If you like."

"It's a nice name. I like it."

He could think of no answer to that which didn't sound ridiculous. "When might your husband be back, Mrs Marriott?"

Evelyn checked the clock on the marble fireplace. "Not too long. Please sit down."

She indicated a long settee. It looked the sort of thing which might be easy to sink into and almost impossible to escape from. Priest perched himself on the edge of it and placed his hat on one of his knees. The living room was as expensive as Evelyn Marriott. There were two bookcases in both of the alcoves flanking the mantelpiece, each one stretching from the floor to the ceiling. There was no shelf space unused. A long, low, glass-topped table was placed in the centre of the room; under the glass, there was a narrow shelf holding a selection of magazines, which were fanned out in such a way that Priest doubted they had ever been read. A white fur rug was in front of the fire. The walls were plain, tastefully decorated with just the right number of framed pictures to make it seem welcoming without being cluttered.

Evelyn sat in the armchair to his right and crossed one leg over the other. "What does a private detective want to speak to my husband about?"

"Something and nothing."

"Is he in any trouble?"

Priest looked into her arched eyes. "Should he be?"

She laughed and Priest wondered whether an angel somewhere had gained its wings. "What a cautious man you are, Alex."

Hearing her say his name seemed somehow to be intrusive, too close to be appropriate, and he felt his anxieties intensify. Something must have betrayed him, his eyes perhaps, or a twist of his mouth, because Evelyn's eyes narrowed and she leaned forward in her chair. "Do I make you nervous? You seem very defensive."

The tip of her tongue ran across her bottom lip again and he watched it with distrust. The ice in his whisky cracked. "Just cautious, Mrs Marriott."

"Evelyn," she said, a smile playing on her lips. Priest sought solace in the whisky.

The sound of the front door seemed to shatter his eardrums. Evelyn stood up and turned her attention to the living room door. Priest rose too, suddenly conscious that he was alone with this woman, casually drinking with her, and giving every impression of sin and deceit. It was his own paranoia, he realised that, tainting and poisoning an innocent situation, but his mind could not divorce itself from the squalid interpretation which it had formed.

Thomas Marriott stepped into the room. His photographs in the newspaper article had done him no justice. The hair was sleeker, the features smoother, and the dark eyes more intense than the camera had been able to portray. He was the sort of man who demanded attention, whose presence in a room commanded comment, and Priest doubted Marriott had ever been ignored in his life. He kissed Evelyn on the cheek and Priest had the sudden impression that it was a proprietorial gesture as much as a romantic one. Marriott looked at him, politely but unquestionably seeking an explanation.

It was Evelyn who provided it. "Thomas, this is Alex Priest. He's a private detective."

Marriott looked at the card she showed him, his eyes only slightly mocking. "Really?"

Priest stepped forward. "I wonder if I could have a few moments of your time, Mr Marriott."

"You have a drink, I see." Marriott looked at his wife. "Evie, perhaps you would refill Mr Priest's glass and pour me one of the same."

She obliged. "Should I leave you in peace?"

Priest was about to respond when Marriott pulled her close to his side. "Of course not. I am sure whatever it is which Mr Priest has to say isn't anything secret."

Priest stared at Evelyn, as if willing her to go, but she was taking none of his silent hints. She smiled playfully, sitting back in her chair and crossing her legs like before. Marriott gestured to Priest to resume his seat and he walked across the room to sit in the chair opposite his wife. As he moved, Priest had the impression of a panther stalking the plains of Africa. Priest remained standing, as if to show he was not owned by these people, and he took out the photograph of Nancy Clayton.

"Do you recognise this girl, Mr Marriott?" he asked.

Marriott looked closely at the image. "Leonard's secretary. I suppose you've been hired to find her," he added, suddenly understanding.

"I understand you're a client of Leonard Quayle," said Priest.

"We're old friends, too."

"Did you know Nancy Clayton?"

Marriott shook his head. "Only as a secretary. She made me coffee several times, took notes of meetings and conferences I might have had with Leonard."

"You didn't know her personally?"

"No." If it was a lie, it was well told.

Priest sipped some of the second whisky, and carefully, in his own time, sat down on the settee. "You wouldn't know anything about a boyfriend?"

Marriott smiled and shook his head. "Nothing."

Priest returned the smile. "You can't think of any reason why she might have disappeared?"

"None. I know that Leonard is concerned about her, as we all are. The police didn't seem to take it very seriously. I suppose that must be hard for the family to deal with."

Priest looked at Evelyn. "Do you know the girl, Mrs Marriott?"

She shook her head slightly. "I'm afraid not. Have the family hired you?"

He gave no reply to that. "Did Mr Quayle telephone you earlier today, Mr Marriott?"

"He phones me regularly, Mr Priest."

"Including earlier today?" Priest tried to keep the sneer out of his voice.

"Yes."

"Did he sound worried or upset when you spoke to him?"

Marriott shook his head. "Not at all. Should he have been?"

"I went to see him this morning."

"I see." Marriott smiled. "I doubt that would be cause for anyone to worry."

Priest rolled with that punch. "I'm just trying to do the job I was hired to do, Mr Marriott."

Evelyn rose from her seat and walked over to her husband. She leaned towards him and kissed him lightly on the head. "Try not to be a bore, darling."

Marriott inhaled her scent for a moment. Then, as if it had worked some sort of magic on him, he rose from his chair. Priest did likewise and accepted the hand which was offered to him. "Evie is quite right, Mr Priest. I am being unnecessarily rude and hostile. I apologise. You caught me off guard, that is my only excuse. I'm not used to coming home and finding a private detective sitting on my settee and drinking my whisky."

Priest shrugged. "The drink was offered and it seemed churlish to refuse."

Evelyn laughed. "I would have been grossly offended, Alex."

She walked behind her husband, her eyes fixed on Priest, peering out from under her lids. Her lips had parted into a subtle, sly smile which seemed to speak volumes, although Priest couldn't hear any of it. He watched her sit back in the armchair, making sure he was aware of every movement she made, as if he was guarding himself against a possible attack from a cobra. Her eyes never left him. They didn't seem to know that Marriott was there. Priest had the urge to run from the room.

From far away, he heard Marriott's voice. "I hope you're not suggesting that Leonard has anything to do with this girl's disappearance, Mr Priest."

He looked back into the man's dark, expressive eyes. "I'm just poking around in a rockpool and seeing what comes to the surface. Stumbling around."

"You're stumbling in the wrong direction with Leonard, I can assure you."

"How long have you been his client?"

The change in subject did not seem to trouble Marriott. "Ten years, perhaps? A little longer, maybe."

"He handles all your legal issues, I presume."

"With discretion and integrity. You've been to his office, you say? Then you'll have seen the awards and certificates on his wall."

"Is he acting for you in the Phoenix project?"

Marriott nodded and swallowed a mouthful of whisky. "Absolutely."

Evelyn sighed. "You may regret that question, Alex. Once Thomas starts on Phoenix, his mouth forgets to take a breath."

Marriott bore the insult with dignity, refusing to acknowledge or rise to it. "It is a vital project. You will have read about it in the press, no doubt."

Priest nodded. "The bare bones."

Marriott raised his eyebrows and inhaled deeply. "We may have won the war, Mr Priest, but we face a new battle now. We must survive our own victory. Nobody comes out of a war unscathed."

"Bombed, bitter, and bankrupt?"

Marriott smiled at the use of his own phrase. "Exactly. We must do something to get back on our feet."

"And how do you propose to do that?"

"New opportunities. Housing estates, schools, employment initiatives. I know what it's like to come from nothing, Mr Priest. Now, for those who haven't managed to escape the slums and the gutters, it will be even harder for them. I see it as a duty to help them." He shook his head, as if rejecting an argument which had not been raised. "I don't mean just with money. I mean with opportunity and hope."

"Money comes into it somewhere. Must do."

Marriott conceded the point. "A sad fact of life, Mr Priest, is that someone always makes money out of tragedy. War is no different. But the overall effect for the country, as a whole, is poverty and destruction."

"There's still no such thing as a clean shilling," said Priest.

Marriott didn't argue, but nor did he continue with the theme. "London doesn't just need to be rebuilt, Mr Priest. It needs to change. This is a time to re-shape it, rejuvenate and reinvigorate ourselves. We should see this not as a time of devastation, but as an opportunity to rise from the ashes."

"Hence, Phoenix?"

"Exactly," preened Marriott. "Phoenix Developments is a renovation initiative, funded and headed up by my company, TGM Investments. I think of it as my legacy," he added, with an intended, but unconvincing, humility.

"And how does Quayle fit into all these plans?"

"TGM Investments is in the process of buying properties across London, buildings which are either damaged or long since abandoned. We'll renovate them, convert them, whatever it takes, to make them useful, profitable, and worthwhile again. As I say, new housing, new schools, factories."

"And Quayle is dealing with the purchases and the legal side of the renovations?"

"A clear view for the future." Marriott grinned and sipped the whisky.

"Sounds easy."

Marriott's eyes had hardened, but none of the smooth politeness had evaporated from his manner. "I believe in giving something back to the country which defended us, Mr Priest."

Priest shrugged. There was no reason to argue for the sake of it. "Was Nancy Clayton involved in the Phoenix project?"

Marriott shook his head. "Not directly. She will have typed letters and memoranda, made telephone calls at Leonard's request, but nothing more. She won't have known any of the intricacies of our work."

Priest poked the inside of his cheek with the tip of his tongue. "Positive about that, Mr Marriott?"

"Absolutely." He frowned and pointed at Priest. "What is it you're trying to say, exactly?"

Priest shook his head. "Nothing."

"Don't lie to me in my own house. What's on your mind, Mr Priest?"

Evelyn had risen from her seat. "For God's sake, Thomas, don't be so aggressive."

Marriott didn't look at her, his dark eyes pinning Priest to the wall instead. "If he's got something to say, he should say it, Evie."

Priest drained his glass and put it down on the low, glass-topped table. "I'll say it to Mr Quayle, assuming I say it to anybody."

Marriott contemplated Priest for a moment, his expression now contorted, as if something unpleasant had crawled into his nostrils. Then, in disbelief, he snorted a humourless laugh. "You think Leonard was sleeping with her, don't you? You think he was having some sort of seedy little affair behind Dorothy's back."

"For God's sake, he doesn't think anything of the sort," sneered Evelyn. But when she looked at Priest, his eyes were filled with intent and the flare of his nostrils could tell her no lies. "It's preposterous."

Priest shrugged. "It's still something I have to consider."

"Consider it somewhere else, then," said Marriott. "Go on, get out. And remember, not everyone's as cheap as you are. Some people have standards."

Priest picked up his hat from the settee and placed it on his head. The words had as much effect on him as rain in the ocean. "I'll see myself out. Thanks for the drink," he added, walking to the door. He paused before opening it. "Do you own a pair of scarab cufflinks, Mr Marriott?"

"No." The answer, when it came, was decisive, but Marriott's smooth control of himself had not been encompassing enough to hide the momentary flicker of recognition which Priest saw flash across his eyes.

Priest smiled, hoping it was both insolent and infuriating. "Very helpful, thank you."

He was on the steps outside when he heard the door open once more behind him. Evelyn Marriott stood framed in the doorway once more, her hair again outlined against the brightness of the hallway. He stared at her directly, waiting for her to speak.

"You're wrong about Leonard, Alex," she said at last.

Priest looked away from her, a movement from the left catching his eye. From the window of the living room, Marriott was staring at him, drinking his whisky so slowly that it almost seemed like an act of malicious intent. Priest broke his gaze and looked again at Evelyn. She was no less intense in the way she looked at him, but he saw no malice in it. He tried to think of something to say in response, but nothing came. Nothing other than a simple, "Good evening, Mrs Marriott."

He touched the brim of his hat and turned away.

CHAPTER EIGHT

It was close to dark by the time he got back to the office. It was the time of afternoon which is neither day nor night, when the shadows are grey rather than black, the streetlamps are lit but not quite necessary, and the traffic and streets are filled with people making their first steps back home after a day of toil. The time of day which is just a little too early for a drink, but far too late for anyone not to be thinking about having one.

Priest felt as if he could have several more than he had already. He doubted that he would have cared much if he had wandered into the first pub he found open, however low and vile it might have been, and poured whisky into his throat without any thought of the consequences. He had thought enough about everything, he told himself, and there was no more thinking to be done. Thinking was for people who want to find trouble. It was better to stop thinking about anything and let cigarette smoke and alcohol cloud any thoughts, numb any part of any brain which was still active. Walking back to the office might change his mood, he thought, but the cool air and increasingly bright lights of London's early evening meant nothing to him. The people he passed on the streets were ghosts, nothing to do with him, because, in Marriott's words, he was cheap. He wasn't one of them. He drank whisky out of a tooth glass, not out of a crystal tumbler. He didn't wear the right suits, and even if he did, the knot of his tie would never be straight enough or intricately tied enough. And when women looked at him as if they wanted to find out what was beneath his hopeless suit and cheap tie, he didn't charm them with champagne and oysters; he withdrew, wanting only to run back to his office and hide under the desk.

His mood was darker than the sky and the whisky was poured into a mug instead of a tooth glass. He threw his coat and hat onto the stand, took off his jacket, and rolled up his sleeves. He pulled the tie further down his chest, the knot constricting so much that it might never come undone again. He sat in the leather chair and put his feet on the desk, crossing his legs at the ankles. His only light was from the small desk-lamp, whose beam was at such an angle that part of it must be shining on the lower part of his face. The shadows across his scowl would have made it seem fiercer than it was, assuming that was possible.

It was Evelyn Marriott, of course. Her blonde hair, her feline beauty, and the barely suppressed allure of mischief within her. He doubted any man would have been repelled by her, although he could imagine many who would be intimidated by her. Himself included.

More whisky.

Intimidated not because of her beauty. He felt more than capable of handling that. He knew where his lips would go, what they would taste, and he knew what her own lips would feel like, how they would explore, how they would caress and harm in turn.

Even more whisky.

It was something else which haunted him. The same old memory, its familiar pain and cruelty. The usual nightmare of the loneliness, the isolation, and the betrayal which had consumed him when that woman, whom he could never think of without anger and bitterness, had walked out for good. Suddenly, she was gone, no word of apology or farewell, just her back fading slowly into the sunlit distance.

Still more whisky, another mug filled.

The words and the memories collided in his mind, like the cymbals in a diabolical orchestra. It was always the same, whenever he thought about that woman and what she had done, how she had hurt him, never once looking back at him as she walked out of his life. Sometimes, he wouldn't think anything of her; other times, he was given no choice, being reminded of her by a passing stranger in the street, a face in a crowd, or by Evelyn Marriott.

That woman.

The shatter of the mug against the wall startled him. The stain of the whisky was already running down the opposite wall of the office, beside the glass-panelled door. He was snorting, spittle running over his lips, his nose streaming with bitter emotion. He was aware that his eyes and cheeks were wet, but he made no effort to clean himself. Not immediately.

"Damn her," he snarled. "Damn the bitch."

He walked to the filing cabinet and got a fresh bottle of whisky, pulling it open in a muffled rage. Walking to the small kitchen area in the smaller, adjacent room of the office, he grabbed the largest glass he could find. He had filled it before he had sat down again. His mind was in danger of wandering, so he tried to focus it. He rummaged in the inside pocket of his jacket and pulled out the bundle of photographs he had taken from Nancy's hidden shoe box. He looked through them again, more slowly this time, hoping to see something which he had missed before. Nothing came to him. As he flicked through, he saw Harry Wolfe's face glancing towards the lens. The dark eyes, like a cornered rat's, seemed to be startled into anger by the flash of the camera, but it might have been Priest's imagination, distorted by the drink and the mood. No useful thoughts came. The photographs had seemed important when he had found them; now, they seemed to mean nothing at all.

The scarab appeared from the bottom of the pile. The cufflink, caught accidentally in a picture which seemed to have been intended to be of Nancy only. Seeing it, Priest's vision seemed to clear. An impulse, unexplained and without any justification for itself, had prompted him to ask if Marriott owned a pair like it. He had denied it and maybe he had told the truth. But Priest was sure, he remembered now, that Marriott had recognised something about the mention of them. If he took Marriott at his word, they were not his, but if so, he had seen them somewhere. Priest's mind drifted back to Leonard Quayle, to those certificates and awards on his wall. Had they been given to him on some sort of function or ceremony, a black-tie dinner being part of the evening? And had Marriott been at one of them, admiring in passing the scarab cufflinks which his friend wore?

Priest's brain, muddled with ideas and drink, tried to slow itself down. He pushed the images away, breathing deeply into his lungs, and running his hands across his eyes and face. He tried to bring his breathing into a slower rhythm, pulling the phone nearer to him. He took a telephone directory from the bottom drawer of his desk and began to make the calls.

On his fifth attempt, he got the right house. "Could I speak to Leonard Quayle, please?"

The woman's voice on the other end of the line was delicate but fussy, almost timid. "I'm afraid he's engaged at the moment. May I ask who's calling?"

"Could I leave a message for him, please?" Priest was trying to keep his voice level. The lady wouldn't be able to smell the drink, but she might be able to hear it.

"One moment." He heard her unfolding a pad and the clatter of pencils. "Yes?"

"Could you ask him to call Alex Priest, please? I'll give you my number." He did. "It's quite urgent, if you could let him know. Any time is fine to call."

"It's late," said the woman.

"Any time," Priest insisted.

"Very well."

He hung up. It struck him that he hadn't asked who the woman was. He was thinking about calling back to see if he could speak to her again. It might have been important, but it might not have been. He doubted he could say what was important and what wasn't. Apart from whisky. Whisky was always important, so he drank some.

The phone began to ring in protest. He stared at it, wondering if the woman from Quayle's house had been having similar thoughts about him. He considered ignoring it, wondering momentarily whether Evelyn Marriott would think it necessary to ring him. He sneered at himself, washing away his vanity with a cruel, sharp mouthful of whisky. The phone was refusing to give up, so he grabbed at it and snarled a greeting. "Priest."

"You on your own?"

The voice in his ear was a man's: brittle, hesitant, almost frightened. Instinctively, Priest felt the effects of the whisky ebb away. "Same as always."

"We need to talk."

"My father told me never to talk to strangers."

There was a snort, which might have been a humourless laugh or a burst of frustrated indignation. "Boyd. Jimmy Boyd. I need to speak to you."

Priest sat back in his chair, his eyes fixed on the shattered mug across the room. "What do we have to talk about, Mr Boyd?"

"I think we can help each other." Boyd barked an address down the line. "Be there at nine tomorrow night."

Priest scribbled the address down. "I don't go anywhere to meet anyone without knowing what it's about, Boyd."

"Be there, Priest."

The call was ended. Priest tore from the notepad the piece of paper where he had written the address Boyd had given him. He knew where it was and there were worse parts of London. Not many, but some. At nine tomorrow night, it would be dark, just as it was now. Whatever Boyd wanted, he didn't want to discuss it in the daylight. Priest thought about everything for a few moments but all he achieved was lost time. He looked down again at his scribbled note of the address and time, then screwed the paper into a small, irregular ball. He picked up the glass of whisky and drank deeply. He poured some more and drank that, but he barely tasted anything at all.

CHAPTER NINE

On the following morning, the stain on the wall had disappeared, but the remnants of the mug remained scattered across the floor. Priest knelt down and picked them up, tossing them into the small wastebin under his desk, and sat down in the leather chair. His head felt as shattered as the mug, only in a hundred more pieces, and his tongue was like a dozen caterpillars. He stood up and walked slowly to the small kitchen and poured himself a glass of water. He drank it down in a single gulp. It did no good at all, so he poured another, which did even less.

He sat back behind the desk and took out the crumpled piece of paper which had Jimmy Boyd's address on it. He spent a few long minutes wondering whether he should know the name, but Boyd meant nothing to him. A search of the telephone directory proved as pointless. Priest checked his watch: a little after eight. He thought he might as well cross the city and go to the address straight away, to see if Boyd was open to discussing things now rather than later. Priest looked around him and shrugged. He was doing nothing else.

But then she knocked on the door. She entered slowly, as if unsure whether it was safe, her eyes peering around the walls as she crept around the door. She was dressed prudently but not cheaply, her woollen twinset set off by a silk scarf at her neck, fastened with an onyx brooch. Her gloves and shoes were black, matching the wide-brimmed hat and veil which she wore over the top half of her face. The eyes behind the lace were wide, pastel blue and innocent, and the lips were painted a delicate shade of red. Her skin was pale and she looked as if walking around the dirty city might damage her forever. Around her throat was a string of pearls which might have been fake, but which Priest suspected were not.

At last, the eyes landed on him, like some blue butterfly landing on a tired, autumnal leaf. "Mr Priest?"

"Come in. Can I help you?"

She closed the door behind her and faced him directly, her shoulders back and her hands clasped with determination in front of her. "We spoke yesterday, Mr Priest."

His brain tried to place her face in his memory, but she wasn't there. "I'm sorry?"

"You telephoned my house last night." She took a step forward. "My name is Dorothy Quayle."

Now, the voice began to sound familiar to him. He had thought it was fussy, but it wasn't, it was delicate, nervous, shy. "Have a seat, please, Mrs Quayle."

She accepted with a slight smile, but she declined the offer of tea or coffee. She removed her gloves and lifted the veil. Her eyes were the clearest he had ever seen, almost transparent, and they carried in their lightness a unique type of coy innocence. Priest sat down slowly and leaned forward, his forearms resting on the desk and his fingers latticed together. "What can I do for you, Mrs Quayle?"

"I hoped I wouldn't have to explain."

"I'm afraid you'll have to." He smiled, although Dorothy Quayle might have called it a leer. "I haven't had much sleep."

She looked at him for a long moment, unsure whether he was mocking her or talking down to her. She watched him light a cigarette and shook her head at his offer to join him. "You called to speak to my husband."

"That's right."

"I'd like to know why you wanted to speak to him."

Priest nodded, a slight smile rolling across his lips. "I can't tell you that, Mrs Quayle."

"I think I have a right to know why a private detective wants to speak to my husband." It seemed to take all her courage to be confrontational.

"You have," replied Priest. "But it's not for me to tell you. Ask him."

"I'm asking you."

"And I'm not saying. I have a client, Mrs Quayle, and that client is entitled to confidentiality."

She lowered her gaze. She had not anticipated this sort of opposition and he could tell that she was not sure how to proceed. He smoked in silence, waiting for her to continue. He had nothing else to say.

"What are your charges, Mr Priest?" she asked suddenly.

"Ten pounds a day, plus any expenses."

"That seems very expensive."

He smiled. "Sometimes it seems high, sometimes there's not enough money in the world for the trouble I get."

She thought about that for as long as she felt it deserved. "I want to hire you, Mr Priest."

The words somehow didn't seem real to him, as if they were just a collection of letters and sounds which made no sense. But her face, with its curious blend of anxiety and fear and humiliation, showed that they were real. He glared at her. "To do what?"

"Find out if my husband is being unfaithful again."

She had expected some sort of reaction, but there was none. His eyes did not flicker, his lips did not quiver, and his hands remained clasped together. The smoke from his cigarette drifted towards the ceiling, as if minding its own business, but it was the only movement in the room, so that it seemed to have nothing to do with either of them. When he moved, it was slowly, so that he wouldn't disturb the quiet. He leaned back in his chair and stubbed out the cigarette. He pulled gently at his bottom lip. Never once did his eyes leave hers.

"Your husband has been unfaithful." It was more of a statement than a question.

"In the past, yes."

"And you think he's at it again?"

"Yes."

"Why?"

She gave a faint shrug of her shoulders. "The way he has been behaving. It's the same as before. Secretive, hanging up the telephone as soon as I walk into the room, staying late in the office but never there when I call. He thinks I'm stupid, Mr Priest. I know he thinks I'm naïve, so he assumes I don't notice things or that I wouldn't act on them, even if I did suspect anything. But he is wrong."

Her lips had begun to tremble, but she kept the emotions contained, and with an effort, she refused to look away from him, as if daring him to think of her as weak. He didn't; that was her husband's job.

"How many times has he done this to you?" he asked.

"Three or four. That I know of," she added with a hollow smile.

"How did you find out?"

"The first time he confessed it to me. I suppose it was a twist of his conscience. He hadn't learned how to live with his own lies. They must still have hurt him back then. He has grown used to them over the years."

"And the other times?"

Her voice shrank, compressed by shame. "I followed him."

Priest stood up and turned his back on her, his familiar but painful memories of that woman and her betrayals swelling inside him. His teeth were clenched together, the taste of bile and disgust heavy at the back of his throat. He glared out of the window, seeming to see the image of her reflected in the glass, her face slightly hidden by the black, stencilled letters of his name, etched onto the pane. She seemed to be mocking him, laughing at him for having to listen to a tale of a wrecked and betrayed marriage, as if she was telling him that it wasn't only her own marriage which had failed and that his hatred of her was unfounded, unnecessary, and unforgivable.

"Why don't you leave him, Mrs Quayle?" he asked, still not looking at her.

"And go where, Mr Priest?" Now, he did turn to face her, looking back over his shoulder. "Living with a man who betrays me is better than living without him. I don't suppose you can understand that, can you?"

He took a moment to reply. "No."

"Perhaps that says more about you than it does about me."

He had no answer to that. "Do you know who the woman is this time?"

Even before she replied, Priest thought he knew the answer. It was never going to be a surprise. "His secretary. A girl called Nancy Clayton."

He moved slowly away from the window and say back down in his chair. "Do you think he knows what's happened to her?"

Dorothy Quayle frowned, her head inclining slightly in confusion. "What do you mean?"

"Nancy Clayton has disappeared, Mrs Quayle."

Her eyes widened and her shoulders began to tremble. She gave a small gasp of air and pulled a handkerchief from her sleeve, which she used to dab away the tears which had started to form. Suddenly, her grip on the lace-trimmed fabric tightened and those eyes, reddened now with fear, darted back to his face. "That's why you telephoned the house. You think Leonard has done something to her."

Priest held up his hands. "Not so fast, Mrs Quayle. I've not got enough facts to think anything yet."

"When did this happen?"

"She's been missing for six weeks. The police have spoken to your husband." He watched her offer no reaction other than the maintain her glare of confusion. "You didn't know anything about it?"

"Nothing."

Priest fell silent for a moment. "What makes you think Nancy Clayton was your husband's latest betrayal?"

"I saw her at his office once," Dorothy said. "She was everything he would find attractive. And she spoke to him in the same way a schoolgirl might talk to a certain type of teacher. I appreciate that isn't much evidence but it's harder to explain than to have witnessed it. I have instincts, Mr Priest. And experience of such things."

Priest shifted in his chair. "What is it you want me to do, Mrs Quayle? You say your husband is having an affair with Nancy Clayton. Not at the moment he isn't, because nobody knows where she is. Even so, you let him do whatever he wants and you don't say a word about it. Why should this time be any different?"

She might have been offended by his words, but she didn't say anything, as if to prove him right about her inability to deal with confrontation. "I wanted to you prove me right, that's all. You won't understand it, but not knowing is worse than being sure of something. How I deal with the truth is my business, but I have to know what truth I am dealing with first. With the other girls, I had proof. Proof of my own eyes and Leonard's own confession. This time, I haven't got any. And I need it."

Priest shook his head slowly. "You're wrong, Mrs Quayle. I understand all that perfectly well."

She gave him a brief, but honest smile of grateful acknowledgment. "Perhaps you're right, though, Mr Priest. Maybe now it doesn't matter. As you say, he can't be sleeping with her if he doesn't know where she is."

Priest pursed his lips. "Maybe not."

"Unless he does know where she is." Dorothy spoke plainly. "That is what you're thinking, isn't it?"

"I'm not thinking anything in particular, Mrs Quayle."

Dorothy pushed the handkerchief back into her sleeve and opened her handbag. From it, she took a leather purse and clicked open the clasp. She took out a folded piece of paper, torn from a notebook. She handed it to him. Written across it, as if it was a reminder, was an address in Southwark. Priest glanced back to Dorothy, inviting an explanation.

"I found that in Leonard's study at home," she said. "I assumed it was somewhere he met her."

"Not a nice area for a respectable woman to go." He shook his head. "This could be anything, Mrs Quayle."

"It's an address which means nothing to me. My husband keeps secrets from me and this address was one of them. It's hardly a district either of us would have any business in, as you said."

"It might be related to his work."

She shook her head, so intently that Priest knew she must have had this argument with herself, perhaps more than once, and had thought of the answers to all the questions. "Anything relating to my husband's work was dealt with at the offices. He never brought his work home. I found it in his private study. That means it is personal."

Priest was still unconvinced. "Don't you think he'd have taken her somewhere better than that?"

She shrugged. "Perhaps he thought it would be safer, less chance of being seen by someone he knew, of being recognised. I don't know."

Priest bit his lip. Perhaps she hadn't thought of all the answers after all. "If so, it doesn't say much for what he felt about the girl."

She sneered. "I doubt he thought anything human for her. His girls are commodities, Mr Priest. Itches he has to scratch. They don't mean anything else to him."

Priest thought back to Quayle, to his ineffective appearance, the grey-streaked hair and the rimless spectacles. It was enough of a stretch of the imagination to accept that he had married Dorothy, let alone that other women would have fallen for him. Priest had no explanation for it. It was all part of life's tapestry. He looked back down at the paper.

"I went there," said Dorothy. "It was a flat, but all boarded up and abandoned."

Priest handed her the paper. "You think he met Nancy in this abandoned flat. Is that your instinct working again?"

She looked down at her feet. "I just felt I had to do something."

For a moment, neither of them spoke. Priest was thinking about Dorothy, about her preference for living with a man who treated her with contempt to being alone, about her need to know what was happening, a need so acute that she had carried out her own investigation of a clue. She might be meek, introverted, and nervous, but she had something he knew a lot of people lacked: guts and goodness. He found himself liking her, pitying her, and admiring her. And he found himself hating Leonard Quayle in return.

"You've got me," he said. "I'll do what I can to help you."

Her face softened with relief. She opened the opened the purse once more and pulled out some bank notes. "Ten pounds, you said."

"We can deal with all that another time."

"Why?" The crease above her nose betrayed genuine confusion.

"I'm getting soft," said Priest. "Leave things with me, Mrs Quayle, and I'll be in touch. Don't say anything to your husband about it."

She rose from her chair, nodding her understanding. "Is Leonard in trouble, Mr Priest?"

"I don't know. Not yet."

She looked at him closely, accepting he had nothing more to offer. She held out her hand and he took it. She held only the tips of his fingers, as if she feared he might break her bones if he squeezed too tightly. She muttered a word of thanks, softly and shyly spoken, but honest and sincere, and he watched her close the door behind herself. Suddenly, he had the idea that the office was lonelier without her. She was good, decent, a change to everyone else Priest met, and almost instantly, he missed her presence. Without it, the world was a colder, crueller place.

Priest shook his head. He hadn't had any breakfast yet, not even a cup of coffee. It was far too early for thoughts like those.

CHAPTER TEN

The place was desolate, as if the world had turned its back on the whole district. The river idled by in the background, minding its own business, oblivious to the devastation of the past few years. It had seen worse before and may do again, but the river would still pass through the city, untouchable and impassive. The buildings which looked out over the river were battle-scarred. Some were still standing, but streaked with the remnants of smoke and fire; others were little more than scattered bricks, their insides scooped out and tossed aside by the bombs. The war might have been raging still here, its wounds still raw, and the smell of burning oil and decaying flesh might have persisted. In the distance, there was the sound of machinery and the distant tolling of bells. Somewhere, life was being lived and time was marching; but not where Priest was standing. There, the world had stopped turning and time was frozen in a moment of bombed despair. Here, the ashes of the fires of combat still smouldered and not even Thomas Marriott's phoenixes rose from them.

The address Dorothy had given him was a jaded building with largely wooden windows. A battered 'For Sale' sign stood in the small yard at the front of the house, the words now covered by a sticker saying 'Sold'. For no reason that he could fathom, Priest made a note of the estate agents' name: Burke & Halliwell. Those windows which were still glass were darkened with mildew and grime. The paint on the door, what was left of it, was red, but its vibrancy had faded and the lock had rusted over, as if in an attempt to match the colour of the door. He knew it would be locked, but Priest tried the door anyway. He turned away from it and looked out across the river, wondering what to do for the best. He tried to peer through one of the windows, but all he could see was his own face looking back at him through the muck. He pulled loosely at his lower lip.

He could have walked away, as Dorothy Quayle must have done, but something inside him forced him to stay. He walked in a small circle a couple of times, his eyes fixed on his feet, his mind racing. At last, he looked back at the house and smiled at it. He ambled around to the back of the property. There was a small alleyway along the length of the building, the cobbles littered with broken bottles and discarded newspapers, which fluttered on the breeze like lost dreams. There was a series of gates at the back of the building and Priest pushed open the one which led to the rear of the tenement in question. He was confronted by a small stone yard, as forlorn as the front of the place. There was a battered door, but it was locked. Under the window, set into the back wall, there was a small set of stairs, fenced off with iron railings, whose black paint was flaking away. Priest could see a small window, not visible from the alleyway. He walked slowly down the steps and peered through the window, but as before, he could see nothing. He glanced above him, just to be sure, and he listened carefully for the sounds of anyone approaching. Nobody was. He shifted his weight and bent his arm. The small tinkling sound of his elbow going through the glass seemed strangely loud, emphasised in his head by his conscience.

In less than a minute, he was in the cellar. The smell of damp was intoxicating and the air was as cold as the grave. Priest brushed cobwebs from his hat and sleeve, noticing a collection of spiders scurrying away from his disturbance. The walls were exposed bricks and a single electric bulb hung from the ceiling. The place gave the impression that the bulb wouldn't work. Tins of half-used paint were scattered around and various tools lay dormant on wooden benches and the floor. A narrow set of concrete steps stretched up from the far corner, culminating in a low archway with a door fixed into it. Two vertical, rectangular glass panels were set into the top half of the door. Priest went up the stairs and tried the door. He must have been surprised to find it unlocked, but it didn't register. He was too concerned with listening for any sound of movement. There was nothing.

A small kitchen was ahead of him, and to the left, there was what might have once been a parlour. Now, it was a forgotten space, a cold, lonely graveyard of torn carpets and empty sideboards. There was the unmistakable stench of desertion, the oddly sweet smell of unwashed fabric and old paper. Further down the hall were two doors, one to the left and one opposite. He looked in both. One might have been a sitting room, the other possibly a dining room. Now, they were shells of their former glory. The stairs stretched up above him. The number of the flat Dorothy had given him meant it was on the first landing. Priest made the climb, the stairs groaning under his weight, as if they had forgotten what their purpose was and were now complaining about it.

At the top of the stairs was a bathroom. There was nothing in there for him. Along the landing was a row of doors, each one numbered with a brass digit, faded and dull. None of them seemed to have been used in months, maybe even years. If Leonard Quayle had brought Nancy Clayton here, there would have been nobody around to see them. Priest walked to the end of the landing and pushed open the door with the number five on it. He peered around the door, not knowing what to expect, but sensing that nothing would shock him. He stepped into the room, leaving the door open.

The window was covered by a red curtain, moth-eaten and torn. He pinched it gently between his forefinger and thumb and slowly pulled it to one side. He looked down into the street he had been standing on minutes before. The river was ahead of him, still minding its own business, still keeping its secrets. The room was furnished, but sparsely. The iron frame of a bed was behind the door, but there was no mattress. Several of the springs had broken. A wardrobe stood in the far corner, but Priest doubted it would hold more than a couple of items before it collapsed. A small fireplace, with a badly tiled surround, was set in the chimney breast wall. A small table and a chair with a broken leg was hiding away in another corner. It would have been a nice place to live for someone who had run out of options and had forgotten what having hope really meant. If Quayle and Nancy conducted an affair here, they must have been searching for squalor. Priest shook his head. The place didn't chime with the intention Dorothy Quayle wanted to hang on it. This was no room for illicit romance. It was a place to hide away if danger was on your track and you had nowhere left to run.

Suddenly, he had no idea why he was there. He walked once more around the place, just so he could say the trip had been worth it. The smell of the house had filled his lungs and he craved the outside air. He tutted once and shook his head for the third time.

"Jesus," he hissed. If it was meant to be a prayer, it went unanswered.

He saw it because his foot caught on a nail in the floorboard, causing him to look down. As he did so, his eyes drifted over the cracked tiles of the fire surround. From there, they drifted to the wrought iron grate. It was dirty and neglected, like everything else, and he doubted that it would ever come clean again. But oddly, there were no webs hanging from it. Priest looked around him, seeing everywhere else the delicate threads left by hidden, silent spiders: the broken chair, the legs of the small desk, the iron frame of the bed, all covered with the soft shimmer of webs. But not the grate of the fire. Someone had wiped all the webs away from that, which meant they had cleaned it. And as he stared harder, Priest could see why.

He didn't need a microscope or a magnifying lens to recognise blood. Whoever wiped the grate had done a good job, but panic and haste had meant it was not quite good enough. Squatting onto his haunches, Priest reached out and dabbed lightly at the stain. It wasn't fresh, but it wasn't exactly ancient either. If he had to guess, Priest would have said it was probably six weeks old. His stomach almost imploded at the thought and he let out a harsh, sickened sigh. He folded his legs underneath him and stretched out on the floor. He placed his cheek onto the floor and glared under the iron frame of the bed. He saw it almost immediately. A thin, gold chain, and even before he stretched out his fingers to retrieve it, Priest knew that it would have a charm hanging from it, a charm in the form of an angel.

He rose to his feet. There was the angel, staring back at him, and there was the broken clasp from where it had been torn from Nancy's neck. A struggle, during which the necklace was wrenched away and perhaps kicked under the bed, unnoticed. At some point, somebody had been hit and blood had spilled onto the grate; or someone had been struck and had fallen, hitting their head on it. He was willing himself not to imagine Nancy lying dead on the very same dusty, dejected floor on which he was standing. He pulled out an old envelope from his coat pocket and dropped the necklace inside it, placing it in his inside jacket pocket. He looked down at the mark of blood once more and then walked away, back the way he came, and away from the house.

He found a public telephone box and lifted the receiver. He shoved some pennies into the slot. He still had a few friends on the official force, but they were a dying breed. He had turned his back on the police after the war and it had cost him several connections whom he had thought were allies. He had never complained; you just never knew who people were until your back was against the wall. It was just a fact of life. But Detective Inspector Frank Darrow had never deserted him, even if he did talk to him as if he were filth.

"What do you want, Priest?" Darrow's voice was gruff and there was a slight wheeze behind it.

"You still need to lose a few stone, Frank?"

"Funny. Remind me to laugh when I remember how to do it."

Priest was smiling. "I need a favour."

"When do you ever call me for anything else? You don't ring to ask if I want to meet for a drink or to see how my allotment's doing."

"You're always too busy for a drink and you haven't got an allotment."

"You think that's the point?"

Priest leaned against the glass panels of the phone box. "Listen, Frank, I need this favour and the sooner you do it, the sooner I can leave you alone."

"Do I need to make notes?"

"No. I just need to know if there are any cases of violent deaths of young girls, say twenty to twenty-five years old, dark hair, and with head injuries?"

"Hundreds."

Priest scowled. "That are unsolved, Frank. And only in the last six weeks or so."

"Give me your number and five minutes."

Priest ignored the heavy sigh and gave the details. He smoked a cigarette whilst he waited, trying not to listen to the thoughts and theories which cascaded through his head. Once or twice, he thought people approaching him were going to use the box, but none of them did. The five minutes seemed to stretch themselves into hours. Finally, the shrill bell of the phone rang. Priest pulled open the door and stepped inside, lifting the receiver. "Hello?"

"Nothing for you," said Darrow. "No bodies like that found in the last six weeks."

"Thanks, Frank. One more thing?"

"What?"

"How's the allotment?" The answer was a severed connection.

Priest stepped out of the box and began to walk slowly down the street. If Nancy had died in that room, her body must have been disposed of, otherwise she would be the subject of a murder investigation. The alternative was that she wasn't dead at all and that was an option Priest would much prefer to take. But if she was alive, where was she? For that matter, if she was dead, where was she? He let his mind wander, but it just seemed to get lost. Something had happened in that room and Nancy had been there. Then again, he was assuming that the blood and the pendant were connected, part of the same incident, and there was nothing concrete to say as much. Nothing at all. Just the tight knot of instinct which had tied around his insides.

CHAPTER ELEVEN

He sat down at the desk in his office and took out the envelope from his pocket. He emptied the pendant from it onto the blotter and poked around at it with the tip of a finger. It wasn't expensive, but it might well have taken a significant part of Margaret Clayton's housekeeping money to buy. That meant it must have been an important gift. A twenty-first birthday, perhaps. Whatever the occasion had been, the necklace hadn't been expected to be left abandoned in a hovel of an apartment by the river. His sentiment told him to call Margaret Clayton and tell her that he had found it. His head told him it was too early, that he couldn't say for certain what finding it meant, or that the blood on the grate was connected. Any argument between head and heart was interrupted by the ringing of the phone.

He put the receiver to his ear. "Priest."

"You remembered our appointment tonight?"

Priest knew the voice. "Why don't you just tell me what you need to tell me, Boyd."

"It's not that simple."

"Can't you make it that simple?"

"Just be there, Priest."

He listened to the click and hum of the disconnected call. He kept the receiver lodged between his jaw and shoulder and dialled a number. It took her some time to answer. "I need to ask you a question, Mrs Quayle."

He wondered if she was not alone, because there seemed to be a delay in any reply, and when it came, the voice was softened in conspiracy. "I hadn't expected to hear from you so early. Have you found something?"

Priest was playing with the broken necklace and the angel charm. "Nothing definite."

"Did you go to that place?"

"Yes."

"And you discovered something?"

Priest closed his eyes. “I just need to ask you something, Mrs Quayle.”

She was silent and he wondered if she was considering either pressing him or terminating the call entirely. It took her a few seconds to make the decision, and when she did, she chose neither option. “What is it?”

“Does your husband own a pair of cufflinks, shaped like a scarab?”

Her voice began to tremble. “You found one in that awful place, didn’t you?”

It was sufficient confirmation. Priest needed nothing more. He said nothing for a while, long enough for Dorothy to grow impatient. “Mr Priest, do you want me to check if they are missing?”

“No. Do nothing, just wait to hear from me.”

Priest dropped the receiver back onto the cradle and sat motionless for a long while. He took the photographs which he had found in Nancy Clayton’s bedroom and scattered them across his desk. He looked at Nancy for a long time, at her wide and delighted smile and the excited, proud eyes staring down the lens of the camera. He looked again at the arm of the man she was with, the wrists decorated by those ornate scarab cufflinks. Dimly, the distant hum of traffic drifted up from the streets below, but Priest paid no attention to it. He was entranced by the photographs and the scarabs. They seemed to Priest to prove that Leonard Quayle was the man in the photographs, which in turn suggested a love affair between with Nancy. Priest was less willing to accept the pictures as proof that Quayle knew either Harry Wolfe or Jack Raeburn, but he was happy to be seduced by the idea. Priest shook his head. He was thinking too much and thinking it too quickly, drowning in suggestions and suppositions. As he looked back down at the photographs, a question struck him. It was an obvious one and he was surprised it hadn’t occurred to him sooner to wonder just who had taken the damned things in the first place.

Priest rose from the desk and made himself some coffee. Strong and black: he needed to give his mind something else to think about, but the coffee was no less powerful and only half as bitter.

There was a knock at the door, confident and assured, and it distracted him from both the photographs and the coffee. He called an order to enter and watched the door open on its hinges. She stepped into the office, took a look around, and smiled. She shifted her weight, placing a gloved hand on one of her hips. “So, this is where you hide?”

"Come in, Mrs Marriott. Coffee?"

Evelyn closed the door and walked slowly towards his desk. He watched her carefully, with a familiar mixture of attraction and caution. Her legs crossed as she walked and she tossed her head with a vague gesture of disinterested insolence, pulling her gloves off her hands. Anyone else would have suggested a deliberate ploy by walking like she did; for her, Priest thought, it was just natural allure. She didn't seem to know he was watching her, which seemed to prove his point. She was walking like that just because she did, not to please an audience. The hairs on his neck prickled with anxiety.

"Does it have to be coffee?" she said, looking back at him over her shoulder.

He looked at his watch. "It's barely noon."

"Does that matter?"

He shrugged. "I suppose the sun must be over the yardarm."

"The sun must be what?" She was smiling, mocking him, but it was only gentle.

He pulled two glasses from the filing cabinets with one hand and a bottle of whisky with the other. He placed the glasses on the desk and poured a decent measure from the bottle into both. He handed her one and raised the other in a toast. "What makes you want a barrel of whisky for lunch?"

"I don't make a habit out of it."

"You only drink when I'm around, is that it?"

She grinned. "I think drinking with you could be fun."

"Isn't it fun with your husband?"

"With him, it's a duty." She sat down without an invitation.

Priest walked to the window and rested himself against the sill. "Meaning what?"

Evelyn's eyes explored the office, but they said nothing about her feelings. "Thomas is always so serious. A drink to him is part of a business transaction. I couldn't imagine sitting in a dive of a pub and drinking the night into the gutter with him."

"And you could with me?"

"I think so."

He tried to smile, but it came across as a sneer. “What do you think you’d be doing in a low dive with me, Mrs Marriott?”

“Having fun.”

“I would have thought somewhere like *The Midnight Pearl* was more to your taste.”

She frowned. “Where?”

“Never mind.” He had watched for a flicker of recognition in her expression, but there had been none.

She was smiling now. “Wherever, Alex, I am sure a drink with you would be great fun.”

Priest tried to drown himself in the whisky. “What do you want, Mrs Marriott?”

She was peering at the photographs on the desk, the space between her eyes creasing slightly. When the cool assurance of her expression was gone, she had a trace of vulnerability which was twice as fascinating as her beauty. Her lips parted slightly and he could see the slight trace of white behind them. He resisted the thoughts about what it would be like to kiss her, but it would have been unnatural for any man not to have them. Even him. He took his hat from the stand by the window and stepped over to the desk, dropping the hat over the photographs. The movement broke their spell on her and she looked up at him, her face that of a child who had been caught stealing apples from a market stall.

“Is that Nancy Clayton?” she asked.

“What are you doing here, Mrs Marriott?”

“Is that all you can ask me?” The vulnerability had faded now and the mischief had returned.

“Until you answer.” He sat down in the leather chair.

Her smile broke into a short laugh which would have buckled his knees if he had been standing. She drank some of the whisky, giving no signs that it was too early. He wondered how much she could take. He had met a woman once in Edinburgh who could drink any man under a dozen tables and still recite Shakespeare to anyone who would listen afterwards. He had thought she was the only one of her kind; now, he wondered if Evelyn Marriott was distilled from the same malt.

“I wanted to apologise for Thomas’ attitude towards you last night,” she said.

"No need."

"He was rude and offensive."

"I've been treated worse than that."

His gaze lowered to the hat on the desk and something about their downward fall struck her. His words might have been a casual dismissal of her apology, but his eyes suggested that there was some darker truth about them. His expression had frozen, as if recalling something from the past, and she suddenly had the idea that holding him would not be dangerously exciting, as she had thought the previous night, but instead would be more tender than anything she had experienced in five years of marriage.

"You're wrong about Leonard Quayle," she said. "He wouldn't do anything to harm Dorothy."

Priest was thinking about scarabs. "If you say so."

Evelyn rose from her chair and walked towards the window. Priest kept his eyes on the hat, but he could feel her close by him. Her scent was hypnotic and so captivating that he felt as if she was close enough that he could feel her nails on the back of his neck. He stood up, just to dismiss the feeling, and stood next to her at the window.

"Doesn't a view like this make you think that what Thomas is doing must be for the best?" she said.

He looked across the city skyline at the half-shattered buildings, the scorched brickwork, and the chasms left by structures which had once dominated the horizon, but which now no longer existed. Somehow, to Priest, their absence was more striking than their presence had ever been. He supposed it was something to do with the loss of the familiar and the realisation that certain facets of London life were taken for granted until they were no longer there at all.

"I don't say what he's doing is a bad thing," Priest said. "The country needs to be rebuilt. Someone has to lay the first brick."

"Bombed, bitter, and bankrupt," she quoted.

"Is he proud of that slogan?"

"Sickeningly so."

She heard him laugh. It was short, but unmistakeable. She looked at him and saw his lips stretched back from his teeth, the creases at the corner of his blue eyes, and the slight tremor of his shoulders. "So, you do smile sometimes."

He looked at her, turning to face her. "When I have to."

She wasn't smiling back. Her mouth was open and her eyes were intense, glaring up at him from under the lids, brimming with guilt and expectation. "It's a nice smile. Too good to keep hidden."

"Lonely men don't have much to smile about."

Without him noticing, she had moved closer to him. "Are you lonely?"

"Isn't everybody?"

"What a sad thing to say."

She spoke so softly that he barely heard it. It seemed to him that the only sound in the room was the blood in his ears, crashing inside his head like waves against rocks. Her scent was now intoxicating, almost smothering, and suddenly the taste of her was on his lips. The waves rolled and crashed with greater intensity, as violent as her lips were soft. They were gentle, like silk, so soft that they might not have been touching his at all. Now, the sensation of nails at the nape of his neck was no product of imagination. Somebody had placed his hands on her hips and was forcing them to pull her towards him. Time had stopped. Hours and minutes meant nothing. There were no sounds in the world except the waves in his head and her delicate gasps between the kisses. There was no sensation other than those lips against his.

He regained control of his hands. He moved them from her hips to her shoulders and pushed her away. She glared at him, her tongue rubbing her bottom lip, as if still trying to have one last taste of him. Her breathing had become deeper and the look in her eyes would have corrupted any man. She brushed a lock of blonde hair out of her face and tucked it behind her ear. Priest watched it all like a starving man watching an orange being peeled. He had no idea what he felt, but he knew that none of it was honest or clean.

"What's the matter, Alex?" Evelyn asked.

"You're a married woman, Mrs Marriott."

"Don't tell me you're shy."

He sat down at the desk, as if it was some sort of protection for him and threw down some of the whisky. It did nothing to erase the taste of her and it couldn't numb the feeling of her lips on his. "It isn't right."

Evelyn laughed slyly and walked back around the desk, running her fingers around the edges of it. She sat down in the same chair and crossed her legs. Avoiding looking at her was like pushing a planet out of orbit.

"You're not that naïve, Alex. A man in your line of work can't afford to be."

"Doesn't marriage mean anything to you?" he asked.

She had lit a cigarette and she now blew smoke into the air. "Once, perhaps. Not as much as it obviously means to you."

He poured another whisky and told the time of day to go to Hell. "Marriage never meant anything to anybody."

It was a curious thing to say, and for a moment, she was troubled by it. He made no effort to explain further, and she was forced to draw her own conclusion. "I suppose I can understand you saying that. You must see a lot of unfaithful husbands in your line of work."

"I don't do divorce work, Mrs Marriott," he said.

"I wish you would call me Evelyn."

"Why?"

It seemed to her to be unnecessarily aggressive and her manner changed because of it. "Why are you so afraid to?"

"I'm not afraid."

"I think that's the first lie I've heard you tell." She leaned forward on the desk. "What happened to you, Alex? Why are you like this?"

"I'm not like anything."

"Lie number two."

He turned the glass of whisky around on its base, the liquid swirling like a whirlpool. He wished he could jump into it and drown. He looked into her eyes and felt himself drown in there instead. A moment passed. "If I ask you a question, would you give me an honest answer?"

She wondered whether she should allow the evasion to pass. In the brief silence before the question, she had hoped that he was about to explain himself to her. Now, she knew that he wouldn't. And in her delay in replying, she had allowed the moment to fall from her grasp, like sand through her fingers. She smiled briefly, and suddenly, she was conscious of the fact that she had never been so captivated by a man before. Because of it, she didn't know if she should love him or hate him. "If I can."

"Is your husband legitimate?"

Whatever question she had expected, it was not that. Her eyes flickered in confusion and her lips quivered with unformed responses. She leaned back in her chair and raised the cigarette to her lips. She didn't smoke it. It was as if she didn't know what to do with it, because the question had somehow altered how she viewed the world. "What sort of question is that?"

"A genuine one."

She laughed, but it was not as pretty as before. "You think my husband is a crook and that Leonard Quayle is an adulterer or worse? Nice view of people you've got, Alex."

He kept looking at her, his expression constant. Their kiss a moment ago might never have happened. "Is he legitimate?"

Now, she inhaled smoke and blew it in his face. "Yes. Why would you think otherwise?"

He shrugged. "I just had an idea."

"It was a bad one." She allowed the silence which fell to linger. "Thomas might not be an easy man to like, but he isn't a criminal. Everything he has, he's worked for."

"All in an effort to escape the slums?" Priest remembered Marriott saying something of the kind.

Evelyn nodded. "His family had almost nothing. The way he tells it, Thomas was little more than a child when he told himself he wouldn't live like it forever. He learned two things at school — how to survive a beating and how to avoid one. Most of the boys he knew went nowhere, achieved nothing. Thomas refused to be like them."

Priest was staring into his drink. "Where was this?"

"Whitechapel. Thomas would see the lights on the other side of the river, hear people talk about the wealth and luxury of that part of London. He says it was like hearing about another city, a far-off land of fantasy and romance. He could never believe it was only a few miles away. And then, his parents died and he was sent to live with his uncle in Aldgate."

"Did that make any difference?"

She nodded. "A little. It was his mother's brother, but they never spoke. There had been a falling out."

"About what?"

She shrugged. "I don't know. Thomas has never talked about it. Anyway, the uncle was better off than Thomas' parents, so things did change. I think Thomas gets his drive and ambition from his uncle. He was always obsessed with money, Thomas says. Money and power. Thomas was determined to build on what his uncle taught him, to turn his back on his past and better himself."

"And he succeeded."

"That's all you need to know about Thomas. When he fixes on an idea, he won't leave it alone."

"Like the Phoenix development?"

She smiled and sipped the drink. "It's like a religion to him. He believes in it absolutely."

"Do you?"

She took a moment to answer. "I can see its benefits. It will provide employment when it is sorely needed and it will give people the chance Thomas says they deserve."

"They're his words," said Priest, "not yours."

"It doesn't mean I don't believe them."

Priest leaned back in his chair. "Does your husband see himself as some sort of messiah, Mrs Marriott?"

She laughed at him, making no secret that she thought his question, and possibly him, ridiculous. "I doubt even he is that conceited. He is using the money he has earned to do some good. What's your problem with that, Alex?"

He shrugged. "No shilling is ever clean, Mrs Marriott. Someone, somewhere, was cheated before it's ever spent by people like you."

She inclined her head, her eyes flashing malice. "Meaning Thomas' money is dirty?"

"Meaning most money is dirty."

"You can be a bastard, can't you, Alex?"

He drained his glass. "I'm glad you're still loyal to your husband, Mrs Marriott."

She rose from her chair. "I came here to be nice. All you've done is push me away and insult Thomas."

He stood up and walked round the desk towards her. "You weren't so protective of him a moment ago."

She moved so quickly that he didn't see the flattened hand arc through the air, so that the sudden fire in his cheek seemed to come from nowhere. His head snapped to the right and the cheek reddened immediately. "Don't make me dislike you, Alex. It would be such a shame."

He rubbed his cheek slowly. "What's on your mind, Mrs Marriott? You come here and act like your husband doesn't exist and we can behave as we please. But when I remind you of him, you get defensive. How do you keep track of your loyalties?"

She ran her tongue along the inside of her mouth, as if she were preparing to spit in his face. He was ready for it. It might even cool down the flames in his cheek. Her eyes were defiant. "You don't have a high opinion of people, do you?"

"I've learned to be cautious."

She was close to him now and the hairs on his neck prickled once again. "Look, I can't make you believe Thomas isn't crooked. All I can do is tell you that he isn't and ask you to believe my word. I don't have to like it when you throw that back in my face and spit on him. But none of that means I feel any differently about him. Or you."

"And how do you feel about him?"

"Not the way I used to. We don't have a marriage; we have an arrangement. I attend parties with him. I speak to people he wants to impress and they like my attentions. I help secure deals for him. He lets me live my life without interfering, in return."

"You want me to believe that's how it is?"

"Yes. Because that's how it is." She held his gaze for a long moment. "Phoenix is more of a wife to him than I am."

"It's his priority?"

Her eyes melted into his. "Above everything else."

The same lock of her hair had fallen across her face. He pushed it back gently, his fingers trembling. "Do you still love him?"

"I don't know."

It had taken her a long moment to reply, but he knew that the truth was often hard to tell. And he could recognise honesty when he heard it. "I'm sorry if I was bastard."

"You were." Her eyes were still entrancing. "Do you always make it so hard for people to like you?"

He shook his head. "Not on purpose."

She leaned towards him and kissed where she has slapped him. When she spoke, it was in a whisper. "I'm not sorry for hitting you."

"I'm not sorry you did either."

"But I am sorry about how Thomas spoke to you."

He shrugged. "Forget it."

She fought for something else to say, but nothing came. Her eyes flickered across his face and he watched them move, shimmering like a mirage. Suddenly, he felt he needed his drink more than ever before. He snatched up the glass and threw some of the whisky down his throat. "Go home, Mrs Marriott. Do whatever it is you do all day."

She seemed determined to stay for a moment, but his face told her that it would be a mistake. She tapped her heel in mild indignation for a few seconds, before conceding defeat with a slight nod of her head. She smiled, if only to show that she was not insulted. "Will you call me?"

The swiftness of his reply surprised him. "Definitely."

"Good."

He watched her walk towards the door. She had opened it before he called her name. She turned back and looked at him over her shoulder.

"Does your husband know a man by the name of Jack Raeburn?" Priest asked.

She took almost no time to shake her head. "Not that I'm aware. Who is he?"

Priest shrugged. For the second time, he had seen no flicker of recognition in her face. "Have a nice afternoon, Mrs Marriott."

She held his gaze for longer than necessary and then, with a smile, she stepped out of the office and closed the door on him. He went back to the desk and collected together the photographs. He walked to the centre of the room, and kneeling down, he pulled up one of the floorboards. Beneath it was a safe. He turned the combination dial, this way and that way, until it clicked. Pulling open the door, he dropped the bundle of photographs inside, slammed it shut again, and twirled the dial several times. He replaced the floorboard and walked back to the desk and sat down. For a length of time he could not determine, he soothed himself with his loneliness.

CHAPTER TWELVE

It was a little after nine when Priest arrived at the house. Night had fallen, the sky almost perfect in its blackness. There seemed to be no clouds and he could see nothing of the stars. The wind was cold but not insistent, so that the black stillness seemed as unnatural as it was profound. It was the sort of night that was impossible to understand, the sort which is quiet enough for lovers and dark enough for killers.

The house was at the end of a grim terrace which ended in a high brick wall. The houses were narrow, the windows little more than slits in the walls, so that very little natural light could filter through them. The doors were drab, ill-painted, offering little security against trespass or the elements. There was the faint smell of coal on the air and the unmistakable stench of dying flames. The street was uninspired, its cobbles chipped and cracked, and its culmination in that morose, brick wall seemed strangely apt. The road had no destination. It went nowhere and it had no purpose. It was as if it spoke for most of this particular corner of London, one so lacking in purpose or value that even the Luftwaffe had not bothered to bomb it.

Priest knocked on the door of the furthest house. The sound was like a thunderclap in the silent darkness and Priest looked up at the windows of the neighbouring houses, expecting to see an inquisitive light in any one of them. Nothing happened. Priest felt a skeletal finger of unease trace its way up his spine. He pushed the door, trying the handle simultaneously, but he could not open it. A small bow window jutted out alongside the door, but he could see nothing through it. Even without the curtain being pulled across it from the inside, the grime on the pane was too thick to permit any glimpse into the room.

He stepped away from the door and looked up at the house. There was no sign of life, no trace of light. Separating the house from the wall at the end of the street was a tall, iron gate set into an archway which led down a narrow alleyway, leading to the back of the terraces. Pushing it gently, Priest found that it swung open. The alleyway smelled of spilt beer and urine, and under his feet, the delicate sound of cracking glass sang out like shrill gunshots, as he walked over discarded, broken bottles. Suddenly, he heard the hissing and screeching of warring cats from somewhere in the distance, as if his own sounds had disturbed them into anger. He moved further into the ink-black of the alley until he stepped out into a grim back yard, which was shared by all the properties which backed onto it.

He saw at once that the back door to the last house of the row was open. A small set of steps led up into the black entrance to the house. It wasn't right. Priest could have accepted that Jimmy Boyd had gone out, ignoring or forgetting their appointment, but he couldn't for a minute believe that he'd have gone anywhere and left the door wide open. Priest climbed the steps, placing his hands on the frame of the door, and he stepped into the darkness.

He could hear nothing. If the outside night had been quiet, the house was like the grave. He paused in the doorway for a moment, allowing his eyes to become accustomed to the gloom. Gradually, he saw that he was standing in a small kitchen. A sink was set under the window and he could see used plates and cutlery scattered inside it. A couple of mugs were placed on the draining board, the remnants of stewed tea still lining the bottom of each. The kitchen led into a small hallway, down which Priest walked cautiously, the naked floorboards creaking under his weight. He was conscious of the shadow of a flight of stairs to his right and the outlines of two doors set into the wall to his left. The shadows seemed to close in on him from either side, oppressing him, and he was suddenly aware of how claustrophobic the hallway was.

Priest pushed open the first door he came to and peered inside. He paused, reaching into his pockets for his matches. He struck one, the sudden hiss of phosphorous crackling in the silence and the glow of the flame illuminating a small section of the room. The room was like the aftermath of an explosion. Papers were scattered across the floor, boxes lay upturned, and files had been opened and discarded. A pile of newspapers had been knocked over. Priest knelt down and looked through them, noticing at once that they all contained articles written by Boyd himself. All about murder, theft, and corruption. Priest scanned a few of them, but they were ancient history. Nothing about Nancy Clayton. He stood up and looked around once more. A bookcase stood in the corner, but its contents had been pulled from the shelves and thrown across the floor. A table had been overturned and the contents of a glass ashtray had spilled out onto the threadbare carpet. Only a small armchair remained in place under the window, looking out onto the same backyard through which Priest had entered. He looked around the chaos. Whoever had been here had been searching for something. He wondered if they had found it.

The match fizzled down towards his fingers and he blew it out. He left the room and walked further down the corridor until he reached the second door. It was slightly open and Priest reached out to place his fingers against it. He glanced towards the stairs, but there was no movement from above him. He felt as if he could taste bile and blood in his throat, but he knew that it was only the bitter, twisted taste of fear. Slowly, he pushed the door and stepped inside the front room.

He saw it at once. It looked even worse in the flickering light of a second struck match. Lying in the centre of the room, silent and motionless, with the particular stillness which only death could have. It was on its front, the arms splayed out to the sides and the legs crossed, as if it had twisted when the knees had buckled and it had fallen to the ground. It was dressed cheaply, the hems of the trousers frayed, the shirt, once white, now a poor shade of grey. The shoes had been new several years ago, but they had long since given up trying to be respectable. The face was looking towards the small fireplace, so that the back of what had once been a head was facing the doorway. Now, it was nothing more than a violent mess of crimson, black, and shattered bone. By the side of it, there was a poker, stained with blood and brains as well as soot and flame. There was a smell in the room, but it was not the smell of the living. The room would never again smell of anything other than death.

Priest moved cautiously into the room. Striking another match, he knelt down by the corpse and lowered the orange oval of light to the face. It was staring blankly at him, seeing nothing, the eyes empty and motionless, like a doll's eyes. The face had that sickening, startled expression which Priest had seen too many times but never grown accustomed to. The mouth was parted in frightened surprise, a trail of blood tracing its way down the angle of the jaw from the wound on the back of the head. The areas of skin which were not tainted by blood were pale, unnaturally white, like the belly of a fish. For all its horror, there was something familiar about the corpse and it was only when he rose to his feet that Priest remembered. The dead thing at his feet had once been a man, the same man Priest had seen watching him outside Leonard Quayle's offices, the one who had run away from him and vanished into the crowd — the man Priest now knew as Jimmy Boyd. He hadn't gone out and he hadn't forgotten about their appointment. Jimmy Boyd had done neither of those things and he would never do anything again.

Priest glanced around, trying to look anywhere but at the battered body of Jimmy Boyd. Like the room next door, this one was in disarray. Papers were thrown about, the drawers of a sideboard pulled out and emptied, and the contents of a desk under the window had been scattered around. An ashtray had been toppled over and the trail of cigarette ends and grey dust took his eyes across the threadbare carpet of the room. There was a camera lying on its side, the flashlight broken and the back pulled open. No sign of any film. Priest walked over to the desk. It was an old fashioned, Victorian bureau, like the one he remembered his grandmother using. Its small drawers had been opened and the contents disturbed. He had no way of knowing whether anything had been taken, and in that moment of realisation, Priest felt powerless. Boyd had wanted to speak to him, but somebody had killed him before that could happen. Whether or not it was rational to feel some responsibility and obligation to Boyd, Priest did not know; but he felt it all the same. And yet, standing there in the darkness, he had no notion of how to honour it.

His eyes drifted over the desk, taking in the battered old typewriter, the notepad with its torn pages, the discarded pencils, the full ashtray, and the untasted glass of whisky to one side. There was nothing to tell any of the story of what happened. Whoever had been here had wanted something and they thought Boyd had it. They had murdered him for it, but whether they had found it or not was impossible to know. Priest took a pencil from his jacket pocket and poked around in the debris of the ransacked papers. It was a gesture, nothing more. Even if he knew what he was looking for, it was unlikely he would find it. He looked back at the body on the hearthrug, but it offered him no help. It was as useless as he felt himself.

Boyd had not called just any private detective and there were plenty of them. He had called Priest specifically. The first call from Boyd had come immediately after Priest had seen him outside Quayle's offices. No coincidence. Priest had thought Boyd was following him, but what if that was wrong? What if it had been Quayle who Boyd was originally interested in and that was why he was at the offices in the Strand that day? If so, Priest's presence there would have been a sheer fluke. The idea was impossible to ignore. Boyd was a journalist. If the story he was working on had intruded into Priest's own investigation, or the other way around, it would be natural that Boyd would want to compare notes. Priest thought back to that first phone call: Boyd had said something about helping each other. Suddenly, in the pit of his stomach, Priest wanted to know what Boyd had to tell him. He wanted to know very badly, almost as if his life depended on it. Just as Boyd's life had done.

For a moment, he lost himself in his thoughts. He looked down at the shattered head of Jimmy Boyd, almost visualising all the secrets the man had kept in there spilling out onto the carpet. His eyes snapped shut. He was surprised to find that his fingers had balled into fists and his breathing had become fierce, like the snorts of a cornered animal. He opened his eyes with a flash of determination. There were things which needed to be done and it was for Priest to do them. He sighed heavily and took one more look at the devastation of Boyd's head. He moved away from the desk and walked around the body, out into the hallway. There was a telephone mounted on the wall. Snatching up the receiver, he telephoned for the police.

Justice had to begin somewhere.

CHAPTER THIRTEEN

Frank Darrow had been assigned the case. They had been the same rank, detective inspector, and they had worked together on several investigations before Priest had walked away from the force. His reasons for doing so were not something he discussed with anybody, but nor were they of any interest to Darrow. He had never questioned Priest about it, and as far as Priest was aware, he bore no malice over it. Priest had been grateful for both, but had never said as much.

They were standing in the hallway while the usual processes of a murder investigation were commenced in the small, tragic parlour of the house. Darrow was a big man, but the muscle which had helped him win several amateur boxing titles was now turning to bulge. His shoulders were still broad and his hands were still large enough to do permanent damage, but the strain on his shirt and coat suggested that his once legendary speed and nimble footing had deserted him. His past was written in his nose and ears, swollen with success and broken with defeat, but nobody would ever mention them to him. Just in case. His eyes were dark, so that the sneer of his lips seemed all the more dangerous. He was smoking a cigarette, which he had lit with the dying embers of a previous one.

"And you don't know who he is?" he was asking.

Priest shook his head. "I know his name and address, but that's it."

"But he called you?"

"Twice."

"And he asked you to come here tonight?"

"Have you forgotten everything I've said already?"

Darrow scoffed. "Don't make me laugh so hard I piss myself. I'm just trying to get the picture straight. You all right with that?"

Priest shrugged. "It's straight enough, Frank. Boyd called me, asked to meet, and he called again to make sure I hadn't forgotten about him."

"He was keen to speak to you. Calling twice, like that."

"Maybe."

Darrow looked down the corridor into the small kitchen at the back of the house. "You got in through there?"

"The back door was open."

"No sign of a break in?"

Priest shook his head. "Like I say, the door was open, but that might not mean anything."

"Killer gets out the same way?"

"He must have done. Crept up on Boyd and took him by surprise."

Darrow turned to face him. "Or Boyd let him in."

"Unlikely. Boyd had arranged to meet me, hadn't he? He wasn't likely to have arranged to meet two people at the same time. The killer was here by chance."

Darrow was frowning. "It could have been that way. Unless…"

Priest laughed, a scornful rasp of amusement. "Don't even think about it, Frank. I didn't kill him and you know it."

Darrow shrugged, but there was nothing conciliatory in his manner. Priest said nothing more. Instead, he watched Darrow pace the hallway, his hands in his pockets and his second chin on his breast. "He was a journalist. You know that?"

"I'd guessed," Priest said. "There's a load of newspapers in the back room with his name all over them."

"What would a journalist want with you?"

"I don't know." Priest held the detective's glare.

"Try again. And don't disappoint."

Priest's eyes did not move. "I don't know. He didn't tell me. Maybe he was about to, but somebody scrambled the back of his skull first."

Darrow was tugging an earlobe. "Could you tell how long he had been dead?"

"I'm not a doctor."

"But you've been around death, Priest. Give me some of that experience."

"An hour? A little longer, perhaps. Ask your quack."

"I will." Darrow sniffed and smoked his cigarette for a moment. "Any earlier and you might have seen the killer."

Priest wasn't inclined to think too deeply about the possibility. Darrow was watching him closely, and in a flicker of inspiration, a thought seemed to occur to the detective. "How did Boyd get your phone number?"

"I'm in the directory," said Priest.

Darrow rolled his eyes. "How'd he know your name to search for it?"

Priest heaved his shoulders and sighed, suddenly tired. "No idea."

"You've never seen him before?"

"Only once."

"Where was that?"

"Outside a solicitor's office." Priest's glare dared Darrow to ask any more.

The inspector smiled. "Which solicitor's office?"

"One connected to a case I'm working on."

"What case?"

Priest put his hands in his pockets. "Missing person."

Darrow took a step towards him. "I don't need to tell you about withholding information in a murder investigation, Priest. You've not been off the job long enough to forget it."

"You'd need to tell me about it if I was doing it."

Darrow smoked heavily and blew the smoke into Priest's face. "This Boyd character wanted to speak to you about something, right? Don't tell me you don't think whatever it was is linked to this case of yours."

Priest conceded the point. "All right, I won't tell you that. It's a reasonable assumption. And it might explain how he got my name and number. If he wanted to know who I was and what I was doing at the solicitors' offices, it wouldn't take a big bucket of brains for him to think to follow me. Maybe he did just that all the way back to my office."

"And the phone directory did the rest." Darrow nodded. "Could be. You never noticed him following you?"

"No."

"He must have been good." Darrow's voice suggested he was marginally impressed.

"Or I was careless." Priest shrugged. "Either way, I didn't see him."

Darrow pointed his cigarette in Priest's direction. "Except that one time."

Priest nodded. "None of it changes the fact that I don't know what Boyd was going to say. And you've no reason to think that whatever it was got him killed. He was a journalist. There could be a dozen reasons for someone to kill him and none of them anything to do with me."

"Or your case, for that matter?" Darrow chewed his lip for a moment, watching Priest give no reply. "If you find out that your missing person and this hack's murder are linked, you come to me first, Priest. We clear?" He jabbed a blunt finger into Priest's chest.

"Don't worry about me, Frank. You concentrate on finding out whatever the killer was looking for. Maybe that'll save us both a lot of time and trouble."

"You don't think this mess was just his natural habitat?" Darrow had brushed past Priest and was staring at the upturned drawers and discarded papers in the murder room.

"Some of it might have been," Priest said, "but not all of it. Someone was searching for something."

Darrow looked back over his shoulder with a less than polite smile. "You any idea what it might be?" He waited for Priest to shake his head before continuing. "Don't worry, Priest. We'll find it."

It was not a dismissal, but Darrow had seemed to lose interest in him. He was watching the activity in the room now, from where the sound of cameras was becoming more insistent. Priest watched men walk to and from the room, trying but failing to overhear whispered conversations between some of them and Darrow. In the middle of the process of murder, Priest stood motionless and alone. None of it was any of his business; it was a job for professionals. A man who was not an official detective had no right to be there. He had keyholes to look through and lost dogs to find. If that wasn't what they were thinking, it was how they were behaving and it was impossible for Priest not to receive the message loud and clear. He waited for another ten minutes only to spite them, and then he slowly and silently walked out of the house.

Outside, it had just begun to rain. He pulled his coat tighter around the lower half of his face and lowered the brim of his hat over his eyes. The alleyway to the side of the house still smelled of urine. He stopped caring. It was better than the smell of murder.

CHAPTER FOURTEEN

The package was delivered on the following morning.

Priest had slept badly, his dreams familiarly vivid and disturbing, so that, when he woke, his body ached and his legs were as heavy as concrete pillars and twice as numb. His shoulders burned, his eyes prickled with unrest, and his head was nothing but a crown of thorns. He took a moment to come to his senses. He was only marginally surprised to find that he was in the office, which explained much of how he felt. He must have slept with his head on the desk, leaning forward in his chair, and his spine was suffering the consequences. The empty bottle of whisky was lying on its side, the glass next to it still containing the last mouthful which he had not been able to drink before he had passed out. And his head was suffering those consequences.

He stood up slowly and walked into the small kitchen to throw water in his face. He drained a couple of glasses of the stuff with an animal fury. He looked at himself in the mirror above the sink, as if seeing himself for the first time. His eyes were dimmed, their blue somehow diluted, and his fair hair had fallen over one of them. He brushed it back over his forehead with his hand. His cheeks were coarse with the lack of a razor and so sallow that they made the scarlet rim of the eyes all the uglier. He rolled his neck for a few moments, hoping that something approaching humanity might return to him. But he felt nothing and no amount of water from the tap could wash away the memory of the back of Boyd's head and the smell of death. He remembered walking home in the rain, so he must have got back to the office cold and wet. That would have been the reason for the first drink: soothing warmth. The previous night's events would have led to the second, third, and the rest.

He shuffled back to the office, conscious of a knocking on the glass panel of the door. One of the commissionaires from the offices below greeted him genially as he opened the door. The man's smile never left his face.

"Morning, Mr Priest," he said. "Package for you."

Priest took the envelope from him. It was large, stuffed with something, and addressed to him in black, simple capitals. They meant nothing to him and there was nothing particular to identify the writer. "Thanks, George."

"Fun night, was it?"

Priest managed a smile. "Every night's a circus, George."

He sat back down at his desk and tore open the envelope. He cleared a space on the blotter in front of him and tipped out the contents. More photographs, dozens of them, but not of Nancy Clayton this time. It was difficult to tell what several of them were at all. Some were so blurred as to be meaningless, little more than flashes of white against black, with indistinct outlines of what might have been hands or faces. Others had more focus, but were no more informative: snapshots of backs of heads, crossed legs, and close embraces. Priest thought back to the photographs of Nancy Clayton at *The Midnight Pearl,* still securely locked in the safe under the floorboards. He didn't need to look at them again to know that they had purpose, some of the subjects posing for the lens, knowing that their photographs were being taken. In these others, there was no sense of any such complicity or consent. Priest's eyes narrowed. He was suddenly unable to dismiss the idea that these second images had been taken secretly. It would explain the haphazard, chaotic nature of them. They were taken quickly, in a brief moment of safety, without posing or deliberation. There was an almost palpable element of risk to them.

Some were clearer than others, but it was not necessarily a blessing. In a few, but still too many, he could see what he thought were naked mattresses and rudimentary bedsheets, legs stretched out, with dark shapes between them, and the occasional arm flung hopelessly out to the side; long hair fell down naked backs and heads were turned away from the camera, with men's legs parted in front of them and encouraging hands on the base of the skulls; numbed, doped, almost sightless eyes of girls staring ahead of them, their cheeks against those same mattresses or sunken pillows, their lips hanging loosely open at one side, with men's hands on the sides of those frozen, helpless faces. Priest could seem to hear the noises which inevitably accompanied the images: the porcine grunting, the moans of sordid pleasure, mixing with the groans of nauseating pain.

He began to flick through them with increasing speed, so desperate to be at the end that he almost overlooked their sudden change of topic. Now, he was not looking at filthy rooms any more, but at open spaces. Trees and snow-tipped mountains in the distance, what seemed like desolate areas of land in the foreground. Some showed the bleakness of the surrounding area in detail, the sense of isolation so complete that the idea of any habitation seemed impossible; others showed the imposing gates of a property of some sort, set into the bleak and unforgiving stone of a long wall, beyond which nothing of the building itself could be seen. A single pathway, leading to the gates, cut through the surrounding emptiness. Now, Priest found himself looking at figures in the distance, indistinct, too far away to have any meaning, but with an overall impression of abandonment. They were standing in groups, no signs of any movement from them, as if they were the soul of whatever place it was. A handful of the pictures showed glimpses of what might have been sunken eyes, bared teeth, and hollow cheeks. These closer images showed what might have been people, but they were blurred and uncertain, so that Priest could not be sure of what he was seeing. He had an impression of propaganda images of places of death which no sane person could ever have conceived. But there was no trace of any Nazi soldiers in these pictures. No gun barrels, no proud smiles over exterminated women and children. Whatever this place was, it was something else, even if it was no less evil for it.

And yet, strangely, the remainder of the photographs were harmless. Abandoned buildings, derelict terraced streets, what seemed to be disused offices. Some had been sold and the name of the estate agents concerned, Burke & Halliwell, stirred a memory in Priest's mind. These pictures had none of the sense of danger behind them of the others, but they had been taken at night, which might suggest that they were still part of some sort of secret endeavour. Priest flicked through them quickly, almost casually, finding none of them of any interest, until he recognised one of the buildings. In the gloom, it seemed even more desolate than when he had seen it, but there was no doubt that it was the same set of rooms to which Dorothy Quayle had directed him in Southwark, where he had found Nancy Clayton's angel pendant.

He leaned back in his chair, trying to force his brain to focus. Two sets of photographs, one found in Nancy Clayton's bedroom and the other delivered in the post. Some pictures taken openly and some apparently covertly. Priest was no expert, but he was willing to bet his grandfather's gold watch that the pictures were skilled, but not professional. The work of a gifted amateur. It was too much of a coincidence to assume that two such photographers were lingering in the fogs of this case. For Priest's money, there was only one man with a camera and all the photographs Priest now held were taken by that man.

Priest stood up and gazed out of the window, recalling suddenly the broken camera which he had spotted in Boyd's front room. Amid the strewn papers and the spilled ashtray, there had been the camera with the shattered flashlight, to which he had paid no attention and which now would be part of Frank Darrow's evidence. Priest remembered that there was no film in it and he looked back at the photographs, wondering if they were the product of that missing film. He could imagine Boyd's killer finding the camera, pulling it apart and finding no film inside, then tossing it to one side in anger, breaking the bulb of the flash. He could imagine the killer searching for the photographs which had caused people to start dying. Priest had the bitter taste of fear at the back of his throat, all traces of his hangover now displaced by panic.

Did the broken camera in Boyd's house mean that he had taken these pictures? Not necessarily. And yet, Priest felt sure that Boyd had sent them to him. Which meant, perhaps, that Boyd knew he had to get rid of them. Priest looked at the postmark on the envelope: dated yesterday. He sat down slowly, arranging events in their proper order. Boyd had seen Priest at Quayle's offices and he had set up a meeting for the following night. Sometime during that period, Boyd had felt compelled to post these treacherous photographs to Priest. It was easy to see a reason for that. Something had happened which convinced Boyd that it would be dangerous to be caught with them. Impossible to say what, but Boyd had got rid of them by sending them to someone he thought could be trusted to keep them secret until he could reclaim them. Boyd could not have known that he would never live long enough to reclaim them.

Priest picked up the envelope and crumpled it in his fists. Immediately, his senses were alive with curiosity. One corner of the envelope was not yielding to his grip. Something hard, unforgiving, was announcing its presence. The envelope had not only contained the photographs, but something else, which had not fallen out initially and which he had missed. Priest shook the envelope again and it fell out onto the desk.

A small square of cardboard, stained with and smelling of alcohol. A beermat, advertising the quality and taste of Burton's Brewery. Priest knew the brewer and its product, but his attention was fixed on neither. He was looking at the crude pencil drawing of a gallows, a matchstick man suspended from it, the noose emphasised around the thin neck. Under the gallows was a single word, obviously a name: Costello. Beneath it, an address. Turning over the mat, he found another name: Jenny. No address, no telephone number. Neither the names nor the address meant anything to him, but the drawing did. Priest knew what it signified immediately. A large number of pubs in London served Burton's beer, and Priest had been thrown out of most of them, but only one of them was called *The Hanged Man*.

Priest leaned back in his chair and ran his hand down his face, pulling his lower lip between his finger and thumb. His eyes flickered over the photographs and the beermat, whilst his mind raced between connections and speculations. They seemed to drown him, like a swamp whose grip was relentless and suffocating. He pulled the telephone towards him, as if it were a broken branch of a tree which he could use to keep himself out of the mire. He shoved the receiver under his jaw and dialled quickly.

"You got news for me, Priest?" asked Frank Darrow.

"Tell me about *The Hanged Man*."

Darrow's voice was full of lead. "You know about it."

"Am I remembering it wrong?"

"Not if you're remembering it was where Clem Murnaugh was last seen."

Priest screwed his eyes closed. "That's how I'm remembering it."

"Are you trying to say that there's a connection between Boyd's murder and Clem Murnaugh?"

Priest bit his lip. "I'm not trying to say anything, Frank. I'm just asking a question."

Darrow's voice hardened. "Listen, Priest, if you've got something on Murnaugh, you need to tell us, even if it isn't connected to Boyd's death. Don't hold it behind your back like a birthday surprise."

Priest opened his eyes. "It's nothing, Frank. If it stops being nothing, I'll call you."

"Don't dance with me, Priest. Nobody has seen Murnaugh for almost three months. If you know where he is, you tell us. And I mean if you know where he is, alive *or* dead."

"What makes you think I know where he is if the police can't find him or his body?"

Darrow snorted. "Is there a connection between Murnaugh and Boyd?"

Priest glanced towards the ceiling. "Not that I'm aware of, Frank."

"Then why are you asking about Murnaugh?"

"I don't know myself."

"What did I say about dancing with me?" hissed Darrow. But Priest had dropped the receiver into the cradle.

Clem Murnaugh.

Priest didn't know much about him, but he knew that Murnaugh had been an associate of Jack Raeburn's. The same Jack Raeburn who owned *The Midnight Pearl*, where Nancy Clayton had danced and dined, before she had likely died in a deserted flat in Southwark. Priest thought about Clem Murnaugh, who had disappeared one night, after drinking in *The Hanged Man.* Nobody knew what had happened to him either, although most suspected murder. Except no corpse had ever been found. Clem and Nancy, both surely dead, but no trace of either corpse.

That was a pattern and not a coincidence, not to Priest. If Jimmy Boyd, certainly dead, had sent these photographs to Priest, he had sent the Burton's beermat too. The drawing might not be proof of a link between Murnaugh and the photographs, but it was close enough, no matter what Priest had said to Darrow. Boyd was telling Priest that Murnaugh had taken the photographs. All of them: the sexual abuse, the strange place in the mountains, and Nancy Clayton in *The Midnight Pearl.*

Priest growled. He packed the photographs back into the envelope and walked over to the centre of the office. He pulled up the floorboard and opened the safe. He dropped the envelope inside and watched them snuggle up with the ones from Nancy's bedroom. They would be safe in there, but Priest didn't feel any better for it. He didn't have the security of a metal door and a combination dial. He walked back to the desk and perched on the edge of it, rubbing his neck. He was thinking about nothing else other than three dead people. Three murdered people, very possibly.

Three people who were killed because of the photographs which he now had in his possession. Alex Priest had no intention of being the fourth.

CHAPTER FIFTEEN

The restaurant was in Soho, the sort of place where a reservation could be granted or denied depending on a man's face or his wallet. The furnishings were extravagant rather than elegant: scarlet velvet, polished brass, and varnished wood, as if the taste of the place was reserved only for the food. And that, like everything else, was proud to be rich. The restaurant seemingly had never heard of rationing, as if the war had never happened or had managed to mind its own business so that the milk wouldn't curdle. British Restaurants, state food halls set up to feed people starved by the effects of the war, were unknown here. Priest could almost taste and smell the money when he walked into the place, but none of it was anything other than bitter and sour to him. People watched him as he walked through the restaurant, all of them hoping that standards had not been permitted to fall to this extent. They remained as thoughts; nobody would have converted them to words. Not in Jack Raeburn's favourite restaurant. A waiter attempted to block Priest's way, but the mention of Raeburn's name had a magical effect. The waiter bowed and requested that Priest follow him. As he passed the tables set into the front portion of the place, conversations were in turn resumed and halted, Priest feeling like nothing less than a pariah.

The back of the restaurant was separated from the rest by a pair of velvet drapes, tied with gold rope to brass hooks, set into two pillars on either side of an archway. It was so luxurious that it was cheap. The lighting was lowered, so that even a lunchtime sitting could feel like dinner. There were only booths in this part of the restaurant, set on either side of a tiled, chessboard floor. Priest's eyes skimmed over the diners, his lips curling into a sneer. He didn't recognise all of them, but he knew enough: judges, barristers, senior detectives, counsellors, union officials. Priest might be a pariah, but at least he wasn't one of their kind.

Two men were standing like sentries on either side of the furthest booth. They weren't carved out of stone, but they might as well have been. They glared at the waiter as he approached, but their eyes were soon shifting to Priest, their stare hardening. In unison, the two men shifted their weight on their feet, unclasping their hands and placing them purposefully by their sides. The waiter bowed and walked away.

Raeburn was still eating what must have been a prime steak. On either side of him were two girls, a blonde and a brunette. The brunette looked aloof, as if she was uninterested in everything around her. It was the blonde who gave away the trick. She wasn't interested in anything either, but only because she couldn't see anything. She wasn't there; she was somewhere else entirely, somewhere Priest never wanted to go. He looked at the girl's forearms, but he could see no signs of a needle. She probably injected the filth somewhere far more private. The blonde had her head almost on Raeburn's shoulder; the brunette was slowly massaging between his legs, almost without knowing she was doing it. Two men sat next to her, one of them trying his best not to be caught staring at what she was doing. He would enjoy reliving it for himself later, Priest thought. His companion was glaring up at Priest, as were both of the other two men sitting opposite, alongside the blonde.

In the centre of it all, sitting in the heart of the booth, was Jack Raeburn. He was short, but his bulk, which he wore with style, made him seem taller. The suits were never strained, the collars of the shirts never looked too tight. Priest had never seen him not wearing a suit, as if it was a uniform, a statement of his pride and position. The hair was dark, unnaturally so, and slicked back from his forehead with an almost vampiric neatness. There was no doubt that it was fake. His eyebrows were similarly black, and just as unnatural, being painted on with thick make up, so that they gave his appearance a grotesque, faintly started appearance. Why he felt the need to emphasise his brows in this way was not known and nobody would have ever felt able to ask, but rumours of an attack with fire had circulated for a long time. The false hair on his head and above his eyes seemed to bear out the theory. Those eyes, peering out from below the monstrosities of the brows, matched the darkness of the hair, but it had often struck Priest that there seemed to be a slight, almost imperceptible, shade of red about them, as if they had soaked up all of the blood he had spilled. He seldom blinked, in case doing so would cause some of that blood to flow out, like leaked secrets and bitter betrayals.

"You don't mind if I finish my lunch, do you, Priest?" Raeburn said in between chewing the meat.

"Be my guest."

Raeburn grinned. "You're *my* guest. I own the place. Have a bite yourself. On the house."

Priest did not reply. A noise from behind him caused him to look over his shoulder. Harry Wolfe had risen from the booth opposite Raeburn's. Priest had not noticed him as he had approached. He hadn't even smelt him. "Hello, Wolfe."

"Pleased to see you, Mr Priest. Would you like to take a seat?"

"No, thanks." He turned back to Raeburn. "I won't be staying long."

Raeburn was looking at him, as if contemplating how easy it would be to have him killed. "You're not looking good these days, if I may say so, Priest. War didn't agree with you."

"Did it agree with anybody?"

"The trick is to take the rough with the smooth."

"Is that what you did, Jack?"

"I've always been able to adapt. It's how a man survives." He shook his head. "You don't look as if you adapted well at all. Maybe you miss the routine."

"Of what?"

"Authority."

Priest laughed silently. "Not likely."

Raeburn returned his smile. "I hear you blame them for what happened to you in the war."

Did Raeburn know about what he had suffered? Priest, not wanting to believe it, found enough of his voice to speak. "Meaning what?"

Raeburn shrugged. "Meaning there's a reason you stopped being a copper as soon as the war was over and became... whatever it is you are now. All I'm saying is, maybe you got sick of being part of the establishment."

Priest looked around him, at the judges, the cops, and the lawyers. "Seems I'm right back into the middle of authority in here."

Raeburn laughed. It seemed genuine. "Just customers, Priest. Some of them at my invitation. Which, incidentally, you're not. Unless you take me up on the offer of that free lunch."

Suddenly, Priest became aware of Wolfe behind him once more, closer this time. He didn't feel the barrel of a gun against his spine, or a blade at his ribs, but he was keenly aware of the threat of either, or both. Raeburn had finished eating, shuffled off the two girls, and was leaning forward, his hands clasped on the table. "How'd you find me here, Priest?"

Priest shrugged. "A few words in the rights ears."

"Which ears?"

"I'm not saying."

"Why?" Raeburn sounded offended.

"You might want to cut them off."

There was a moment. The consequences of the remark could have been one thing or another. Laughter or pain. There were no other options, and in that moment which passed, Priest did not know which to expect. Raeburn's face was impassive, but in the end, he broke into a laugh. Even that was not without the prospect of danger.

"You're a funny kid, Priest." The *kid* was an insult. Raeburn had no more than a few years on Priest. "So, you found me. What do you want from me after all these years?"

Priest did not reply immediately. He had placed his hands in his trouser pockets, having pushed back the tails of his overcoat; now, he slowly pulled them out, in case he was going to have to move swiftly and use his fists.

"I want to know what happened to Clem Murnaugh."

He spoke the words as blandly as he could. They contained no threat, no suspicion, and no accusation. They were simply a statement of detached, undeniable fact. They were nothing to be feared, nor were they cause for retribution. Raeburn was silent, however, although the quiet was somehow not peaceful. He seemed to be expecting Priest to say something more, but nothing came. Priest had nothing else to say for the moment.

Raeburn leaned back in his seat. "Is it true you're a private detective now, Priest?"

The question threw him, but he didn't show it. "Yes."

A smile broke across Raeburn's lips. The blonde shared it, but she had no idea what was funny. The brunette carried on taking no notice of anything. She was happy being nowhere.

"Don't tell me Murnaugh had family and they want to know what happened to him, so they've hired you," said Raeburn. "Is that what this is?"

Priest felt as if razor blades were beneath his feet. "Maybe."

"His family are your clients?"

"I don't reveal the identity of my clients." Priest placed his hands back in his pockets. If a storm was going to break, it would have done so by now. "Who the client is doesn't matter. And it doesn't alter what I want to know."

Raeburn chuckled to himself. "Nobody knows what happened to Clem Murnaugh."

"Somebody must do."

"Meaning me?"

Priest inclined his head. "I didn't say that."

Raeburn's smile refused to fade. "Murnaugh liked a drink. Putting it mildly. He could knock back a bottle and still throw a dart into a bullseye. One night, he drinks more than even he can handle. He walks it off, loses his feet, falls in the river. That's it."

"You think that's what happened?"

"Tell me something better."

Priest knew it was a trap, but he didn't try to avoid it. He had come here to walk into it. "Someone murdered him."

Raeburn laughed, the blonde following his lead, but still without any idea why. The men sitting at the table broke into grins and laughs, too. The sentries at the booth remained impassive. Priest looked over his shoulder. Harry Wolfe was not laughing. His eyes were flickering like bat's wings, a muscle in his cheek pounding like a pumpjack. No smiles for Harry Wolfe. To Priest, without question, he was assessing a threat.

Priest looked back at Raeburn. "Is it a stupid idea?"

Raeburn leaned forward, a finger tapping on the surface of the table. "Why would anybody want to kill a slug like Murnaugh?"

"He was one of yours, Jack."

Raeburn closed his index finger and thumb until they were almost touching. "Little, tiny cog in the wheel, Priest. He meant nothing. An errand boy. If somebody was going to try to hurt me, they wouldn't kill Murnaugh. I'd hardly notice he was gone."

It was said with an authority which made it almost impossible to refute. "What if he wasn't killed to hurt you?"

"Why, then?"

"To protect you?" Priest could sense Wolfe take a step closer to him.

But Raeburn remained amused by it all. "From what?"

Priest hesitated. There was still no barrel or blade behind him, but the razors under his feet were getting sharper. The hairs on the back of his neck raised in caution and he became suddenly aware that this was not his moment. He realised now how impetuous it had been to force this confrontation. What had he expected? That Raeburn would succumb to the effects of Priest's instincts and conjectures? That he would be intimidated by a private detective with a few ideas? Except that Priest had more than a few ideas. He had the photographs. But without knowing what they proved, they were useless as a weapon against Raeburn. Mention of them now could only be dangerous.

But Priest could not allow himself to surrender completely. "I still think he was killed, Jack."

Raeburn nodded. "Fine. You make sure you find out who did it and I'll gladly pay your fee."

"Why?"

"He was one of my boys, like you said. Not much of one, but still one of them. Think of it as helping out his family." There was nothing for Priest to say to that. He looked behind him, finding that Wolfe had moved away and sat back down in the opposite booth. Raeburn sat back. "Anything else, Priest?"

"Leonard Quayle. Ever heard that name?"

"No."

If it was a lie, it was well told, but Raeburn was a master. Priest offered no reaction. "Nancy Clayton?"

Raeburn shook his head. "Random names, Priest. What have they got to do with me?"

"They were both customers at *The Midnight Pearl.*" Priest smiled. "You recognise that name, yes?"

Raeburn raised a finger and began to massage his temple. "Are you asking me if I know two people who might have once gone to one of my clubs?"

"Yes." Priest made no apology for it.

The voice from behind him seemed to come from nowhere. "What were you doing at the club a couple of days ago, Mr Priest?"

Priest looked across to Wolfe. "Just following some ideas."

"About these people?" Wolfe's eyes slowly rose to meet Priest's. "I forget the names."

"Leonard Quayle and Nancy Clayton. I haven't forgotten the names."

Raeburn slammed his hand down on the table. It sounded like a gunshot. "Whatever they're called, we don't know these people. Now, is that all?"

Priest shrugged. "They were at the club, Jack. Together, as a couple."

"So what?"

"Quayle is married."

Raeburn held out his hands, showing his upturned palms. "Again, so what? It's a matter for him and his wife."

"The girl has disappeared. A married man is having an affair with her, they go to your club, and she vanishes."

"Coincidence." Raeburn was smiling, but his eyes were as deadly as bullets. "There's nothing in it, Priest. Now, are you going to have that free lunch or not?"

Priest shook his head. "I don't think so."

He made a move to leave, heading back to the archway with its lurid, velvet drapes. He had taken only a couple of steps before he stopped, raising his hand to his mouth and tugging at the bottom lip. He turned on his heel and walked back towards Raeburn's table. Wolfe rose and crossed the floor to meet him, but Priest took no notice. To him, in that moment, there was only he and Raeburn in the room at all.

"One last thing, Jack," he said. "If the names Quayle and Clayton don't mean anything, what about Costello?"

If Priest had expected an explosion to follow the grenade he had thrown into the room, it was not to come. There might not have been any blast, but there was something. Despite his impassive, cold exterior, Raeburn's twitch of an eye showed that a nerve had been sliced somewhere inside him. He rose from the table of the booth and pointed toward Priest. The eyes were alive with violence, but the voice was benign, almost benevolent. And all the worse for it.

"You're starting to bore me, Priest," he said. "There's nothing for you here, not even that free lunch. Now, Mr Wolfe will show you out."

The pain was immediate. A sharp, malignant spark of electricity flashed across his kidneys, arching his back and snapping back his head. One of the two motionless sentries was now active and he took a step forward, his fist curling upwards through the air, causing a second flash of agony in Priest's stomach. A different type of pain to that in his back, but no less effective. He felt his arms being pulled backwards suddenly, without warning, and the sentry who had hit him was now behind him, his arms locking Priest's in place. The movement had been so swift, so smooth, Priest had not noticed it. The second guard was now in front of him. With a similar, equally devastating speed, his fist had connected with Priest's jaw. Once, knocking his head to the left; twice, without any time for recovery, and with such force that Priest's knees buckled.

And then, he was moving. No, being moved. They were dragging him away, towards the back of the building, so that none of the more innocent customers in the front would have their lunches disturbed. Priest's feet could barely move of their own accord, so he let them fall limp, scraping along the floor as they dragged him through the rear corridors of the place. They seemed to drag him for miles until, at last, they stopped at a dirty, greasy door. Wolfe pulled it open and Priest could see the alleyway behind the restaurant. For good measure, one of the sentries took Priest by his lapels and slammed him against the wall. A further blow into the pit of his stomach forced out whatever air was still left in his lungs, so that he was little more than a bundle of loose, cheap clothes.

"Throw out the rubbish," said Wolfe, with no suggestion in his voice that he thought it was a joke.

They obeyed. Priest landed on the cobbles of the alleyway with a sound which struck him as nasty, but he did not seem to feel any pain. He was too numb now for pain. He lay still for a moment, allowing his senses returned to him. He could feel the cold wet of a puddle against his face and the coarseness of discarded newspapers and cardboard under his fingers. In his nostrils was the smell of old vegetables, cooking meat, and urine.

Somewhere in the distance, he could hear motor vehicles. Above all, he could feel the dull throbbing of malice in his back, legs, and face. He spat out a ball of blood and pulled himself to his feet.

He took a moment to catch his breath, steadying himself against the wall. He coughed up another small pellet of blood and ran his fingers around his mouth. No teeth were loose. He breathed in, deeply but carefully, and allowed his lungs to become accustomed to the idea of working once again. Then, he walked away from the alleyway and the restaurant. Back to the office and the bottle.

Still the best medicine he knew.

CHAPTER SIXTEEN

The address which Boyd had written on the beermat was by the sea, on the northern side of the Thames Estuary. Priest had never been impressed with places like this. He had never felt any sort of affinity with the human desire to lie on the sands or swim in the seas. He was urban, a creature of the city, and the appeal of the open spaces of beaches, the salty smell of shingle, and the vast expanse of the ocean was alien to him. In his mind, it was associated with holidays with his father and sister. Helen was happy to play on the beach, building castles of sand and paddling by the water's edge. For Priest, each day was one step closer to the return home, away from stewed tea and scones of marble. The exposure to the elements, the openness of the beaches, and the rolling dunes had only seemed to emphasise his personal isolation. Perhaps it might have been different if his mother had been with them, so that he wouldn't have had to worry all the time that his father was as lonely as him. To Priest, every holiday was just another reason to curse that woman for leaving them.

His father had let her go. He hadn't begged, pleaded, or argued. Priest had never understood why, but he could never recall a complaint from him, never a tear shed, no criticism or curse against that woman who had left him alone with the two children. If there was any of that, and Priest supposed that there must have been, it was done in private, so that the children never saw or heard. Priest could remember his sister, Helen, two years older than him, asking the question once. At the time, Priest wondered whether Helen understood more than he did, as if age could grant some deeper understanding of what had happened, and more cruelly, why. Helen had asked when mummy would be coming back. Priest's father, his voice controlled but lowered, had replied only after a pause: "Eat your dinner, girl." *Mummy*: the word had never seemed appropriate to Priest. She had never been one to him. To him, she was only that woman who had gone out and never come back. He knew he would never be able to forgive her, despite what Helen now wanted and hoped for, and he knew that he never wanted to see that woman again.

"Whatever she did," Helen had said the last time they had spoken, "she must have had reasons and I think it's time we listened to what they were."

"No."

"She's still our mother, Alex."

Not to Priest. To him, she was nothing more than that woman who walked out. Who was never there on birthdays or at Christmas, who was never there when he or Helen was ill, who was never there when they woke in the night after yet another nightmare, and who was never there to play in the sand or the sea in towns like this one.

Except that this particular town, ravaged by the war, seemed even bleaker than those of Priest's childhood holidays. Its shops, which might once have sold ice cream and novelties, were boarded up; guest houses were abandoned to decay; a major hotel on the main esplanade of the town was in bombed ruins. The remnants of wedge-shaped battlements, topped with coiled barbed wire, still lined the front. Kiosks and beach cafes were still boarded up, as if life could never return to normal and opening up was nothing more than a clamour for a bygone era which could never be recaptured. Some shops had forced themselves back into life, but Priest's overall impression was of a town so battered and defeated that it could never resurrect itself. He was unable to prevent Thomas Marriott's slogan from crashing into his thoughts: *Bombed, bitter, and bankrupt.*

A swift search of the telephone directories had given Priest the full name of Patrick Costello, to go with the address on the beermat. It was one of several bungalows in a small crescent, set above the town. The day wasn't warm, but Priest still had to remove his coat and jacket as he made the climb up the hill from the front to the housing estate. There were perhaps six or seven bungalows, each set back from the road and hiding behind neatly trimmed hedges. There was the clear suggestion of money, so that Priest felt as if he could smell it over the scent of the sea and freshly cut grass. And yet, there was something artificial about the arrangement, as if the affluent tranquillity of the estate somehow had been protected from the horrors of the war, not simply by their distance from the main town, but by their wealth. He took a moment to savour the quiet, allowing himself to believe for a short while that the world was gentle. It was easy to do there.

Unlike the streets below, the war seemed a long time ago on that crescent. But it was just another false impression, more of the fakery suggested by these quaint houses in their ideal gardens. The reality was the boarded-up hotels, the abandoned shops, and the beaches of barbed wire.

Priest walked up the small garden path and knocked on the door. It took several further knocks to elicit any response. Eventually, the door was pulled open by a fraction of an inch and a single eye peered out from behind it. The rims were reddened and the whites had faded to the colour of stale milk. It took a moment for the eye to rest on Priest and he doubted it could focus on his face. He had seen the eyes of enough drunks to recognise the glassy, detached glare.

"Patrick Costello?"

The door opened further, revealing more of the face. It was unshaven, but there was not yet a full beard. The cheeks were sallow, emphasising the dark patches which hung beneath the cold, wicked eyes. The hair was white, unruly, but tinged with yellow streaks of tobacco. His shirt was open at the neck, the collar stained with grime, and a small bush of wiry hair sprouted from within. The trousers were frayed at the hems and held up by a pair of ancient braces, years beyond their prime. From them, there protruded a pair of small feet inserted into threadbare carpet slippers. The man had obviously been coughing badly, because there were flecks of spittle at the corners of his mouth and he was clearing his throat in short, coarse rasps.

"What do you want?"

Priest caught the distinct stench of alcohol, both stale and fresh, and it was blended with that familiar twist of tobacco, likewise both stale and fresh. There had been times, little more than brief moments perhaps, when Priest had thought that his life had been dominated by whisky and cigarettes, but he knew that it had never been to this extent. He had seen people in the gutter, but none of the gutters were as low as wherever it was Patrick Costello was forced, or had chosen, to fall. Of all the people Priest might have expected to live in this small corner of luxury, Costello was not one.

"I'd like to have a quick chat," said Priest.

Costello looked over him, his lips sneering. "Got anything to drink?"

Priest shook his head. "Sorry."

"Piss off to Hell then." The door slammed shut.

Priest stood for a moment on the doorstep, looking at the glass panels of the door. He turned away, glancing at the hedges and lawns. He looked across the street to the other bungalows. It was hard to imagine Costello being welcome at neighbourhood parties. Priest doubted Costello saw any of the people who shared his immediate space, unless he bumped into one of them on the front, assuming he ever left the house at all. Priest smiled to himself. Of course, Costello had to leave the house sometimes; there were whisky and cigarettes to be bought. Priest ambled down the pathway and back onto the main arc of the crescent. He looked around him once again, trying to understand how and why a man like Patrick Costello had come to live in this respectable, almost exclusive exile by the sea.

Half an hour later, Priest was knocking on the door again. He had found somewhere to buy a bottle of whisky, and by the time he was back at Costello's house, he was craving a glass himself. Costello pulled open the door, his malevolent eyes now widened with fury and an uneven line of discoloured teeth snarling from between the thin, broken lips. Priest held the bottle like a trophy.

"Can I come in now?" he asked.

Once inside, Priest found that the smell was far more toxic than he had imagined. The slovenliness and filth which were so obvious in Costello himself were echoed in his home. The furnishings themselves were of good quality, possibly even expensive, although Priest was no expert, but they were layered with dust, tarnished by cigarette burns and aged alcohol stains. At the end of the hallway, through a partly opened door, Priest could see the kitchen and the unwashed, discarded mugs and plates, which he somehow knew had been there for weeks rather than days. The room into which he followed Costello was protected from the outside world by the closed curtains across the front window, so that it seemed as if Costello lived in perpetual darkness. Perhaps he preferred it that way. Ashtrays were scattered around the room, filled beyond their capacity, and empty bottles and abandoned glasses kept them company.

"Get a glass." Costello mumbled the command so harshly that Priest was not sure he had understood it. He looked at Priest, one eye half closed and the other's focus indistinct. He indicated a glass-fronted sideboard in the corner of the room. Priest looked inside, surprised to find a clean glass waiting for him. It looked forlorn, somehow, as if it had been the last choice in a parade of prospective players for a drunken, hopeless team. He took it in his hands and walked over to Costello. He had already poured an unhealthy measure of whisky into a glass which looked as if it had never been washed since its first use. He handed the bottle to Priest. "Don't waste it and don't be selfish."

Priest poured only a small amount of the whisky into the glass. It might have been clean, but he didn't want it near his lips for longer than necessary. Costello watched him carefully, and when Priest handed it back, he snatched the bottle to his chest with that particular possessiveness which only an alcoholic can understand.

"Who are you, you bastard?" The insult meant nothing; Priest doubted Costello even knew he had used it.

Priest took out a business card and placed it on the small coffee table which was set in front on the fireplace. Costello ignored it. He might continue to ignore it forever.

"I'm a private detective," said Priest. "I think you might be able to help me."

Costello said nothing. He was tipping the glass to his lips, drinking the whisky in strange, avian slurps. Priest could see his nostrils flaring and he realised that he was smelling it too, so that all his senses were intoxicated by it. Finally, he threw it down the back of his throat and filled the glass once again.

Priest wondered how much the old wreck could hear or understand. "Do you know a place in London, Mr Costello, a pub called *The Hanged Man*?"

Costello's eyes, screwed shut for the most part, struggled to open. He ran a whitened tongue along the chapped, reddened lips. Noises which might have been words fizzled out of the lips, but they were mostly indecipherable, little more than incoherent mumblings which had their own bizarre, meaningless rhythm.

"Do you know it?" pressed Priest.

The low rambling continued for a moment, increasing in volume and violence, until it ended with a sudden and shocking clarity. "Bloody snake pit."

For a moment, Priest thought he had misheard the words. Costello was consoling himself with the whisky, his eyes rolling around in their sunken sockets, and his tongue searching for any stray drops of the drink which might have escaped his mouth. He poured himself another glass of the stuff and the mumbling began again. Incessant, like the groans of the suffering or the insane.

Priest leaned forward in his chair. "You used to go to *The Hanged Man*, is that right?"

"Whores and bastards," snarled Costello.

"Clem Murnaugh." Priest said the name carefully and clearly. A brief spark of recognition flashed in Costello's eyes. "You know the name. He went to the same pub."

"Leave me be, bastard."

"What about the name Boyd, Jimmy Boyd? Know him?"

Costello coughed back phlegm. "Don't know you, I know that. So... go on. Piss off."

But Priest was going nowhere; he had more names to try. "What about a girl called Jenny?"

Costello coughed and spat out something unpleasant onto the carpet. He wiped his nose across his sleeve. "Piss off."

"Jack Raeburn?"

This time, the same flash of recognition as before sparked in the narrow eyes. "Monster."

Priest wasn't about to disagree. He was about to say something, but Costello's eyes were fixed on him and his lips had curled into a cruel, malicious smile.

"All monsters," he said. He gave a short, rasping laugh and Priest had the impression of a malevolent memory, fondly remembered. "Killed them. For money."

Priest felt his spine stiffen. "Killed who?"

Costello seemed not to have heard. "All of us... Forced them all into it. And just for the cash."

"Forced who into what?"

"Dead. Every one of the bastards. All the bones...bodies... skulls." Costello's eyes had glassed over now, but the nasty smile remained. He threw some whisky down his throat. "Dead, the minute they arrived. Didn't matter, none of 'em. No use to nobody."

Priest could make nothing of the rambling words, tumbling into each other on account of the drink, so that they almost meant nothing at all. "Did Clem Murnaugh laugh about it?"

Costello spat onto the floor at his feet. "Weasel, little bitch."

"What happened to him?" Priest waited for an answer which was never going to come. "Where can I find him?"

"Dead. All of them, dead."

Priest's eyes had narrowed. "Is Clem Murnaugh dead?"

Costello sneered once more at the name and spat again on the carpet. "Little bitch."

Priest rose from his chair and emptied his own glass down his throat. Costello would say nothing more about Murnaugh other than what he had. Priest was going to have to change his direction. He was fighting back the urge to admit that he was wasting his time. He was getting nowhere, it seemed, and yet something about these jumbled phrases, these spasmodic references to death and skulls, struck him as important. But only one idea seemed to him to be anything near explaining them all.

"Concentration camps?" he asked, his voice never more serious.

Costello looked at him, as if seeing him for the first time. His mouth was moving but no words came and his eyes darted around the room, as if they were looking for the words he needed. He gave a vague shake of his head. "No… never them."

"What, then?" Priest was kneeling by the side of the man's chair now.

"Not them…" Costello mumbled to himself.

Priest had his hand on the old man's arm. "What about the skulls and the bodies, then?"

It took a moment for the words to come. Costello's eyes had frozen again in one of his blurred, fragmented memories. He began to rock gently in his chair, the whisky in the glass trembling as he did so. When he spoke, the words were soft, barely audible, but they possessed a definite sense of cruelty. "House of skulls."

Priest inclined his head, not certain he had heard correctly, but sure he did not understand at all. Costello drank what was left of his whisky and poured the remainder of the bottle into the glass. Priest walked around the chair, so that he was facing the shrunken, drunken husk of a man sitting in front of him. He spoke his name three times before Costello raised his eyes to meet him.

"A house of skulls," said Priest. "What do you mean by that?"

There was a still silence for several seconds. Then, without warning, the empty whisky bottle was spinning through the air towards Priest. He ducked down onto one knee, covering his head with his arms. Costello had seemed harmless, too drunk to be of any threat, but there was a power behind the throw, one fuelled by something more than physical strength. Something like fear, anger, or hatred. The bottle smashed against the sideboard, shattering into pieces, each one sharp enough to have caused serious damage to Priest if it had connected with his face or head. And that had been the intention. If Priest was in any doubt about that, the malevolence which now twisted Costello's face dispelled it.

"Leave it alone, you bastard," hissed the old man. "Leave it alone."

"Leave what alone?"

With a scream of rage, Costello launched the still full glass of whisky at Priest, forcing him back onto his knees, covering his head once more with his arms. With surprising speed, Costello was now on his feet, marching towards Priest with a lumbering, drunken stumble of a walk.

"Bloody filth." He spat the words and began to bring his fists down on Priest's back as hard as he could manage. They were not the most powerful blows Priest had endured in his life, but they were dangerous enough for Priest to have to fight to stand beneath their onslaught. Certainly, he wouldn't have liked to fight Costello when the man was younger and sober.

Priest was moving now, out of the room and into the hall. Costello had stopped hitting him, but was still behind him, too close and too angry, shouting ceaselessly for Priest to leave it alone. Priest was retaliating, making assurances he had no intention of honouring, but his voice was lost in the violence of Costello's. By the time Priest was outside and the door had been slammed shut once more, he was breathing heavily. He stared back at the house for a moment, expecting the front room curtains to be parted and Costello's sneering face to appear in the window, satisfying himself that Priest had left. But the curtains did not move. Had Priest been able to see inside the room, however, he would have seen Patrick Costello lying exhausted in his chair, wheezing breaths inflating his chest, and in between them, his mouth whispering that it should all be left alone.

As it was, Priest turned away from the house and made his way back to the town. He was not sure what he had achieved by coming here. Nor was he sure what he had learned. Only one phrase stuck in his mind, with the tantalisingly clear impression that it was important: *house of skulls*. Whatever it meant, it dominated Priest's thoughts as he walked back into the town, so wrapped up in himself that he almost did not notice the black car which followed him, then drove slowly past him, before gathering speed and disappearing from view.

CHAPTER SEVENTEEN

When Priest returned to his office, he found Thomas Marriott waiting for him. He was leaning against the wall, one ankle crossed over the other, and his hat twirling on the tip of a finger, like someone without any cares in the world. Priest found it impossible to accept at face value, meaning that he found the casual attitude nothing less than sickening. He felt like swiping Marriott's legs from under him and bringing him to the ground, where Priest felt sure he belonged. As it was, Marriott pushed himself off the wall and stood to attention.

Once inside, Priest took off his coat and threw it onto the stand, his hat following with a similar carelessness. Marriott was standing in the doorway, looking around, just as Evelyn had done the previous evening. The memory stirred in Priest's mind, and with it, came the sudden suspicion that the two visits were not coincidental. Where Evelyn had been gently mocking about the office, her husband was overtly dismissive.

"I don't suppose you make much money being a private detective," he said, running his finger along thc top of a filing cabinet and examining the results.

"Enough to get by."

Marriott smiled, as if to say that the office suggested otherwise. "Have you found Leonard Quayle's secretary yet?" He looked up at Priest when no answer was forthcoming. The expression on Priest's face suggested that an answer would never be forthcoming. Marriott pointed to one of the chairs reserved for clients. "May I sit down?"

Priest nodded, sitting down himself in the leather chair. Marriott sat down and lit a cigarette, casually but deliberately, failing to offer one to Priest. He didn't mind. He had his own cigarettes, but nothing in the world would induce him to light one now, in case it was taken as any sort of response to Marriott's rebuff. Priest remained silent, but his eyes never left Marriott's face and the ice in them never came close to melting.

"I believe my wife came here last night," Marriott said at last. Priest said nothing. "Are you going to answer me?"

"You haven't asked me a question yet."

Marriott smiled, but it was clear the response hadn't amused him. "Is it true?"

"If she said so, it must be."

"What did she want?"

Priest shook his head. "I might not be a priest in anything but name, Mr Marriott, but what's said in this office might as well be said in a confessional."

Marriott picked a stray strand of tobacco out of his mouth and flicked it away. "I'll take that as a yes, then."

"Take it wherever you like."

"She's already told me why she came here."

It was a cheap trick and Marriott's eyes betrayed it. Priest leaned back in his chair. "You don't need me to repeat it then."

Marriott pursued his lips. "Is there something between you and my wife, Priest?"

"No."

"You're a liar," hissed Marriott. "If I find out you've done anything to her, I'll ruin you."

Priest smiled dangerously. "Stop trying to scare me to death."

"I'm warning you, that's all."

"Should I hide under the desk?"

Marriott's smile was sinister and his voice was filled with knives. "Don't underestimate me, Priest."

Priest rose from his chair and turned to the window. He leaned on the sill and peered out over the streets below. "What's this all about, Marriott? You're too in love with yourself to be jealous of anybody. What are you really doing here?"

Marriott lowered his head, his voice suddenly solemn. "You're wrong about me, Priest. When it comes to Evie, I am jealous."

Priest turned round to face him. Marriott was looking at him from under dropped lids, so that his eyes seemed vulnerable, almost saddened, both at his confession and the truth of it. Priest searched for some signs of deceit, anything which might unveil dishonesty and reveal the performance for what he suspected it to be, but there was nothing. Marriott inhaled deeply on the cigarette and stubbed it out in the ashtray on the desk.

"So, some things do matter more than the Phoenix development project?" said Priest, hating his own churlishness, but doing nothing to apologise for it.

Marriott nodded. "I suppose I deserve an insult like that. Perhaps I have allowed Phoenix to dominate my life since I began it. And perhaps it took you being in my house to make me realise that Evie was a casualty of that commitment."

It was as if a bullet had been fired into Priest's conscience, but he had fired the gun himself. He didn't know what he felt for Evelyn Marriott, but he knew it might go some way to proving he was wrong about love. His mother's desertion had taken its toll on his belief in it and very few had come close to shaking or melting the cynicism, but Evelyn Marriott had come closer than anyone. And now, whatever that might have led to was a pointless speculation, all because Priest had somehow opened Marriott's eyes to his marriage. He felt suddenly sick, worse than ever before.

"Glad to be of service," he said. Marriott's only response was a smile. "How has she taken this revelation of yours?"

"Happily."

To Priest's ears, it sounded sordid. "You won't be abandoning Phoenix though, will you?"

Marriott shook his head. "Of course not. I still have faith in it and I still believe it can benefit everybody."

"So, she still doesn't mean more than it."

The muscles in Marriott's jaw clenched, as if suppressing an angry retort. His voice remained placid and engaging. "She understands its importance. Anybody with optimism and compassion does."

"Would your uncle approve?"

It unnerved him. Priest had no idea why he had asked the question, but its effect was interesting. Marriott hadn't expected him to know anything about his personal life and the emotion on his face progressed from surprise to anger. "Evie had no right to discuss my private life with you."

"I understand you're annoyed," said Priest. "I would be myself. Yes, she did talk about it. I didn't ask her to. I think she was trying to tell me how proud she is. But I've been wrong before."

"I see." Marriott seemed instantly ashamed. "For what it's worth, I think my uncle would be proud, yes."

Priest nodded aimlessly. "These properties which Leonard Quayle is buying for you, so that you can renovate and reuse them… How many have you bought, would you say?"

Marriott was still momentarily distracted. He looked back at Priest and shrugged. "It's an ongoing project, but perhaps twenty, thirty."

"Over how long?"

"Phoenix has been active for six months."

Priest whistled softly. "That's a high number for such a short time."

"Quayle is very efficient." Marriott crossed his legs. "As are the estate agents he appointed on my behalf."

A memory stirred in Priest's mind: an estate agent's board in a small yard in Southwark, the same name appearing in some of the photographs which Jimmy Boyd had sent and which Clem Murnaugh had taken, the same photographs now locked in the safe under the office floorboards. He looked at Marriott, his expression innocuous and the query seeming irrelevant and bland. "Which agents?"

Even before Marriott replied, the hairs on the back of Priest's neck were like spiders crawling over his skin. "Burke & Halliwell. Do you know them?"

"Never heard of them," lied Priest.

"I'm surprised. They're fairly well known."

Priest shrugged. "I don't buy many properties, Mr Marriott. As you said, you don't earn much as a private detective."

"I suppose not." Marriott moved. He uncrossed his legs and leaned over the desk, clasping his hands in front of him. "I haven't told you the full truth, Priest."

The spiders on Priest's neck went into a frenzy. "About what?"

"Evelyn."

"What about her?"

Marriott held his gaze. "She didn't tell me what she was doing with you last night."

Priest smiled. "I never thought she did. Does it bother you that much that she was here?"

Marriott laughed. "If she was your wife, wouldn't you worry if she was with another man in the evening?"

Priest had no answer to give to that. "She came to apologise to me."

"For what?"

"For you." Priest watched Marriott frown. "She thought you were rough with me when I came to your house the other night."

"Was I?" It seemed a genuine question.

Priest shook his head. "I've had worse scratches from a kitten."

Marriott did not seem to be offended. "Thank you for being honest."

"Is that why you came here? To find out what your wife wanted me for?" Priest waited until Marriott had nodded. "And all this because you're jealous?"

"Is that so hard to believe?"

"I just didn't think you'd be that easy to rattle."

"We all have our weaknesses, Mr Priest. Including you."

"No argument there." Priest leaned back in his chair. "Mine is never believing what people tell me."

"Meaning I'm lying about why I came here?"

"People lie about all sorts of things, but it isn't always any of my business." Priest gestured to the door and lit a cigarette. "Go home to your wife, Mr Marriott."

Marriott rose to his feet and placed his hat on his head. He seemed about to say something more, but he didn't. He looked down at Priest for a long moment and then simply nodded, as if satisfied by something which had occurred to him. With a firm word of farewell, he turned on his heel and walked out of the office.

Priest remained where he was, wondering. He wondered about a lot of things. Most of all, he wondered why Marriott had come at all. It hadn't been to find out why Evelyn had been there, he was sure of that. Which meant that Marriott had come for another reason entirely. For the moment, all Priest could do was wonder about it. And about Evelyn herself. Had Marriott been needling him, by saying Priest had bridged the gap in their marriage? He could easily believe it. It would seem like a victory to a man like Marriott, a reassertion of his status as Evelyn's husband. He might not love her, nor she him, but that was no reason to allow anyone else to have her. Not that Priest wanted her. He was sure of that. If he hadn't been sure before, he was now. Positive of it, in fact, just as he was positive that God existed. But he had long ago stopped being sure of that.

"Damn it," he snarled, slamming his fist against the desk. It solved nothing. He picked up the phone and dialled. Darrow answered almost immediately. "It's me, Frank."

"Got something for me?"

"I might have."

The surprise in Darrow's voice was impossible to conceal. "One of these day's you'll kill me outright, Priest."

"It might be nothing, Frank, but have somebody look into Burke & Halliwell, the estate agents. See which properties they're buying and how much for."

"Anywhere in particular?"

"Southwark," said Priest. "But anywhere in London, concentrating on abandoned offices and broken-down houses."

"What's this about?"

"Just an itch I can't scratch."

"I know all about them," said Darrow, before hanging up.

In the couple of hours which passed, Priest did nothing. He sat back in his chair and let his mind go for a walk in the woods. Outside, the sky eventually turned to a dull, slate grey colour as the late afternoon sun finally surrendered and the night began to exert its power. Priest had taken a whisky from the filing cabinet bottle, then another, and was contemplating a third when the phone rang again.

"This itch of yours means nothing to me," said Darrow. "The agents are legitimate. Nothing funny about them at all. Quite a respected firm, in fact."

"I didn't think there was anything funny about them," said Priest. "But I thought there might be about the property sales."

"Nothing there, either, apart from the fact that some of these burned-out places are being bought for big money."

Priest's hand tightened on the receiver. "For more than they're worth?"

"Definitely."

"Can you find out who was buying them?"

"Not without an official reason for asking them to disclose their files. And your itches don't count as official reasons."

"But someone is buying up worthless properties at high prices?"

"That's the gist of it."

Priest smiled. "I'll give you the name of one possible buyer. TGM Investments."

Darrow snarled a laugh. "The Phoenix development? That's no secret, Priest. You can't escape from it. But I, for one, believe in Phoenix and I say we need it. The war did more damage than any of us have been able to understand so far."

"I'm not disputing that, Frank."

"Right. So, the Phoenix scheme is a good thing. But if TGM is paying more than it should to get these places back up and running because of it, that's their business and not mine. And I still say good luck to them."

There was some sense in that, after all, but Priest was shaking his head. "Why pay over the odds?"

"Why should I care?"

"Perhaps you shouldn't. Thanks, Frank." Priest dropped the phone back into its cradle.

He drained the third glass of whisky. Maybe he was seeing ghosts where there were none. Darrow was right: if TGM, or anybody else for that matter, was spending too much of its own money in property purchases, it was nothing to do with the police or Priest. Except Priest had a deep suspicion that Nancy Clayton had been killed in one of the apartments which Burke & Halliwell had sold. And Clem Murnaugh had photographed other properties which the same agents had handled, the sales being dealt with by Leonard Quayle, Nancy's secret lover, who took her to nightclubs owned by Jack Raeburn.

But none of it meant anything definite and none of it was proof of anything. Coincidences rather than connections, just more itches he couldn't scratch. But those itches weren't going away.

Darrow would do nothing without evidence and he wouldn't go looking for that evidence without having good reason. That left Priest on his own, with nothing more than his head and instincts. Same as ever.

He got up and crossed the room. He pulled up the floorboard and unlocked the safe, rummaging inside the envelopes until he found the beermat which Boyd had sent to him. He put it in his jacket pocket. Then, rising from the desk, he put on his hat and coat, walked out of the office, and locked the door behind him.

CHAPTER EIGHTEEN

Priest had never been in *The Hanged Man*, but he had been in many pubs like it. As he pushed his way through the crowd, which had already formed in the short space of time since the doors had opened, he felt strangely accustomed and comforted by its surroundings, at once unfamiliar and yet reassuringly recognisable. The haze of smoke through which he moved, the faint tinkle of a distant piano, its sound smothered by the rumble of conversation and laughter, and the sweet smell of freshly poured beer were all old friends to him, even if their particular details and expressions were appearing before him for the first time. The pub was homely, if not quite welcoming, but its furnishings had seen better days. The brasses needed a polish and the varnish on the chairs and tables was still dark enough to assert itself, but it no longer glistened with vibrancy. There were holes in some of the stools' upholstery, but these went by either unnoticed or ignored. The floor beneath Priest's feet was unpleasantly sticky, the effects of too much spilled beer and gin, if not worse, and attempts to clean it which were too lethargic to be of any use. It was a place with no elegance, no pretence, and no desire to be anything except what it was. In that, at least, it had its own honesty.

He stood at the bar with the pint of beer which he had ordered and let his eyes flicker around the room. Men watched him from darkened corners, their hats pulled low over their eyes, and some of the women, even the ones who were not prostitutes, fixed him with interested glares. In one corner, oblivious to anything else around them, two old men played dominoes. There was nothing for them but the game and the glasses of beer and whisky which were placed at their respective elbows. They were old enough to have seen everything which could happen in life. Nothing which happened in here could surprise them and Priest doubted any of it would interest them. One day, perhaps he would be old enough to let the world pass him by, for it to offer no more surprises or betrayals, for it to mean nothing more to him than an old game and a couple of glasses of beer. He hoped so; that day seemed like a good day to be alive and he hoped that, when it came, he would recognise and enjoy it for what it was. But it was not today.

Priest ordered another drink, this time with a whisky to follow. "Anyone in here called Jenny?"

The barman placed both down in front of him and took Priest's money. "You a friend of hers?"

"Friend of a friend," lied Priest.

The barman pointed toward a small alcove in the far wall of the pub, beneath one of the frosted windows set into it, where a girl was sitting alone. "That's her."

On instinct, Priest ordered a gin and walked away from the bar. The two domino players did not notice him pass by. As he approached, he saw that the table was filled with glasses, all empty, except one being nursed by a girl of indeterminate age but undeniable status. There were no chairs at the table, except for the wall seat built into the alcove itself. The other chairs had been taken away, to other tables, by people who didn't care about the girl or what she was. Priest placed the three drinks on the table and gestured to the spare space beside her.

"Mind if I take the weight off?"

She looked up at him. "It's a free country."

"It nearly wasn't," said Priest.

The girl raised an eyebrow. "Are you always this much fun?"

"Most of the time." He pushed the gin towards her. "Sorry if I was presumptuous in ordering that."

"No problem. Changed your mind about taking the weight off?"

He smiled and sat down beside her. She drank silently for a few moments. If life had been easier for her, he supposed she would have been attractive. Her age was still impossible to say, but she was younger than he had thought. From a distance, she had seemed to him to be about his own age; up close, he doubted she was much past twenty. Her hair was blonde, fashionably but not professionally styled, and her lips were a vibrant, almost garish red. Her eyes were blue, but the creases at their corners were a consequence of that particular type of premature aging which hardship and trouble never fail to produce. They watched him out of their corners and he knew that she was assessing him, wondering whether he wanted what she suspected, and if so, whether she would feel safe obliging him. When she drank, the glass quivered slightly, so that he knew that the prospect was still unpleasant to her. She was in that period of transition, balancing between the hope that things could still get better and knowing for sure that they never would. Suddenly, Priest felt manipulative, cheap, and overwhelmingly sad.

"My name's Alex," he said.

She snorted, her red lips breaking into a smile. "No one usually cares about names."

"That's not what I want." He drank some of the beer, hoping it would wash away the bitter taste which had formed on his tongue.

She looked across at him. "It's all anyone ever wants."

He shook his head. "Not me."

She was looking directly at him now and it took all of his determination not to look back at her. Finally, she held out her hand. The nails were long but not unpleasant, although the varnish was chipping away. "Jenny."

Priest took her hand. She gave him a small smile, which broadened into a wider, more assured one. He returned it as best he could. They drank for a short while in silence. Now, it seemed nobody in the pub was paying any attention to Priest, as if they assumed that he had found what he was looking for. Before, he had been a stranger, something to suspect; now, he was sitting with one of the girls, just another sad man looking for a cheap thrill away from home, daring to look into the dangers of risk, instead of confining himself to the safety of the marital home. *The Hanged Man* had seen men like it before, could recognise the signs, even when they were not there.

"Is this your usual pub, Jenny?" asked Priest.

She shrugged. "Closest to where I live, if that's what you mean."

"Do you like it?"

"As much as I like anywhere else."

It seemed as good an answer as he was likely to get. They sat in silence for several minutes, drinking, and watching the pub go about its business. Whether either of them found the silence uncomfortable, they did not show or admit it. Several times, young men approached the table, clearly interested in Jenny; some not for the first time, Priest thought, and others excited by the expectation of their first taste of her usual services. When they saw she was not alone, their eager and expectant expressions evaporated, transforming into spurned, disappointed, and malevolent glares. But something about Priest's own stare must have suggested that any argument would be unwise. The men, little more than boys some of them, would go back to the darkened corners of the pub, staring over occasionally, beating up Priest with their private, whispered insults, because it was the best any of them could do.

"Some of these kids don't know when to stop," said Jenny.

"They give you any trouble?" He smiled privately at her use of the word *kids*. She was one herself.

She shrugged. "Nothing I can't handle."

Despite himself, Priest could believe it. There might have been a vulnerability about her, but he thought Jenny would have been more than capable of dealing with boys like those; it was the older men, he thought, who would give her trouble. He took out one of his cards, ignoring his internal warnings that it was a bad idea. He slid it towards her. "If you ever get in trouble, call me."

She looked at the card as if it might be a trick. After a moment, she twisted it towards her, so that she could see it more clearly. Her eyes narrowed as she read it, and for a moment, Priest wondered whether she needed to wear glasses. She smiled, as if she didn't believe what she had read. "A private eye? Like in the films?"

"Not exactly."

Jenny bit her lower lip, picked up her glass, and leaned back in the window seat. "So, you didn't come to speak to me because you liked the look of me."

"Not entirely," confessed Priest. "But I did want to speak to you."

"What if I've got nothing to say?"

Priest shrugged. "I can't force you. All I can do is buy you another drink and leave you alone."

"That sounds fine."

Priest smiled, nodding his head. "My problem is that some people have died and I want to know why."

She looked at him sharply. The red lips had parted in surprise and the eyes had widened initially but then, almost immediately afterwards, they narrowed in suspicion, as if he had accused her of something. "What's that got to do with me?"

Priest did not reply. Instead, he reached into his pocket and took out the beermat. He pointed to her name on it. "Your name, this pub."

"So what?"

He turned over the square of cardboard and pointed to Costello's name and address. "Know him?"

She squinted to read the words. Then, the creases above her nose smoothing out and her eyes opening wide again, she shook her head. "Never heard of him."

Priest turned the beermat over in his hands for a moment, trying to decide whether she was lying or not. Costello's name on the beermat must have meant that Boyd had been given it and had made a note of it on the first thing which came to hand. But Jenny's name was on the beermat too, which meant either that someone else again had given Boyd her name or that he had written it down to remind himself of it, in case he ever needed to speak to her again. If the first, Priest had a lot more looking to do; if the second, Jenny was lying. And only one of those options seemed likely.

"I think you have heard of him, Jenny," he said.

She twisted in her seat so that she was facing him. "I told you, I don't know him."

"Not knowing him personally is different to never having heard of him."

"Meaning what?"

Priest felt certainty running through his veins in place of blood. "I think you know something about Costello and I think you told someone else what you know."

She inched away from him, as if now sensing that he was somehow dangerous to her. "What you talking about?"

Priest was staring down at the table. Now, he moved his head, so that he was looking sideways into her face. "Clem Murnaugh."

She glared at him, as if he had made a lewd suggestion in the confessional. Her blue eyes had widened, not this time with shock, but fear. The red lips parted again and he saw the tip of her tongue run itself across her slightly crooked front teeth. She turned away from him and grabbed at her drink. The glass reverberated against the table and some of the gin trickled down the side of her jaw as she drank. It would take some time for the trembling in her hand to subside.

"Who are you?" she whispered. He pointed to his business card, still lying between them on the table. "You been hired to find Clem?"

Her eyes were filled with something strange to him, a blend of fear and hope which installed in him a desire to put his arms round her and assure her that everything was well. He remained still, refusing to lie to her or himself. "No."

The hope vanished from her eyes and her teeth clenched together, her features hardening, as if he had led her to believe that life could be better, and now, he had sold her into something worse than she was living before. "Then what do you want from me?"

"Answers."

"To what?"

"To whatever the other man was asking about." He watched her frown in bewilderment. "Another man came looking for Clem Murnaugh. You spoke to him. He wrote your name on that beermat, Jenny, after you'd told him something. And whatever it was, it involved this man, Costello, because you gave him that name, too. He wrote it on the same beermat. See for yourself."

She had become childishly stubborn, her lips pursed in defiance, but the eyes incapable of matching the courage. "So, what if I did?"

"Was the man's name Boyd?"

Jenny shrugged. "Don't remember."

Priest moved closer to her, turning so that he was facing her. "It was, Jenny. And now, Boyd is dead. Someone killed him."

Tears globed in her eyes and she wiped them away swiftly, as if refusing to allow anyone to see anything which might be taken for weakness. "Killed him how?"

Priest shook his head. "You don't want to know."

"I don't know nothing about anyone being killed," she said, forcing back the tears.

"I know that," he replied. "But you did tell Boyd some things, didn't you?"

It took a moment for her to give a nod of her head. "He said he was a friend of Clem's. I asked him if he knew where Clem was, but he didn't."

"Do you?"

She gave a violent shake of the head. "I can't help thinking the worst. If he was all right, he'd have got in touch. I know he would."

"Were you and Clem a couple, Jenny?" Priest asked it with as much tenderness as he could muster.

She let a tear roll slowly down her cheek. Eventually, she shook her head sadly. "Nothing serious. I think he wanted there to be more, but there never was."

"Did you want more?" When she nodded her head, she began to cry properly, and Priest had to look away, suddenly embarrassed by his position. "When was the last time you saw Clem?"

It took her a moment to respond, and when she did, her voice was broken with sobs. "In here, the night he disappeared."

That would make it almost three months ago. Meaning that if Murnaugh had sent the photographs to Boyd, he had done it at least three months ago, before he disappeared. The Phoenix scheme had been underway for six months. Priest wondered: if everything was connected, Murnaugh could have spent three months taking his illicit photographs, from the moment the Phoenix project commenced to when he vanished, and after receiving the photographs, Boyd had spent the subsequent three months trying to uncover whatever Clem Murnaugh had discovered. And now, Boyd had passed it all onto Priest himself.

Priest doubted he had ever felt more helpless than in that moment.

"After Clem vanished, did anybody come to see you?" he asked.

"Mr Wolfe came to see if I was all right."

"When?"

"A couple of days after Clem went missing."

"Did Wolfe ask you anything?"

She shrugged. "He was checking on me, that's all."

"Did he know where Clem had gone?"

"He didn't say. He asked me what Clem and me had talked about recently."

Priest was smiling encouragingly, just an interested friend. "Which was what?"

"Nothing much." She began to pick at a nail.

"Nothing about his work?"

"No."

"And you told Wolfe that?" He watched her nod. "Did he say anything else?"

She shook her head. "Just that I wasn't to worry about anything."

Priest thought about that for a moment, but there didn't seem to him to be anything else to add to it. "When you last saw Clem, how did he seem? Was he worried about anything?"

She shrugged, the tears coming under her control now. "Not on your life. If anything, it was like he had no care in the world."

It made sense. Clem had sent the photographs to Boyd; he would think they were out of harm's way, safely protected. They weren't in his own possession, if anyone did question him or search him. But it had been a false sense of security. He had left the pub and they had been waiting for him. Priest could understand exactly what had happened, to that extent at least. All of which meant that, whatever the photographs showed, whatever they represented, they were worth killing for.

"Did Clem ever mention taking photographs to you?" he asked.

She looked confused. "Of what?"

Priest shrugged. "Of anything. People, buildings."

She was already shaking her head. Priest wondered if Clem had not told her anything on purpose. The less she knew, the safer she would be. "When did Boyd come to see you?"

"A couple of weeks ago, maybe."

"Was he asking about Clem?"

She nodded. "Amongst other things."

"What things?"

"About how well Clem knew Jack."

Raeburn. "What did you tell him?"

"I just said Clem worked for him, but that I didn't know what he did." She looked earnestly at Priest. "And I don't, I swear. Clem always said that he was well respected, that he was going places. Do you think that was true?"

The expectation in her eyes was so intense that he could only have disappointed her, so he said nothing in reply. "Did Boyd ask about Costello?"

She shook her head. "I gave him the name."

"So, you do know him?"

Jenny was adamant. "I don't. I just told that man, Boyd, that it was a name Clem had started talking about recently. I don't know nothing about him, like I said."

"Did Boyd recognise Costello's name?"

Jenny shook her head. "I wouldn't have said so."

"What did Clem say about Costello?"

Jenny seemed unsure how to respond. She tried to form words, but none of them came, and she began to concentrate very seriously on her glass. "He was frightened of him."

Priest's spine stiffened and his nerves crackled. "Why?"

She shook her head violently. "I don't know. It was just an impression I had. He would say that if anyone by that name came asking for him, I was to say I had no idea where he was. And he said that if I ever met a man called Costello, I wasn't to go with him anywhere. Not anywhere, not ever."

Priest thought back to the drunk wreck of a man he had met. "I don't think that's likely to happen now."

"Is he dead too?"

"As good as."

Jenny lowered her gaze, in relief rather than sorrow. "Clem was ill one time. Nothing serious, but he was bad for a few days. And he was rambling, talking to himself, saying things I didn't understand, but he kept mentioning this Costello over and over. And he said something else." She looked at Priest now, her eyes wide with fear. "Something about bodies."

"Bodies?"

But she had begun to correct herself. "No, not bodies. That's what I thought he meant but it wasn't actually what he said. Bones, it was. He was going on and on about bones, skeletons."

Priest suddenly felt as cold as the grave himself. "And skulls?"

Jenny nodded, her eyes wide. "And houses. Skulls and houses."

Priest was shaking his head. "Not houses. Just one. A house of skulls." His mind was back with Costello himself now. The old drunk had used the same phrase.

"Do you know what it means?"

"Did Clem not tell you?"

Jenny's eyes dimmed with sadness. "When he got better, after the fever had passed, I asked him what it meant. It was the only time he ever hit me."

Instinctively, Priest put his hand on hers. She didn't discourage it, not at first, and when she did, it was only the gentlest of movements, as her hand slid out from underneath his. She looked at him, smiling gently, and placed her hands in her lap.

"That other man, Boyd, he asked me about that, too," she said.

"About a house of skulls?"

"I think he knew what it was. He told me never to talk about it to anyone." She sighed, her brow creasing with frustration. "And here I am, doing just that."

"Don't worry about that," said Priest. "Telling me was a wise thing to do. But don't mention it to anyone else. Boyd was right. You know nothing about it."

She looked at him, her expression pleading with him for honesty. "Was Clem mixed up in something bad?"

He nodded slowly. "I think he found something out."

"And he told Boyd?"

There was no sense in deceiving her. "I think so."

"I'm frightened." The silent tears which fell down her face were proof enough of that, as were the wide, flickering eyes. The words themselves were unnecessary.

Priest looked around. Nobody seemed to be paying any attention to them. "I don't think you need to be. I think Wolfe came here to reassure himself as much as you. Maybe Clem had convinced them you didn't know anything and Wolfe was making sure." He knew that people like Wolfe had techniques, ways to make sure someone wasn't lying to them. Wherever he was now, Clem Murnaugh had experienced something of those methods, Priest was sure of that. "I don't think you need to worry, Jenny, but it might be an idea to stay with a friend for a few days. And avoid coming in here."

"What's going on, mister?" She was trembling now, her face little more than a scared child's, as if the years and the brutality of her life had been a mask which was now slipping away and revealing her frightened innocence. "What did they do to my Clem?"

The words were like knives in his ribs. He tried to find a way of replying, but whatever he said would either terrify her or break her. If he voiced his own suspicions on what had happened when Clem Murnaugh walked out of *The Hanged Man* on that last, fateful day, she would not be able to bear it. He could hardly do so himself. But he knew now, even if he could not prove it, that Murnaugh was dead. He had stumbled onto something and he had documented it in photographs, but they had found him out. Clem had kept his secrets and they had killed him. What Clem had discovered remained a mystery, but he had made sure they understood that Jenny knew nothing about it. For that, at least, Priest could be grateful. He suddenly found that he respected Clem Murnaugh more than he might otherwise had believed possible.

Priest pointed once more to his card. "Get to a friend's house and stay there. Just until I sort everything out. And phone me tomorrow morning, to let me know you're all right."

She nodded, taking the card and placing it in her pocket. "Why are you doing this?"

Priest stood up and stepped out from behind the table. He looked down at her, but said nothing. Perhaps all the answers he could think of were too unconvincing. Or perhaps he just didn't know the answer at all. He tried to smile but found that he couldn't. Instead, he lowered his gaze, turned on his heel, and walked away.

CHAPTER NINETEEN

He was almost back at his office when it happened.

The night was pitch, like the darkest of all the blackouts. The moon was not visible, covered by a bank of cloud which rolled across the sky with an oppressive determination. There was a stillness about the ominous lack of sound, as if life had somehow taken itself away, leaving behind a silent, suffocating nothing, which made their sudden movements seem all the more terrible.

He had not quite reached the door of the office building before they were on him. They took hold of his arms, linking him like lovers, forcing him to walk in the direction they chose. Any attempt on his part to resist was met with a tightening of the grip around his elbows. It was trouble, he knew that, but there was nothing he could do while his arms were pinned and his movements were not his own. He looked across to each of their faces, recognising neither, but knowing only too well the sort of people they were. The faces were masked by shadow, the same sort of darkness which had inked its way across the sky. He could imagine the soulless, dark eyes and the impassive, calm faces surrounding them, the sort of faces which show no shame, no regret, and no pity in their filthy work, but which show no pleasure or reward in it either. They were faceless, nameless beings with only one thought, to obey orders, and only one mission, to inflict pain.

Several cars passed by and he thought about raising the alarm. He doubted it would have achieved anything. Even if his voice reached anybody's ears, and even assuming that anybody took any notice, the way the two men were flanking him meant that a passer-by would see only three men, three friends no doubt, out walking in the night air, possibly after a night of drinking and reminiscing. There would be no way for any one of the drivers of those passing cars to know that the opposite was true. A cry for help would only give them further reason to hurt. It would not help him, and if anybody did chance to interfere, it would not help them either.

They threw him into an alleyway, causing him to stumble over the cobbles, but he didn't fall to the ground. They were swift, but he was prepared. He had time to balance himself, arcing his right arm back and bringing it forward with speed and power. As his fist connected with the nose of one of the men, he could feel the warm, tacky liquid on his knuckles, which told him that some damage had been done. First blood.

But it came with consequences. The other man had circled around him as he was tumbling, and whilst not quick enough to stop this initial attack, he was able to prevent another with a short, sharp, but effective blow to Priest's back. His kidneys erupted in pain and any air in his lungs exploded out of them in a dull, guttural roar. His knees deserted him almost entirely, but he managed to stay on his feet. It was the second blow to the spine which brought him to the ground. His ribs screamed in agony from a kick to his side. Instinctively, but somehow foolishly, Priest covered his head against any assault.

None came. In this position, a kick to the face and head would be simple, but it never happened. From somewhere in the muddled mix of pain and anger which he was registering, the thought occurred to him that they were avoiding his head because the order had not been to kill him. Whatever they did, he would survive it. It might have been an isolated flash of optimism, but it was something he could hold onto. It seemed vital that he did.

He was hauled to his feet again and held in position by a pair of powerful arms snaking through his own. The second man went to work on his stomach. He could hear himself groaning in protest at each strike, and as if in punishment for the noise, the man turned his attention to his nose and jaw. Priest tasted the metallic sharpness of blood in his mouth and he spat some of it out onto the cobbles, angry with himself for not aiming well enough to make sure some of it splattered onto the shoe of this front assailant. His nervous system was in action, sending out its electrical pulses to register the pain in his stomach, face, and back. His kidneys felt the way they had done at the end of a three-day drinking binge, after a particularly successful conclusion to a major enquiry in his life as an official detective, with the exception that, prior to that pain, he had spent three days of drunken happiness. Here, now, there had been no previous joy to compensate for the pain. He was coughing, his breathing short and erratic, and he suddenly felt exhausted.

Without warning, he was in the air, moving at speed. He struck the wall of the adjacent building with a force which he felt sure should have done some serious damage. Breathing now was almost an impossibility. He sank to his hands and knees and the two of them towered over him. One of them kicked him in the side, turning him onto his back, so that he was lying beneath them, staring up into their shadowed faces. It didn't matter who they were. All that mattered is what they were doing. A foot stomped on his groin, sending a lance of fire through his body and causing a wave of uncontrollable nausea to overwhelm him. He heard himself crying out in pain, but the voice sounded unreal, barely human, as if it was nothing to do with him at all. Now, he was nowhere. He was nothing but a bundle of clothes, blood, filth, and agony.

He became aware that one of them was kneeling over him, his weight planted on Priest's chest, so that the rasping breaths became even more laboured. Big hands took hold of his head and Priest feared that his skull would burst like a watermelon. The grip was unforgiving, absolute, but it did not intensify. Instead, it lifted his head slightly from the ground. Priest uttered a single grunt of protest, horrifyingly aware of what was about to happen, but his sounds meant nothing to anybody. With just the right amount of pressure, the man shot back Priest's head, striking it against the stone of the ground. There was no danger of death, even of permanent damage; the calculation had been exact, the product of years of sickening experience.

A flash of lightening exploded behind his eyes, before they rolled back in his head and the lids fluttered like distracted moths in the moonlight. Priest heard the dull, terrible thud of his head against the cobbles, and something which might have been a snigger of satisfaction from a place far away, but then he heard no more. The weight on his chest alleviated, and in the final moments, Priest saw the two hulking shadows rise above him and then disappear. Finally, the night seemed to grow darker than ever and all of his senses faded into the blackness.

CHAPTER TWENTY

He had no idea how long he had lay there, but he stayed still long after his eyes had opened. To move would have been to exacerbate the already intense pain which coursed through him. He breathed carefully, testing for any traces of broken ribs, but there were none. His tongue ensured that there were no loosened or missing teeth. The back of his head reminded him of the trauma it had suffered, and when he tried to move, it screamed at him, pleading for him to remain motionless. He didn't listen. He refused to listen. He had to move, to stand, and he had to keep going. He'd been hit before; this was no different. He was luckier than some. He was bruised, battered, and beaten, but he was breathing. And that meant he was alive. Some people couldn't say as much. He had to do nothing more than stop complaining and get himself moving. Anything less would be a defeat.

In the office, he turned on only the desk lamp. Too much light would be unbearable. He sat for a moment at the desk, a whisky poured out in a glass by his elbow, and he let the aches in his body settle. The walk from the alley to the building, through the foyer to the lift, and from the lift to the office had been a struggle. Someone had been dragging his destination away from him, so that the outside entrance to the building, the concrete steps, the lift doors, and the office door had all seemed to get further from him than closer to him. Now, sitting in his chair, he was able to allow all the dust to settle. And the whisky helped. The whisky always helped.

He had taken off his coat and jacket and now he pulled off his tie, unbuttoned and removed his shirt, and gently pulled off his vest. He walked into the small kitchen and turned on the light. It was a single bulb, just bright enough but not powerful enough to hurt. Priest approached the small, grimed mirror which hung over the sink and stared at the ghoul which confronted him. There was nothing in the face which he could recognise. It wasn't the bruise to the left eye or the dark, almost black trail of dried blood from the now discoloured nose to the broken lip. It wasn't the livid circles of purple and dirty yellow which mottled his torso and ribs. It wasn't even the older wounds, the hardened white lines of scars which latticed the whole of his back and chest, and which extended down further to the backs of his calves, the terrible remnants of agonising days under the lash of a sadist, all suffered and endured in the name of King and Country. It was none of that. It was the pale cheeks, the hollow eyes, and the general expression of disenchantment and futility which stared back at him from a face he knew he should recognise, but which meant nothing to him. What he saw was not the man he thought he was. And that was more painful than the lasting effects of any fist, boot, or whip.

He bathed his face in cold water, dabbing away the excess moisture with an old towel, limp and pathetic, only just suitable for the purpose. He walked slowly out of the kitchen, his mind focused on the bottle and the glass. He had not heard anybody knock on the door and he had not heard the door itself opening. Perhaps the ringing in his ears was worse than he thought. For a moment, they stood in silence, staring at each other, neither able to find any words of immediate worth. He was conscious of her eyes, filled with horror and concern, as they passed over his injuries, both old and new.

"God in Heaven," said Evelyn Marriott. "What happened to you?"

She was walking towards him now, her arms outstretched, desperate to touch him, to help him. At once, his limbs and muscles stiffened in defence. "I'm fine."

"You look it. Sit down. I'll get you a drink."

She walked across the office as if she owned it, grabbing the bottle as if she commanded it, and poured the drinks as if their lives depended on it. They drank in silence, Priest sitting in his chair, the leather soothingly cold against his naked back, Evelyn sitting on the edge of his desk, twisted so that she was facing him.

"Who was it?" she asked.

He shrugged. "Doesn't matter who they were. What they did is what counts."

"I can see what they did. Why, though?"

He smiled, but only briefly. "One question too many."

"But I want to understand."

He shook his head. "I didn't mean you. I meant me."

Her eyes widened. "This is something to do with Leonard Quayle's missing secretary?"

"Partly."

"What could she be involved in which would make someone want to do this to you?"

The question was asked in a tone of voice which suggested that it was a genuine enquiry. Her expression was earnest, the eyes narrowed by the creases of confusion on her brow and the slight parting of her lips provoked a suggestion of innocence. For a moment, fuelled perhaps by the pain and the drink, Priest had a sudden desire to kiss her, to abandon and defy all his anxieties and preconceptions about the legitimacy of love, to spite his mother by showing her that he was capable of something approximating it. Instead, he sipped at the whisky and rolled it around his mouth.

"Have you ever heard of a man called Clem Murnaugh?" he asked, without warning.

She thought about it, but shook her head. "I don't think so."

"Has your husband ever mentioned him?"

"Not that I can remember." The voice was harder now, but only fractionally. "I know Thomas came to see you today."

Priest drained his glass and poured another. "Is that why you've come now? You two need to talk more openly with each other. He comes to see what we talked about and now you come and do the same thing in reverse. It's funny." Except he knew that it wasn't; it was anything but funny.

"As a matter of fact, that's exactly right. And if you want to know the truth, Alex," she added, "I was worried about you. Imagine that."

"No need to worry about me."

"You say that, but I called again and again today and got no answer. So, I came in person. And this is how I find you."

"It's been a long day." He watched her not respond. "Are you sure you don't know the name Clem Murnaugh?"

"Positive," she hissed. "Who is he?"

He shrugged casually. "Just a crook."

She sneered at him, placing the whisky down on the desk. "He's a crook, but you think my husband knows him?"

Priest stood up and pulled his shirt back on, buttoning it up as he spoke, but leaving the tie coiled on his desk. "Look, I don't know exactly what's going on, but there are a lot of coincidences which trouble me. First, Nancy Clayton goes missing. She works for Leonard Quayle, the man who is helping your husband with the purchases of properties for the Phoenix project. Quayle instructed an estate agent firm called Burke & Halliwell to buy those properties. That same estate agent is also selling derelict and abandoned buildings to someone for far more than they're worth. That might be your husband, or it might not. I've no way of knowing. What I do know is that Clem Murnaugh was taking secret photographs, pictures of prostitution and gangsters on the one hand and the same buildings Burke & Halliwell were selling for extortionate prices on the other. Murnaugh vanished about six months ago. Before he did, he sent his photographs to a journalist called Jimmy Boyd, who I found murdered last night." He counted off each point with his fingers. "So, that's Nancy and Murnaugh, both missing, both likely dead; photographs taken by Murnaugh are sent to Boyd, also dead; the same photographs show a direct connection to the agents used to buy properties, on behalf of your husband, by Leonard Quayle, the man I can prove was Nancy's lover. How does that all strike you, Mrs Marriott?"

She stared at him for a long moment, her eyes flickering with indecision, and her lips quivering with unformed questions. She drank some whisky, but whether it was to steady herself or to delay responding, Priest could not say. "Are you telling me that my husband might be involved in murder?"

Priest shrugged. "Unwittingly, maybe. I can't be sure, not yet. But I do know that there's a connection between the Phoenix properties and some very dangerous people."

"Who, exactly?"

"I'm not going to tell you that, for your own good," said Priest, shaking his head. "But I think that somehow the Phoenix project has been sabotaged and turned into a front for something much nastier."

"I just can't believe it."

"You don't have to believe it and there's nothing I can do about that. It doesn't stop it being true."

She got up from her chair and began to pace the office. "Are you sure, Alex? About any of what you're saying?"

"You think I'm just a paranoid private detective who's been battered once too often and drank one glass too many to make any sense. Is that it?"

"I'm not saying that, Alex."

He rose from the desk and walked across the office towards her. Her stared down into her eyes, as if he could hypnotise her into believing what he was saying. "I might be a little drunk, Mrs Marriott, but I don't think I'm paranoid."

"All right," she said, looking up into his eyes. "If you're right, why haven't they killed you?"

"Because they don't know how much I've found out. If I'm no real threat to them, my murder would be a step too far. The police would look into the death of one of their own, even one they've lost faith in. A beating the police would take as an occupational hazard for a man like me. Killing me is too dangerous right now. So this," he gestured to his face, "this is just a warning to keep in line."

"Do you think Thomas had anything to do with that?" She pointed to his face. He didn't reply and she tried not to read anything into his silence. "It doesn't make any sense, Alex. Why would Thomas allow anybody to cajole him into allowing the Phoenix project to be sabotaged?"

"They must have some hold over him."

She was denying it with her glare. "Never."

"How well do you know him?"

"I know he isn't a criminal."

Priest spread out his hands, almost conciliatorily. "Then answer your own question. Why is he allowing it to happen?"

But there was no answer to give. She shook her head vigorously, lowering her head so that he could not see the tears well in her eyes. But it was too late for that. He stepped towards her and stroked her hair, then her cheek, feeling the dampness against his palm. Gently, he forced her to raise her head. It was shocking to see her so helpless, so out of control of the situation, given her usual confidence and assurance.

"I don't want to make you cry," Priest said. "I just want to know the truth, a few more days to look into things further. If your husband's being used and exploited, let me see if there's any way that I can help him."

She tossed her hair out of her face and tried to smile from behind the tears. "And why would you do that, Alex?"

"Because if he's innocent, he's going to need a friend."

"And if he's guilty of anything?"

"Then I'm not the friend he gets."

She looked into his damaged face. "Why do you do this? What do you get out of any of it?"

"Ten pounds a day and expenses." He held her gaze for a long moment. "And the chance to sleep at night and look myself in the eye every morning."

The kiss was inevitable. They both knew it was going to happen and neither of them stopped it. It was Evelyn who pulled him towards her and it was her hands which clutched at him. If she worried about why his own hands were less assured, she did not break the moment to ask. If she had, he doubted he could have answered satisfactorily. For once, there seemed to be no spectre of his mother looming over him, no bitter taste of her betrayal and desertion. There was only the taste of Evelyn, the touch of her lips, and the scent of her perfume.

"You bastard," she said. "Why do you make me feel like this? Why did you ever have to come to my house at all?"

He did not reply. Her hands had moved from his shoulders to the base of his spine. Her nails probed his back through his shirt, tracing their way over his spine and either side of it. She was breathing heavily, and intermittently, she planted small kisses on his cheek. He remained motionless, neither encouraging nor refusing, as if any motion would break the spell and force him to confront the reality of the situation.

"What happened to you?" she asked.

For a moment, he did not understand the question, framing it in his mind only with reference to the beating he had suffered. But in an instant, he was aware of her fingers on his back, moving around all over it, running their way along the horrible roadmap of scars which she now knew were under his shirt. With a sudden ferocity, he gripped her wrists and pulled them away, dropping them in her own lap. He took a step backwards from her, but she knew that it might as well have been a country mile. His eyes were so sharp, so hard, that they could have cut glass.

"Nothing," he said. "Nothing which matters now."

"I've seen them, Alex. I can't forget them."

"They're just what they are."

"War wounds?"

He nodded. "And not as bad as some. Leave it."

"They look bad enough to me," she said. "Alex, they're whip marks."

"I said, leave it." His voice was even more distant now. Whatever the moment had been between them, it was over now and she had lost him.

"Don't be alone, Alex. Whatever has happened to you in the past, please share it with me. Or don't you trust me enough?"

"I don't need to share it."

"You were starting to trust me, weren't you? That's why you told me about your suspicions about Thomas."

"Maybe I made a mistake." He picked up his glass of whisky. "Too much of this bloody stuff."

She was smiling at him. It was a smile of kindness, but the pity which accompanied it was only too obvious. "No, it wasn't. Whatever you think, Alex, you can trust me."

He pointed to the door. "You should go back to your husband."

She did not move. "Let me help you, Alex."

"I'm the one helping you, Mrs Marriott," he said. "Go back to your husband. I'm too damned tired for all this now."

He sat back down in the chair, raised the glass of whisky to his lips, and leaned back. He closed his eyes and said nothing more. Conversation over.

Evelyn Marriott watched him for a long moment, expecting him to open his eyes once again, but he didn't. Even when he took a drink, it was as if she was not there and that all he had was his own thoughts. She walked to the door and pulled it open. Looking back at him, she found that he had opened his eyes and was watching her.

"Go to Hell, Alex," she said, slamming it shut.

He waited for a moment, in case she returned, but she didn't. He wasn't sure how he felt about that, but he wasn't prepared to do anything about it. He rose from the chair and turned to face the window. It had begun to rain and the pane was covered with flecks of water, which seemed to distort his face even more than the bruises. Below him, the streets glistened, the headlamps of the cars were blurred, and people ran for shelter. Or perhaps they were running for their lives. It was impossible to tell. He placed his forehead against the cool pane and closed his eyes. His breathing became shorter, fiercer, and the sensation of the desire to leap from the window, to fall down with the rain, was almost frighteningly overwhelming. He slammed his palm against the glass and swore bitterly. Evelyn had told him to go to Hell and perhaps she had meant it. She was too late, though. To Priest, it seemed that he was already there and he wondered whether he would ever find the way back.

CHAPTER TWENTY-ONE

On the following morning, the pain was no better. He had avoided sleeping in the office and had gone home to the single room he rented, but which was no more of a home to him than a hotel room was. It was an adequate place and he had no complaints about it. The bed was comfortable, as far as cheap mattresses and blankets went; the amenities were cleaner than he had a right to expect; the rent money was manageable and the landlady was amenable and unintrusive, her cooking impressive, on those rare occasions when he had sampled it. He had no complaints at all about the room; it just wasn't the office. It didn't speak to him like the office did; it didn't know him like the office did. It didn't comfort him like the office did.

Nevertheless, he slept better than he had for some weeks and he rose early on the following morning, bathing immediately, making sure that he could be dressed and out before any other lodger, so that he didn't have to engage in common pleasantries or explain his battered appearance by similarly engaging in troubling unpleasantries. The bath had been soothing and his muscles were grateful for it. His broken lips and bloodied nose were less thankful. He shaved, the razor slightly too blunt for the task, resulting in an incomplete but adequate job. He drank two glasses of cold water from the tap in his room, made his bed by picking up a dislodged pillow, tossing it on the mattress, and dragging the blanket untidily into place.

He had been in the office long enough to brew a pot of coffee when she knocked on the door. She did not wait for him to invite her to enter. Instead, she pushed open the door and kicked it shut with a flick of her heel. Priest didn't know her, but her knew her type. He had seen too many like her in too many shop doorways, too many corners of disreputable pubs, and too many street corners. Her skirt and jacket were dark, but not as dark as some of her encounters would have been, and they were not yet quite past their best, still smart enough to pass off as respectable. Her hair was a vivid shade of red, like the roaring fires of the war, and in its own way, just as devastating. Her features were pale, making the blue of the eyes seem all the more astonishing. She was pretty, not yet looking older than her years, but not far from it, and the scarlet pout of the lips suggested no fear of confrontation, a symptom of the life she had been forced to lead for too long.

"Alexander Priest?" she said.

"That's what it says on the door." He pointed behind him. "And the window."

She rolled her tongue along the inside of her lower lip, as if she was tasting the retort and was preparing to spit it back at him. "My name's Latimer. Mary Latimer."

He pointed to the client chairs. "Have a seat, Miss Latimer. How can I help you?"

As she walked towards the desk and chairs, she took in his face with more care than previously. "You had a row with someone?"

"Something like that." He touched the bruises automatically.

"Don't tell me," she said, "I should see the other fella."

He smiled, despite himself. "I gave a good account of myself."

"Yeah?"

Priest nodded. "I just about managed to break one of his fingernails."

Her smile, and the subsequent laugh, was reluctant, but no less honest for that. "She said you were a nice bloke."

He frowned slightly. "Who?"

"A friend of mine, Jenny Barlow."

The spiders began to crawl over Priest's neck again. "Is she all right?"

Mary watched him carefully. "That's what I came to ask you. Last night, she came to see me, to ask if I could put her up for a couple of days. She told me about you."

"Did you say she could stay?"

"Jenny and I are good friends. I'd never let her down."

In spite of the spiders on his neck, Priest leaned back in his chair and shrugged, aiming for nonchalance. "So, why are you here?"

"Jenny left my house to go back to hers, to get a few things," said the girl. "I told her she didn't need to, but she insisted. Didn't like to think she was imposing, like as not. I waited for her to come back. All night," she added, after a pause.

The spiders had turned to icicles, melting on the warmth of his neck, so that small rivers of fear flowed down his spine. “She might have changed her mind.”

Mary shook her head. “I went to her lodgings this morning. I asked one of the blokes who lives there if he’d seen her. He hadn’t, not since yesterday afternoon.”

“This man,” said Priest, cautiously, “is he reliable?”

Mary sneered at the question. “One of Jenny’s regulars, if you must know. And he’s as reliable as any of us get.”

“Did you ask him if he knew where Jenny might have gone?”

“He didn’t know.”

Priest took time to frame his next question as delicately as possible. “Is it possible she met a client on the way back to her lodgings? Been persuaded to go with him, maybe?”

“On business, you mean? You know how it works for girls like us, Mr Priest. Anything like that, we let each other know details. It don’t just happen straight off like that. A garbled message with someone or a scrawled note delivered somewhere. There’d be something. And I’ve had nothing from Jenny.”

Priest shifted in his chair so that he was leaning forward, his elbows on the blotter. The smoke from the cigarette which he had lit curled in front of his face. “Did she tell you what she and I talked about?”

“Not much. That’s why I’m here now, to find out what I can from you.”

Priest said nothing for a moment. “Did you know Clem Murnaugh?”

Mary hesitated before replying. She pointed to his cigarette. “Can I have one of them?”

He pushed the packet and matches across to her and watched her light it. Her hands didn’t tremble, but it took an effort. “You know what Clem was, then?”

She nodded, blowing smoke out of the side of her mouth. “I know who he worked for, if that’s what you mean.”

“Did Jenny ever mention a man called Boyd to you?”

“Not that I remember.”

“What about Costello, Patrick Costello?” Another shake of the head. “Did she ever mention something called the House of Skulls?”

Mary smiled. “That a club?”

"No."

"I never heard of it, whatever it is."

Priest smoked for a long moment, but his eyes never left her. She had no reason to lie to him and he couldn't say that she was doing. Her eyes had remained open, fixed on him, and her voice had remained constant, with no trace of the cautious hesitation which comes with deceit. All of which meant that what she said was true; in turn, that meant that Jenny had vanished. Like Murnaugh, like Nancy; the only difference being that Jenny had disappeared almost immediately after speaking to Priest. Cause, effect, and all his fault. Suddenly, the beating hadn't seemed anywhere near severe enough.

Mary broke the silence. "So, what's all this about then?"

Priest glared at her. "I can't tell you."

"Can't? Or won't?"

"Take your pick."

She gave him two fingers. "I want to know where she is."

"So do I."

"Then let me help you."

"No."

The same two fingers. "Thing is, clever bastard, Clem Murnaugh might be nothing to do with it."

He tried not to betray any sense of the sudden, chill wave of anxiety which had swept him onto the coast of concern. "Why not?"

"Because Jenny ain't the only one to disappear." Her eyes were serious beyond her years. "There's been others."

"You mean Murnaugh?"

She shook her head. "Other girls. There one minute, gone overnight, without a word said."

Priest took the cigarette slowly from his lips and crushed it in the ashtray. "Gone where?"

Mary shrugged, almost petulantly, and began to pick at a fingernail. "I don't know. They just stopped coming in the pub. It was the same during the war. Some of the girls, older than Jenny and me, seemed to have given up on the game. Just like that, without a word. We'd not see them no more. No one ever knew where they went."

"When did it start again?" He felt he could predict the answer.

She shrugged, as if the question was irrelevant. "A good few months ago."

Six months ago, if Priest was any judge. "Anybody been to the police?"

She laughed, scornfully and bawdily. "Course we have! Straight to the top of their list, we went. What do you think? Bloody hell."

"There must have been rumours," persisted Priest.

"A few."

"Such as?"

"Some folk said they'd heard that the girls had moved on to better things. Gone up in the world."

"Meaning what?"

She stubbed out her cigarette. "Got off the game, like as not. It happens, you know. Some of us get saved. Sometimes."

Her wish that it would happen to her was palpable and Priest felt a sudden desire to grant it, regardless of how impossible it might be. "And you think Jenny's got off the game overnight?"

She could tell that he was not convinced. "Struck me as a possibility."

"But you don't believe it, do you?"

"I don't know what to believe," she replied. "I just know that Jenny didn't come back to my house last night, when she said she would, and that it was your idea she should stay with me in the first place. I'm just trying to understand what's going on with her."

"Me too," he replied.

But the truth was that he felt that he was beginning to understand. The property purchases through Burke & Halliwell, Clem's photos of the buildings, the secretly taken pictures of rape and abuse, prostitutes leaving the slums for better things: Priest saw it all. The places were being bought, renovated, and turned into brothels. The girls were being moved out of the East End to service them, except they thought their fortunes were changing. The Devil alone knew what stories they were told, what empty promises were made, but they had been silky enough to make sure the girls went willingly. Once there, as Clem's photos suggested, they were pumped full of dope and put to work. Welcome to going up in the world. It was naïve to think that Jenny wasn't now part of that nastiness. Priest thought about the apartment building in Southwark, suddenly knowing for certain that it had been intended to be one of these brothels, one of many soon to be scattered across London, infiltrating and polluting wealthy suburbs as well as deprived ones, all so that the rich hypocrites didn't have to risk a visit to the slums of the East End to satisfy themselves.

Mary Latimer was watching him as he thought, her eyes widened with confusion and desperation. He smiled at her, but nothing in his mind was pleasant or amusing. The more he stared at her, the more he could picture her in one of those places, like Jenny must be now, her eyes glassed over, and her will crushed under the weight of artificial control, slowly melting into dependency and death, her emotions and nerves numbed by the endless intrusions of the rich and the powerful, the filthy and the depraved. It was bound to happen at some point.

Priest snatched up the phone. He was connected quickly. "Frank, I need a favour."

"When did I become your secretary, Priest?" asked Darrow.

"I've got a witness with me." He lowered his voice. "I need someone to take care of her for me. Just for a little while." He ignored Mary's attempts to resist, the waving of her hands in protest, and the silently mouthed refusals to co-operate.

"Why?"

Priest turned his chair to face the window and lowered his voice. "I think she needs protection."

"From what?"

"Jack Raeburn."

There was a long silence. When Darrow spoke again, there was an undercurrent of caution in his voice. "You need to bring this witness to me and you need to come with her, Priest."

"Can you send a car for her?"

"I can send one for both of you."

"Just her, Frank."

"I'm not asking you, Priest. I'm just letting you know how it is. Don't touch Raeburn without me knowing what's going on. I can only protect you so far."

"You're all heart, Frank."

The voice was becoming more insistent. "I mean it, Alex."

Priest was shaken by the use of his first name, not something Darrow had done in a long time, and even back then only very rarely. Of all the things said and done, that use of his name troubled him the most. What might normally have been a sign of friendship, now seemed to Priest to be a warning of danger.

"Ten minutes, Frank," he said. "We'll be ready in ten minutes."

When the police car arrived at Priest's building, it drove off again with only one passenger in the back. As Mary Latimer looked out of the back window of the car at Priest, she found herself hoping that a few bruises to his face were the only damage he would suffer.

CHAPTER TWENTY-TWO

They had arranged to meet after lunchtime, which suited Priest fine. The call had not been friendly, but it had served its purpose. Leonard Quayle had been defensive, as Priest might have expected him to be, but Priest had been as diplomatic as he could manage.

"I don't see what you can have to say to me, Mr Priest," Quayle had said. "Certainly nothing which might affect me in a personal manner, as you put it."

"You will, if you give me the chance to explain it, Mr Quayle," Priest had replied. "I just need to tell you some things which I've learned."

"Tell me now."

"Better in person," Priest had insisted amiably. "Believe me, Mr Quayle, I'm trying to help you."

So, the arrangement had been made. Quayle had suggested his office but Priest, with as much neutrality as he could inject into his voice, and said that his own would be better.

"I feel I should insist on neutral ground," Quayle had said.

"Right now, Mr Quayle, my office is as neutral as it gets."

Quayle arrived punctually. He accepted the offer of a chair, declined a coffee or anything stronger, and placed the leather briefcase which he had been carrying at his feet. He was looking at Priest's wounds, with the eye of a man who was wondering how much they had hurt and hoping for the worst.

"Well, I'm here, Mr Priest," he said, crossing one leg over the other. "What is it you want? I can't spare you a great deal of time."

"Then I won't waste it." Priest leaned forward and clasped his hands together on the desk. "Tell me about the properties you're buying on behalf of Thomas Marriott."

Quayle shrugged, but it was not as careless as he had desired. "It's part of his Phoenix project, to rebuild London after the war. We're buying derelict and abandoned office blocks, apartments, and so on, with a view to renovating them for the future."

"And you're buying them through Burke & Halliwell?"

Quayle was surprised to learn that Priest knew it, but he was able to hide it well. "Yes."

"Are you buying any of them at a higher price than they're worth?"

Now, Quayle's eyes became daggers behind the lenses of his glasses. "What's this all about, Mr Priest?"

A moment drifted by unnoticed. "Do you know a man called Clem Murnaugh, Mr Quayle?"

"No."

"Jack Raeburn?"

Quayle shifted in his seat, making a show of trying to place the name. "I know of him, of course. By reputation."

Priest smiled. "You know what he is?"

"What he is alleged to be, yes." Quayle managed a smile, but it had been like pushing water up a hill for him. "Are you suggesting, Mr Priest, that this Raeburn character is somehow involved in the Phoenix project?"

"Would that make you think that my brain had fallen out?"

"I would have to caution you against making any such statement publicly. Any damage to Thomas Marriott's reputation, or TGM Investments, even the Phoenix scheme itself, would result in a very unpleasant writ being served against you." He looked dismissively, around the office. "Could you afford that, Mr Priest?"

Priest leaned back in his chair and cocked his head to one side. "Let's leave Marriott out of things, then. Let's talk about you and Nancy Clayton instead."

Quayle's eyebrows rose slightly, his nostrils arching, but retained his composure with only a small struggle. "I've told you everything I know about her."

"I don't think so. I think you know everything about her."

"You're wrong."

"Intimate details, I'd say."

In order to disguise his outrage, Quayle laughed sardonically. "You've been knocked about, Mr Priest, anybody can see that. You've obviously hit your head."

"You'd better hope I don't hit yours." Priest reached into his desk drawer and pulled out an envelope. He tipped out the angel pendant. "I've been to the flat in Southwark, Mr Quayle. I found that under the bed."

Quayle's eyes were glaring at the pendant and almost invisible specks of sweat had begun to glitter like night stars on his upper lip. "What of it?"

Priest took out a photograph of Nancy Clayton and pointed to her neck. "It belongs to Nancy."

"There must be hundreds of them sold in the country."

Priest smiled dangerously. "True. But I bet not all of those hundreds end up under beds in apartments sold by Burke & Halliday, who you've also instructed on behalf of Thomas Marriott. And only one of those hundreds of pendants belongs to your own secretary. See my point, Mr Quayle?"

Quayle's expression was insolent rather than defiant. "I'm afraid I don't."

"You don't see any connections here?"

"No." The defiance was becoming more clearly emphasised now.

Priest raised his eyebrows and sighed, as if he had experienced an inevitable but significant disappointment. "The pendant shows she was in that flat, in a building sold by Burke & Halliwell. You're a direct connection between the two. And I know about your trips to *The Midnight Pearl* nightclub."

Quayle's composure was in place, but cracks were showing in the dam wall, the pressure of the water behind it building up uncontrollably. "I don't know what you're talking about."

Priest's eyes had become malevolent. "I know all about you, Quayle. Nobody would think it to look at you, but you've got a problem with women. In the sense that you can't keep away from them. If you see a girl you want, you have to have her. Never mind your wife sitting at home, wondering where you are, but knowing what you're up to."

"Leave my wife out of this," warned Quayle.

Priest was relentless. "You wanted Nancy, didn't you? And she wanted you, though God alone knows why. Maybe you represented power, money, and influence, a way for her to escape the dreary homelife she hated. You took her dancing, to clubs like *The Midnight Pearl*, gave her champagne, cocktails, and anything else she wanted to try. All courtesy of Jack Raeburn, no doubt."

"I don't know Raeburn," insisted Quayle.

"I can place you in the executive areas of *The Midnight Pearl*, with Nancy on your arm, your little scarab cufflinks showing themselves off in the lights."

Quayle's face had whitened as Priest spoke, his mouth dropping open in silent and ineffectual protest, and the lenses of his spectacles seeming to shimmer with guilt. He uncrossed his leg and began to rub his palms slowly across the length of his thighs. "I don't know Raeburn."

"He owns *The Midnight Pearl*, Quayle."

"I don't know him."

"So, how did you get into the executive areas with Nancy?"

"I don't know him." It was all he could say, as if repeating it would convince Priest of its truth. "What you say about Nancy is true, but I don't know Raeburn."

Priest leaned back in his chair. "Let's concentrate on Nancy, then. You were having an affair?"

Quayle nodded meekly. "Yes."

Priest sneered. "You must be a lot more impressive in private than you are in public."

Quayle, unexpectedly and violently, slammed his fist against the desk. Priest didn't budge, but his eyes burned with fascination.

"Don't mock me, you grubby little man," seethed Quayle. "You've no right to be so sanctimonious when you earn your sordid living from peeping through keyholes."

"Don't frighten me with big words and clichés, Mr Quayle," said Priest. "Tell me about Nancy instead."

Quayle spread his fingers, as if he hoped to see some sort of escape in the palms, but all he saw were the small beads of sweat which had formed on their surfaces. No answers there. "The others were a bit of fun, a distraction from my marriage. I don't have a complete marriage, Mr Priest. I suppose, in your line of work, you hear a lot of stories about loveless marriages. Mine is no different to any of them. Dorothy loves me, I know that, but any fire between us burned out long ago."

"And you enjoy the fire, is that it?"

Quayle looked up to meet his glare, refusing to be patronised. "I'm only human, Mr Priest."

"You are that," said Priest, bitterly.

Quayle did not rise to the argument. He was too busy living in his memories. "Nancy was different. She had such wonder about her, so eager to experience life. You talk about her life at home being dreary and I think it was. Certainly, she felt it was."

"And you rescued her from it?"

"I don't claim to have done anything of the sort."

Priest took out a cigarette and turned it over in his fingers, giving no thought to lighting it. He just had to have something to occupy his hands, to keep them busy. "What went wrong?"

Quayle took a long, slow intake of breath. "She had become rather demanding. Of my time and my attention. She was becoming less and less discreet during working hours. I told her it had to end, that we had run our course."

"Meaning you'd had your fun and the sparkle had dimmed?" It was a petulant remark and Priest knew it. "Did she accept it was over?"

"I think so."

Priest thought the opposite, but he said nothing. He pointed to the angel. "So, how did that come to be under the bed in a flat in Southwark?"

Quayle fought against his unease. "Finding private places to go when you are meeting secretly can be difficult. I abused my position as a solicitor on a number of occasions."

"Including using the properties you were buying for the Phoenix project to meet Nancy." Priest did not frame it as a question; he did not need to. Quayle nodded. "The flat in Southwark was a rat hole. Didn't Nancy deserve better than that, at least?"

Quayle shrugged. "It added to the risk for her. She would say what we were doing was sordid, as well as thrilling, so it should be done in sordid as well as thrilling places. Cheap, seaside hotel rooms; abandoned apartments. Once, even, against the wall of a darkened alleyway." He folded his arms and crossed his legs, as if to prevent his apparent shame from cascading out onto the desk. "Sometimes, you understand, not always."

"Don't look so embarrassed. You loved every minute of it."

Quayle's flick of the eyes, like a snake's tongue sniffing the air, was rapid and filled with malice. He pointed to the angel. "That must have fallen from her necklace during one of our meetings."

"That would suggest they were fairly violent encounters."

"Passionate, Mr Priest."

"I prefer to say violent," purred Priest. "That way, I can account for the blood I found on the fireplace grate."

The effect on Quayle was both immediate and profound. His eyes did not widen, but they burned with startled horror and his lips tightened in silence, as though any words would be incriminating. His body froze almost entirely, with only the muscles in his throat rising and falling in swift, tense movements, as if he was fighting back the urgent need to vomit. "Blood?"

Priest nodded. "On the grate."

Now, there was a flicker of agitation in the corner of Quayle's eyes. "Nancy's blood?"

A shrug of the shoulders from Priest. "I don't know, but it seems likely to me. It'd explain her disappearance, wouldn't it? If she was dead, I mean."

Now, slowly, Quayle's arms unfolded and his legs unwrapped themselves. He leaned forward in his chair, resting his hands on the side of the desk. "Are you accusing me of murder?"

"I'm saying where there's blood, there's some sort of injury. I'm saying pendants like this don't break easily. I'm saying that it's easier to get rid of a dead body than a living one. And I'm saying that Nancy hasn't been seen for six weeks."

Quayle had slowly pulled himself out of his chair. He was steadying himself by gripping the edge of the desk with his fingers. His eyes were moving quickly, unable to focus on anything for longer than a few seconds, his mouth quivering with silent words of protestation.

Priest was watching him. "Something hit a nerve? What part of all that makes sense to you, Quayle?"

"None of it.".

Priest stood up and leaned into his face. "Had she become dangerously indiscreet? Or had she given you some terrible, much more personal news?"

Quayle seemed confused by his words. "Terrible news?"

Priest lowered his voice. "I can think of a dozen reasons why a man would have to kill his secret lover, Mr Quayle. I don't need to go through them all, do I?"

It seemed to pull Quayle out of himself. "I haven't killed anybody."

"So who did?"

Quayle seemed about to reply, but no words came. His eyes had hardened, as if he had made a crucial, final decision about something and with it, there came a return of his self-assurance. "Do you have anything further to say to me, Mr Priest?"

Priest was still leaning over the desk. Not for the first time, he felt as if a joke was being played and everyone but him was involved in it. Except nobody was laughing. Instead, people were dying. "You're involved in all this, Quayle. Murder, prostitution, maybe even worse."

"You'll need proof, Mr Priest. Remember that writ I mentioned." He turned his back and began to walk towards the door.

"Where will I find it, Quayle?" Priest called after him. "In the House of Skulls?"

Quayle stopped dead in his tracks, the door half opened, so that the light from the corridor turned him into a half-silhouette. "If you have turned over enough stones to find that name, Priest, you had better be careful or else those bruises to your face will seem like a stroll along the beach."

"You'll have to get up earlier than you do to terrify me."

There was the sound of a low, disturbing snigger. "Perhaps it isn't me you need to be frightened of."

"What is the House of Skulls?" asked Priest.

Quayle did not reply. He repeated the gentle but sinister laugh, stepped out of the office, and shut the door behind him. Priest remained motionless, still leaning over the desk. Somewhere far away, somebody was beating a bass drum. It wasn't music, just a sombre rhythm. Priest listened to it for a moment, wondering where it was coming from and what purpose it was supposed to serve. It took him a long moment to realise that it was his own heartbeat.

CHAPTER TWENTY-THREE

The buildings which Clem Murnaugh had photographed, if it were possible, looked worse in reality than they did in the pictures. Somehow, seeing the faded colours of the paintwork, the mildew on the panes of the windows, and the burnt amber of the dead bushes in the ill-kempt plots of unprepossessing gardens was more depressing than the black and white representations of those things. Perhaps it was that the chipped and distressed colours of the paint on the doors and gates were a reminder that, at one time, there might have been hope and vitality behind them. Now, there was only the suggestion of decay, not only from abandonment but also from the effects of the conflict which had only recently come to its end. For some people, perhaps even Priest himself, the war might as well still be raging, since its presence could still be felt so keenly. Its sounds, smells, and destruction could still be seen and felt, and not for the first time, Priest couldn't help thinking that one way or another, there would never be peace again. Not truthfully, not absolutely.

After Quayle had left his office, Priest had spent half an hour plotting a route across London, using Clem's photographs, a telephone directory, and a map to identify the various locations. The pictures had been identical in terms of the depiction of the bleakness of the sites, but the places themselves were varied: dance halls, bingo halls, blocks of apartments, abandoned pubs, derelict houses. A bingo hall would be too large to convert into a whorehouse, thought Priest, but it would make a suitable casino and the dance halls could be returned to their former glory more easily than anything else. The only difference would be that they would be owned now by Jack Raeburn, which meant that with every glass of champagne would come a free dose of cocaine or a bullet to the brain, whichever way your fortune fell.

What he was hoping to achieve by visiting them, Priest could not tell. It was something to do other than to scramble his brain trying to put everything together. At times, he could have enough of thinking and his legs would itch for movement, his lungs scream for air, and his mind clamour for physical activity rather than mental exercise. It was the human desire to feel as if something were being done, of being practical, rather than sitting in a chair with your feet on the desk and your brain in your hands.

Proof. It was what Quayle had said he needed and Priest had no argument with it. He wouldn't get it by turning ideas over in his head; he would get it by going out and searching for it. People like him weren't called gumshoes for nothing. And so, he had got out a selection of the photographs, the map, and the directory, and he had started with the pencil and pad. A call to Frank Darrow had assured him that Mary Latimer was safe.

"She keeps asking to see you," Darrow had said.

"Tell her I'll come as soon as I can."

"Why's she so special, Priest?"

He had not known what answer to give, not initially. "Maybe she's one we can save, Frank."

Darrow had laughed coldly. "Make sure you don't cut yourself on that armour of yours, Lancelot."

Priest had dropped the phone back onto the cradle without another word. He needn't have felt so offended. What was a bit of friendly mockery on top of everything else? Maybe if he had been in a better mood.

He was thinking of giving up when he saw them. They were outside one of the old dance halls, a place which had once been known for its exclusivity, but which now was nothing more than an outgrown chrysalis, whose butterfly of elite entertainment had spread its wings and flown away. The domed roof, its windows broken and damaged by age and conflict, now looked so pretentious in its neglect that it was pitiful; the velvet of the curtains behind the darkened panes of the front of the place had fallen victim to moths, the torn strips of fabric which hung from the rails now seeming hopeless in their despair. The doors had been opened to their extreme, like welcoming arms spread to greet an awaited saviour, except that the impression given was that the fresh air would turn the insides to dust, like an archaeologist exposing a mummified corpse to the elements. Priest thought back to Clem's representation of it, at his capturing of the forlorn and forgotten shell of what had once been the opulent and elitist *Cavendish Club*. Now, it was nothing, a distant memory, and piece of old newspaper on the breeze, even if it was soon to be restored to its former glory, albeit as a gangster's paradise. Somehow, Priest seemed suddenly to prefer it in its present state of sombre disrepair.

Leaning against a lamp post, Priest lit a cigarette, watching as men carried boxes and crates through those welcoming arms of the front entrance. The sound of a car door, opening and closing, distracted him. Wolfe had seen him before Priest could have had any chance of walking away. Even before the thought had occurred to him, and he had rejected it, Wolfe was approaching him. Neither of the two mountains who had got out of the car with him followed. They didn't need to; there would be no trouble on a public street in the middle of the afternoon. Wolfe was confident enough about that and Priest had no intention of disappointing him. If he had, there would be only one loser.

Wolfe stood in front of him with his hands clasped behind his back. Anybody looking at them would see what looked like a businessman in tailored clothes and a battered nobody in a crumpled suit, one step away from a tramp. One respectable, the other far from it. Priest was only too keenly aware of the irony.

"You look as if you've been in the wars, Mr Priest," said Wolfe.

"You wouldn't know anything about it, would you?" Priest did not expect a reply and he was not provided with one. He pointed to the trucks and the open doors of the club. "Moving in?"

Wolfe looked casually over to the work being undertaken. "New business premises, Mr Priest."

"Bought through Burke & Halliwell, no doubt?"

Wolfe smiled. "I don't know any of the details."

Priest tossed away the butt of his cigarette, the end still burning. "I think you know all the details, Wolfe."

Wolfe let out a small, oddly delicate laugh. It other circumstances, in a different place, it might have terrified Priest. "You flatter me."

"I'd hate to think how many secrets you keep."

Wolfe looked towards him, as if seeing him for the first time and suddenly being aware that he was not at all what he might have expected. It was more than the bruises, more than the twist of obvious disgust on his lips, and more than the malevolent glare of his eyes. It was the sudden impression, one which Wolfe had never been aware of previously, that perhaps he and Priest were not so different, that their capacity for hatred and violence might not be so far removed. When they were stripped down to their souls at a time of atonement, assuming either of them believed in such things, Wolfe had the clearest idea that there would be little to differentiate them.

"Are you not also a man of secrets, Mr Priest?" asked Wolfe.

"Meaning?"

Wolfe shrugged. "All those questions you ask, you must receive some answers. But none of us ever know what they are, do we?"

"The answers I get only lead to more questions, Wolfe."

"Is that so?"

Priest shrugged. "Like that poor bastard who kept rolling a rock up a hill only to watch it roll back down again."

Wolfe inhaled slowly and exhaled silently, but Priest was still aware of the suppressed malice underlying the breath taken. It was the calmness of it, the stillness in Wolfe's being, which was so unsettling. His manner was always the same, one of unruffled, almost soothing serenity, even when he was employed in the most unpleasant of tasks. There had been a rumour, never wholly verified but no less frightening because of it, that Wolfe had once broken the toes of a man with a pair of pliers, sliced off one of the ears, and begun work on the other, before the man began to give the information required; all of which done without Wolfe breaking a sweat and without any external display of aggression or effort. Priest had doubted his heart rate had increased much higher than it would if he had run up a flight of stairs. Blood pressure and pulses only intensify when the body is under stress; but there is no stress when doing what comes naturally.

"Mr Raeburn might have a few questions," said Wolfe. "Come with me."

"Jack's here?"

Wolfe pointed to the club. When Priest took a step forward, an arm snapped out like a switchblade. "Make sure his answers don't lead to more questions. Hear what I'm saying?"

Like bells tolling for the dead, thought Priest. But it wasn't the words which troubled him; it was the smile which had come with them.

Inside, the club smelled of rooms left too long without air and the sounds of their shoes echoing on the wooden, parquet floors only added to the sense of desolation. From a distance, Priest could hear the sound of saws against wood, furniture being shifted around, and voices in turn arguing and laughing. Without people to fill it, the club seemed enormous, almost overpowering in size, so that it seemed impossible that it could ever be filled, no matter how many bodies moved on the dance floors or sat on the stools at the bar. Without the sound of music, of singing, and of chatter, the acoustics of the club seemed tragic and forlorn. It was as if a world had come to an end, its population decimated, and only the ghosts of its former glory left to roam around unheeded. Perhaps it was no different to anywhere else, no matter how keenly Priest felt its particular sense of despair.

Wolfe led him up a flight of stairs, curling from one of the bars to the upper echelons of the club. Several alcoves, lined with booths, branched off from the corridor which stretched out ahead of them, areas which once would have been reserved for prominent and important guests. Priest had a sudden recollection of Nancy and Leonard Quayle in the equivalent sections of *The Midnight Pearl*. At the end of the corridor was a door, which Wolfe approached casually, knocking once when he reached it. He didn't need to wait for a reply, so he pushed open the door and beckoned for Priest to enter.

Jack Raeburn was standing in the centre of the room. He had removed his jacket and rolled up his shirt sleeves, so that the thick forearms were exposed. It was not done in order to enable him to participate in any of the physical labour which was taking place around him. Priest suspected that it was more to do with reminding people that Raeburn was still able to do some damage with those arms, if and when he felt the need. He turned to face them as they approached, the false black hair and thick, painted eyebrows as startling as ever, their unreality all the starker, somehow, when set against the harsh truth of the abandoned room.

"You're seeing history be made here, Priest," he said, throwing wide his arms. "You remember the old *Cavendish Club*?"

"Not my kind of place," muttered Priest.

"It was great in its day," said Raeburn. "Fell on hard times during the war, of course, but I'm going to restore it to its former glory."

"Good for you."

Raeburn's smile faded slowly. He walked over to Priest, his eyes glancing swiftly but meaningfully to Wolfe for the briefest of moments. "You don't sound too excited."

Priest shrugged. "As I said, not my kind of place."

Raeburn touched Priest's cheek, just below the crimson and blue of the bruising around his eye. "A bad knock. Obviously not thinking straight."

Priest returned the smile. "What do you want me for, Jack?"

Raeburn frowned. "Did I want you?"

"Wolfe dragged me in here, because he said you had a few questions for me. I was minding my own business outside."

"I doubt that." Raeburn turned away and began to walk towards one of the alcoves. "Come and have a drink, Priest."

"No, thanks." There was a sharp, brutal shove in his back, propelling him forwards and off balance, so that he nearly stumbled onto his knees. He turned to look at Wolfe, who was pointing at the table at which Raeburn was now sitting. Priest smiled without humour. "A drink. Good idea."

He sat down opposite Raeburn. From somewhere, seemingly without any order being given, a girl had arrived with two drinks on a silver tray. The girl might have been one of the two who had been with Raeburn in the Soho restaurant, but Priest couldn't be sure. All he knew was that the distant, vacant expression in the almost lifeless eyes was the same. He felt a curious sensation of nausea. She handed him one of the glasses. It was a champagne flute, chilled by the look and feel of it, and the liquid inside was a dull yellow colour. Priest assumed it was champagne, but the twist of lemon zest on top of the foam seemed incongruous. He waited for Raeburn to drink first, a crude but seemingly necessary precaution. Raeburn savoured the mouthful he took and Priest followed the example. Almost immediately, he felt as if he had been shot in the chest by a cannon.

"Christ," he gasped.

Raeburn was laughing. "Never had a French 75 before, Priest?"

Priest had put down the flute, as if it was something lethal, something so dangerous that only distance could save him from it. "What the hell is it?"

"Champagne and cognac. A French-American fighter pilot in the Great War invented it. Champagne wasn't enough for him, so he tossed in some cognac. He named it after the French 75mm field gun, because it seemed to him to pack the same amount of power. Keeps you on your toes, doesn't it?"

"It puts you on your bloody back," hissed Priest.

"What's the matter with you? I thought you were tough."

Priest glared at him. "I can take a baton, a sap, or a pistol butt any time. They're easy. That thing is for maniacs."

Raeburn was smiling to himself. "You'll get used to it."

Priest sipped some more of the cocktail and tried to keep the top of his head in place. "Did you bring me up here just to poison me with this stuff?"

Raeburn was admiring his champagne flute, staring almost lovingly at the small globes of condensation on its surface. "They don't serve anything like this in *The Hanged Man*, do they?"

It was spoken deliberately, the tone of voice heavy with implication. Priest was staring down at his glass, suddenly conscious of both Raeburn's and Wolfe's eyes on him, daring him to say he didn't know or that he didn't understand. He picked up the flute and drank slowly, prepared this time for the effect. On second taste, the cocktail wasn't half bad, which meant that the bitterness and the bile in his mouth must have been the result of something else, something worse.

He looked up slowly into Raeburn's eyes. He did not speak immediately, but allowed a moment to pass by in silence. He pointed to the bruises. "These show you know I was there, Jack, and I never doubted it. So, why don't you tell me something I don't already know."

"You being there doesn't matter to me. What interests me is why."

"Any ideas on that?"

The thick, fake eyebrows rose and a smile parted the bulbous lips. "I don't need ideas, Priest, because I know. I just want to hear you say it."

Priest shook his head. "Where's Jenny Barlow, Jack?"

"You don't need to worry about her."

Another shake of his head. "No deal, Jack. Your monkeys see me talking to her, word is passed along, and I get a boot in my face. Next day, she goes missing, along with a whole bunch of girls over the last six months."

"People come and go," said Raeburn, shrugging.

"You're moving them out. You're using Leonard Quayle to buy up abandoned flats and houses, under the cover of the Phoenix Development run by TGM Investments. You're converting them into brothels and filling them with girls from the streets, all there to service any clients who don't want to be seen slumming it in the East End."

Raeburn was smiling, but his eyes didn't share the joke. He signalled to Wolfe. "Take away his drink, Harry, it's going to his head."

Priest clamped his hand around the flute, his eyes pinning Raeburn to the back of his seat. "You think I was talking to Jenny Barlow about Clem Murnaugh. That's why you've shipped her off to one of your new places. You'd discovered that Murnaugh was leaking secrets to a journalist, so you made Murnaugh vanish. When that journalist came round to follow up the scent, you had someone batter his head in for him. Is this stirring any memories, Jack, or am I whistling in the wind?"

Raeburn had been still throughout Priest's speech; now, he simply shook his head and shrugged his shoulders. "You're not just whistling. You're wailing a whole fucking opera. Clem Murnaugh drank his own weight in booze and fell in the Thames. End of story. If you've been hired to find him, you're burning your client's money."

"Who says I'm looking for him?"

"Can't see any other reason for you talking to his whore girlfriend."

Priest resisted the temptation to launch himself across the table. "If I was looking for him, would it bother you, Jack?"

"Bother me? By about ten buckets full of nothing."

"What if Murnaugh was leaking secrets to the press?"

Raeburn barked out a laugh. "Why do you keep saying that? Leaking secrets? What secrets?"

Priest lost none of his certainty. "About sabotaging the Phoenix project, about using it to bankroll brothels."

Raeburn laughed silently. "I don't need to hijack Tommy Marriott's little school project, Priest. If I wanted to buy properties and turn them into something like you're saying, I'd just do it. Besides," he added, shrugging, "if Murnaugh had the brains and the guts even to think about doing something like that, he'd have proof, right? Because without it, he's just a bag of wind with loose lips."

Priest sipped more of the drink, now grateful for its punch, its relentless sharpening of his senses. He was thinking about the photographs under his office floorboards. "Maybe he did have proof."

"But you don't know for sure, am I right?" Raeburn watched Priest nod swiftly. "So, you and Murnaugh are the same, two bags of fucking wind with loose lips."

"Someone still killed the journalist, Boyd," Priest felt obliged to say.

"So what if they did?" Raeburn drained his glass, clicking his fingers for a second. Now, he was pointing at Priest, his finger like a dagger. "You say it was me. All right, for the sake of argument, say it was. What motive do I have? These mott shops you're obsessed with? You're better than that, Priest."

"You're saying they're not a motive?"

"Damn right. Who do you think the rich and powerful are in the city, Priest? The politicians, the lawyers, the senior coppers, the bankers, the union leaders, the newspaper owners. Who do you think these whore houses, if they exist, would be designed for? If some greasy little spiv thought he'd have a news story about it, it'd be shut down before he licked the tip of his pencil. See? I wouldn't need to kill anyone if they found out about a scheme like that, because it wouldn't get past the first word. Too many people would be implicated in it before I was even mentioned and those same people would be denied a certain avenue of pleasure. Follow me?" He sipped at the new drink. "Then there's you."

Priest's eyes narrowed. "What about me?"

"Well, if anything like that was going on and you rumbled it, as you think you have, why'd you only get away with a tap on the head? If a hack was worth killing for it all, wouldn't an ex-copper private 'tec be worth it?" Raeburn was smiling. "You need to get your thinking cap back on, old lad. You're like a polar bear in the Sahara. Well off track."

He sniggered, but Priest didn't share the amusement. He drained the remainder of the drink, promising himself that he would never touch one again, and stood up. No hands gripped him by the shoulders and there was no command to sit back down. The interview was over and the damage had been done. Priest's certainty, his assurances of his own theories, was soaked up and left behind, like the twist of lemon zest in the remnants of the champagne foam in his flute. Only his stubbornness, and his refusal to believe that Raeburn could be innocent of anything, prevented him from walking back to the office, shutting the door, and never contacting any of them ever again.

He stepped away from the table and brushed past Wolfe, making sure he did not meet his glare. Priest had nothing to say to him. When he got to the door, he turned back and called out to Raeburn. The eyebrows, ridiculous and black, rose in response.

"That cocktail tastes like shit, Jack," Priest said, "but I'd drink ten of them before I believed a word you said."

Nothing more was said, but Priest could hear Raeburn laughing loudly to himself long after he had left the room.

CHAPTER TWENTY-FOUR

Priest had been walking for so long that he had not noticed that the skies had darkened and the air had dropped into its familiar, autumnal temperature. He hadn't thought he had been wandering for long, but the elements made a liar of him. He hadn't had any particular destination in mind; the walk had been aimless, without any other purpose than to allow him time to think. Ordinarily, he would have thought with a drink, his preferred combination, but it had seemed inappropriate. Drink could inflame his ideas, send him into directions which he had not anticipated, and he felt sure that he had to keep his thoughts concentrated on facts, without allowing them to go dancing through the moonlight with attractive, distracting theories.

But now, he was suddenly aware that he was both hungry and thirsty. His instinct was for the drink more than the food, but his body was telling him that he needed some form of nourishment. It might have been true, he thought, but his need for food seldom worked in tandem with his appetite for it. As he walked across London, heading for a small café he knew, a small distance from Euston station, none of the options for an evening meal which he considered seemed to appeal to him. All his mind could think of, all his taste buds and stomach could react to, was the lethal blend of champagne, cognac, and deceit.

The corned beef fritters and overboiled carrots did nothing to alter his mood, but he ate them dutifully, if reluctantly, and washed them down with a glass of lukewarm water and a mug of hot, strong tea, which had almost as much impact on him as the French 75. He left a few shillings more than the price of the meal and made his way back to the office. By the time he was sitting back at his desk, the bottle opened and a drink poured, he had been forced to turn on the desk lamp, as the evening had now descended with all its black emphasis.

Priest tried to empty his mind, to force all images and speculations out of its boundaries, but he was only partially successful. He managed to make them less distinct, but they still swirled around his brain, a kaleidoscope of blurred images, like a child's wanton experiment with different coloured paints, a turmoil of indistinct images, shapes, and colours, without anything coherent to bring them together into a recognisable whole. He closed his eyes and let out an involuntary sigh. His muscles ached, his brain buzzed, and his head and limbs suddenly felt as if they were carved out of lead. He was not human, not any more; he was a golem, without thoughts or feelings, just a faceless, emotionless slab of something which had nothing to do with breathing air and pumping blood. Slowly, he opened his eyes and sneered at the reflection of himself in the glass of the office window, the leering face of a stranger, of someone who had nothing to do with him, and nothing worthwhile to say. His sneer intensified and he toasted himself with the whisky, using it to drown his own depression. He shouldn't have had those fritters. He poured another whisky, just to lighten his mood.

When the phone rang, he felt like throwing it across the room. The best he could do was bark a greeting into the mouthpiece and wash it down with the whisky.

"You sound like a drunkard's privy," said Darrow.

"Are you going to ruin my night, Frank?"

"Doesn't sound as if it was too good to begin with." Darrow waited for some sort of reply, but got none. "Someone to speak to you."

Priest sat up in the leather chair, taking his feet off the desk. He could hear the rustle of movement across the connection of the phone, the hushed sound of whispered voices. Then, Mary Latimer's voice was in his ear. "All right of me to call?"

"Where are you?"

"At your pal's sister's house." Her voice lowered. "I don't think she's too happy at me being here. Think I'm putting her out."

"Frank will have explained why it's necessary."

There was a trace of shame in her voice. "I don't think he's told her what I am."

Priest smiled weakly. "She doesn't have to know."

A pause. "Anyway, I just wanted to let you know where I am. That I'm all right, like."

"Thanks. And I'm glad," he added. "Don't make a nuisance of yourself."

If he had expected a laugh, or a curt response, he was to be disappointed. "How long do you reckon I'll have to stay here?"

"I don't know."

She sighed gently. "At least you're honest. You still think I'm in some sort of danger?"

He tried to make his voice amiable, dismissive of her fears. "I'm just being cautious."

"And paranoid?" She was mocking him and he allowed her to do so. "Are you still carrying on? Looking for Jenny and Clem, I mean."

He rubbed his eyes with the tips of a forefinger and thumb. "Yes. But I can't promise any answers. Or happy endings." There was a small delay, tinged with instant regret. "I didn't mean that to sound cruel."

"It did," she said, without any hurt or anger in her voice. "But I know what the world's like, Mr Priest. I live in it, after all. If you do your best to find out what happened to Jenny, I can't ask for no more. And if whatever has happened is horrible… Well, just got to live with it. Right?"

"Right."

"So, don't you worry about me, Mr Priest. You just do what you need to do, so I can go home. Got that?"

"Loud and clear." Irrationally, stupidly perhaps, he wished in that moment that she could see the smile which formed on his broken, scabbed lips. He took a breath, intending to speak, but she denied him the opportunity.

"Best go," she said. "I'll have to pay for the call, so can't be on long."

And before he could ask her to call again, she had whispered a hurried goodbye and the line had gone dead.

CHAPTER TWENTY-FIVE

They arrived later that night. Priest was still sitting alone at his desk, the office in almost total darkness, as if no time at all had passed. His muscles had stiffened, so that when he shifted his position in the chair, it was like something close to agony, forcing a hiss of discomfort to escape through his teeth. They had knocked only once on the glass panel of the office door and they didn't wait for him to offer any sort of reply, so that they were inside the office almost before he had time to register anything.

They looked like exactly what they were. To Priest, it was pointless calling them plain-clothed anything. The overcoats, the broad shoulders beneath them, the angle of the hats, and the self-assured strides of arrogant authority were as much of a uniform as the blue tunics, custodian helmets, and truncheons of their counterparts. There was no hiding who and what they were, no matter how far over their eyes they pulled the rims of the battered, misshapen hats. And the most tragic thing of all was that Priest was one of them, no matter how many times he told himself otherwise. It didn't matter how inconspicuous he thought he was, or how different to them he felt; he was the same. He still shared their characteristics, their attitudes, and just possibly worst of all, their arrogance.

"The inspector wants you to come with us," one of them said. It didn't matter which one; it would have sounded the same coming from either of them.

"Where?" There was no reply and Priest gave a tired, knowing smirk. "Tell Frank Darrow that if he wants me, he can come and get me."

One of them shook his head. "Not how it's going to be, swabbie. You come with us. One way or the other."

Priest leaned back in his chair. "I see Darrow sent two of his best. You two should get into films. You'd make a fortune."

If they were insulted, it was harder to see than dust in the wind. "Just get on your feet. Or we arrest you."

"For what?"

"We'll decide afterwards." It was designed to be a threat.

Priest smiled. "Give me a minute to change my underwear."

One of them leaned over the desk. There was no way he wouldn't smell something of the whisky Priest had been drinking. "The inspector wants to see you. That's just how it is."

"About what?"

The shadow pushed itself away from the desk and resumed its previous position. "A body. Someone you know."

Suddenly, there was nothing amusing about any of it. "Who?"

One of them remained still, staring blankly at him; the other calmly walked to the office door and pulled it open, standing to one side. "Let's go," said one of them. Again, it didn't matter which.

Priest knew who had died long before he saw the body. The direction in which they drove, the building outside which the car stopped, the lift in which they ascended, and the corridor down which they walked all sang together to tell him. If Frank Darrow had hoped for an element of surprise, he had gone about getting it in the wrong way. When Priest walked into the room, his face was already wearing an expression of inevitability and his teeth were clenched in the same futile anger which was so evident in his eyes.

Darrow was leaning against one of the bookcases of legal texts. He was chewing on an unlit cigarette. "Thanks for coming, Priest."

There was no immediate answer, as if Priest himself was as dead as Leonard Quayle. The solicitor lay on his stomach in the centre of the room, his arms spread out to the side and his feet uselessly, almost comically, splayed out beneath him. He was wearing no jacket, only the white shirt now mottled and stained with the dark red of death. His spectacles had come off somehow and were lying to the side of his face. The one visible eye stared widely at the ceiling, sightless, and not just because of the discarded spectacles. The other eye was buried in the carpet. But it was the back of his head which held Priest's attention. It had been more than one blow. No man, however strong, could inflict this level of disaster with a single strike. Priest, as hardened as he feared he was, still felt his stomach and throat protest at the sight, contracting and expanding so quickly and violently that he thought he might retch there and then, adding to the wreck of the head, with its confused, sickening amalgamation of grey, white, and red, once a skull and brains, but now nothing more than a violent mass of matter and waste.

Priest put his hands in his pockets, as if to conceal their shaking. "When?"

Darrow shrugged. "Waiting for confirmation, but only a few hours ago. It's still fresh, as you can see."

Fresh. It was one word to use, Priest supposed. "Who found him?"

"One of the cleaning women."

"What was he doing here at this time?"

Darrow shrugged. "It wasn't unusual for him to work late, apparently."

"Any sign of a weapon?"

Darrow pointed towards the desk. Priest stepped around the body and sank to his haunches, his eyes fixed on a marble ashtray, square and heavy. The smears and stains on the edges were proof enough and its size and weight could do nothing but confirm it. "Not a premeditated killing, then. The killer saw his chance, and a handy weapon, and took both."

Darrow was noncommittal. "Unless that's the impression we're meant to have. Whoever it was could have come with the intention of killing Quayle, but of making it seem otherwise."

Priest was unimpressed. "What would the point of that be?"

"I don't know. When we find whoever it was, we'll ask him."

"Him?"

Darrow pointed to the body. "You think a woman could do that?"

"We've both come across women who've done exactly that, Frank." Priest's voice was flat, bearing in it neither conflict nor condescension. Darrow took the unlit cigarette out of his mouth and stuck it in the band of his hat, as if that somehow addressed or conceded the point.

Priest turned his back on the whole thing and walked behind the desk, staring out of the window but seeing nothing other than his own reflection in the dimly illuminated glass. What he could see of the night sky outside was the same as his mind. Empty, a black mass of nothing, with no sparks of illumination or explanation, either in the form of stars or ideas. Priest felt numb, as if his brain was a slab of concrete, impassive and obstructive, allowing nothing to pass into or out of it. Of all the people he might have predicted would turn up dead, Leonard Quayle hadn't been one of them.

If Priest was right about the Phoenix development, and Raeburn was financing his sex trade through it, he needed Quayle and Priest doubted that Quayle would have had the courage to declare himself done with any such deal. Every glass of complimentary champagne which Quayle had sank at *The Midnight Pearl*, and any other pleasures he had enjoyed under Raeburn's hospitality, would have had a price eventually. There was no way Quayle was ever going to be able to walk away it all, which meant there was no reason for him to be lying dead now.

"Remind you of anything?" Darrow asked. He was kneeling beside the body now, one arm crooked on his raised knee. He pointed to the wound on the back of the head with his other hand.

"Similar injuries to Jimmy Boyd," said Priest.

"Right." Darrow stood up and walked over to him. He was inches away from Priest's face, his breath a toxic dose of coffee and tobacco, both designed to keep his obvious exhaustion under control. "I want the truth, Priest. All of it."

The antagonism instantly put Priest on his guard. "I don't know what you mean."

Darrow smiled, the same sort of a smile a thug might give before he breaks a man's knees with a crowbar. "We're friends, Priest, right? I stayed your friend through the war and after it, when you couldn't take it any more, for reasons of your own. Didn't I?"

"Yes."

"And I've never pressured you to tell me what happened to you in the war to force you to turn your back on the rest of us. Right?"

"Right."

"Because we're friends."

"Right."

The smile was still on Darrow's lips, but Priest felt sure the crowbar was aimed at his knees. "Just know that I'll do whatever I have to, even if that means locking you up and not giving a damn about that friendship."

Priest stood his ground, determined that his knees wouldn't be harmed. "Locking me up for what?"

"Withholding evidence, for starters. Who knows what else I'll find? Something tells me I'll have a bit of fun digging around."

"Withholding what evidence?"

"I told you before not to dance with me, Priest." Darrow's voice was barely under control now. "We've got two bodies, both with their heads smashed in. You said Boyd's killer must have gone to his place by chance, not knowing Boyd had an appointment with you. To me, that says a lack of premeditation, just like we seem to have here. To a simple thinker like me, those two things say the same killer. You told me, when we met at Boyd's place, that you'd seen him when you were watching a solicitors' office in relation to a case you were working on. Then, you asked me to find out about an estate agent, Burke & Halliwell. I haven't been sitting here with my thumb up my arse waiting for you to get here, Priest. I've looked through the desk."

He leaned down swiftly and pulled open a drawer in the desk. He took out a collection of files, slamming them down on the surface of the desk. He opened them angrily, spreading out papers, receipts, invoices, and letters, all of them with the Burke & Halliwell letterhead and logo on them. Priest felt a sudden desire to vomit.

"You were watching Quayle's offices," said Darrow. "Your missing persons case involved him somehow. You thought he was a lead, maybe you even questioned him. And Boyd was following you. That makes you a link to both victims."

"Is that more of your simple thinking, Frank?"

"Is it wrong?"

Priest did not reply immediately. "The missing person was Quayle's secretary."

Darrow slammed his hand down on the files and the papers. "What's that got to do with Burke & Halliwell?"

"I'm not sure."

The inspector leaned against the side of the desk and put his hands in his pockets. "And Clem Murnaugh?"

"I've no proof of anything, Frank," cautioned Priest.

Darrow looked around him. "I thought this was a solicitor's office, not a court room."

Priest smiled, reluctantly. "I think Murnaugh was leaking information about some of Jack Raeburn's operations. I don't believe Murnaugh fell drunk into the Thames. I think he was killed and his body disposed of."

"And Boyd was killed for what he knew?"

“Or might have known.” Priest tried not to think about Murnaugh’s photographs, still locked in his safe in the office. He had to say enough to placate Darrow, keep him on side, but there was no reason to tell him everything.

“And how does Quayle fit in?” asked Darrow.

Priest held up a warning finger. “No proof, remember.”

“We’re just chewing the fat, Priest. We can go and do it over a mug of tea or a beer, if you prefer.”

Priest knew that a point, and not an offer, was being made. “I think Raeburn is sabotaging the Phoenix project. I think he’s somehow muscled his way into TGM Investments and he’s forcing Thomas Marriott to let him use the development as an alibi for something else.”

“How would he do that?”

“How does Raeburn do anything?”

Darrow nodded. “And Quayle?”

“He was Marriott’s solicitor. He’d have to be in on it.”

“And now he’s dead.” Darrow bit his lower lip. Priest said nothing, allowing personal conclusions to be drawn. “What about this girl I’ve got staying with my sister?”

Priest shrugged. “A precaution, that’s all. She’s a friend of Murnaugh’s girlfriend. She disappeared, Frank. You could do worse than ask Mary Latimer about girls going missing during the war and again over the last few months.”

“Whores, like her?”

Priest nodded. “Which explains why nobody was looking for them, right, Frank?”

Darrow sneered, but refused to engage. “What’s the connection to the rest of it?”

Priest clicked his tongue. “Work it out. The Phoenix project, buying properties, Raeburn, missing whores. What does it spell to you?”

He walked away from the desk and back to the door of the office. He tried not to look at what used to be Leonard Quayle. It wasn’t something he wanted to see again, even if it did seem to fill the room, to diminish everything in the place simply by its own oppressive horror. In the moment, Priest could imagine the noise, the dull thump of the blow and the wet snap of smashing human bone, and he seemed to smell the stench of blood and death. Suddenly, he needed to be outside, as far away from all this as possible.

At the door to the office, he paused and turned back to Darrow. "Need me for anything else, right now?"

Darrow shook his head. "But don't go to the seaside without telling me."

The remark was facetious and Priest largely ignored it, although the mention of the coast reminded him of Patrick Costello, who lived, albeit barely, by the sea. And who had first mentioned something called the House of Skulls. Priest would have dismissed it as a drunkard's rambling, if Leonard Quayle, now lying with his head in his own brains and blood, had not recognised the name and understood something of what it meant. Suddenly, Priest was unable to look at anything other than Quayle's remains.

"Can I save you a job, Frank?" he asked. Darrow inclined his head in a brief, taciturn gesture of agreement. "Let me tell the wife."

"Why?"

Priest forced himself to look into his old friend's eyes. "She's a client, of sorts. I think I owe it to her."

"You've got no argument from me," said Darrow. Priest bowed his head and made to step out of the door, but Darrow called his name. "You think Raeburn killed Murnaugh and Boyd? Must follow you think he killed Quayle, right?"

Priest stared at him for a long moment, then smiled. "Good night. Let's have a drink sometime, when our minds aren't poisoned by stuff like this."

Darrow watched him leave. He could have called after him, commanding him to remain where he was. There was still much more that Darrow wanted to know and that he was sure Priest could tell him. But Priest wouldn't respond to any such commands. He had left them behind in the dust kicked up by him as he fled from his past. The corridor seemed like a long, barren road between Priest and him. So, he didn't call after Priest. It would have been too much like shouting into an empty valley.

CHAPTER TWENTY-SIX

"I'm sorry for calling you when it's so late."

"It's not that late, not really."

"It's past ten."

"I don't think for a second you call that late, Alex."

They were sitting in his office. They had finished what was left of Priest's opened bottle of whisky and had opened a second. They were sitting beside each other on the battered, leather settee which was set against the far wall, opposite the small kitchen. Priest had taken some persuading to move from his office chair, to come out from behind the protection of the desk. Evelyn Marriott had never doubted he would comply. She knew how persuasive she could be. It was, she thought, something about the almond shape of her eyes which made men so compliant. And some women, on far less frequent occasions.

His call had surprised her, both by its spontaneity and its abruptness. It had announced itself without warning or invitation, like a black sheep at a wedding breakfast.

"Will you come to the office?" he had asked.

"Now?"

"Is it inconvenient?"

"Not really."

"Then will you come?"

And that had been it. She had not thought about it. She had put her hat and gloves on, hailed a taxi, and gone to him immediately. Why, she couldn't say, not precisely. It was not that she found him attractive, or that he intrigued and fascinated her. Evelyn had never run to a man for those reasons alone and because he merely said so. She had only ever answered a man's summons if she chose to do so. Nothing, especially not Alex Priest, was going to change that. Perhaps it had been the desperation of it. If he thought he had no alternative other than to call her, he would think he was desperate. And maybe that same desperation made her need to know what had prompted him to ring her without warning. And so, she had gone and now she accepted his offer of a drink and persuaded him to come and sit beside her on the cracked, distressed, leather settee.

"Won't your husband wonder where you are?" he asked now.

"He isn't home himself, so why should I worry?"

"Where is he?"

"At his club, I suppose. He usually is if he doesn't come home straight away. I left him a note to say I was going out and would be back later, so he can make do with that." A pause. "You didn't call me to ask about my husband."

In response, he drank. The glass rattled gently against his teeth. Evelyn sat upright, twisting to face him, and placed her hand on his knee. Instinctively, he recoiled, a spasm of his leg muscles, as if she had touched his skin with a naked flame. Her hand withdrew, but only momentarily, and she replaced it, more slowly this time, so that he could have no reason for being surprised or alarmed by the action.

"Alex, what is it?" Her voice was soft, reassuring rather than seductive.

He leaned his head against the wall. A sudden shock of pain from where it had been struck against the cobbles of the alleyway coursed through him, but he closed his eyes against it, betraying it only with a brief but expressive exhalation of air. Evelyn watched a vein in his neck pulsating, his chest rising and falling, as if sitting motionless was a long-awaited relief. She wondered just how tired he really was. He looked like a shadow of the man she had first met. It wasn't only the bruises, now settling into their usual black and blue stains across his eyes and cheeks; nor was it the broken lip, which had now formed a deep, crimson crevice in his mouth. It was more than both these physical signs of trauma. There was a sadness behind the swollen eyes, which had replaced the shy cynicism which she had noticed on their first meeting, and his shoulders were slumped under an invisible weight which they were not broad enough to bear. He looked as if he had become estranged from sleep, as if there had risen between them differences which went beyond being irreconcilable. His cheeks were pale, shrunken somehow, and she dared not think about how he had been living or whether his only nutrition had been alcoholic. He looked beyond exhausted, as if he were ready to lie down and never get up again. Without knowing it, she had begun to stroke the back of his neck, and surprisingly, he had not flinched on account of it.

"Leonard Quayle is dead," he said.

She stopped stroking his neck, but the nails remained against his skin, like the tips of daggers. "Dead?"

He turned his head to look at her, dislodging the knives, which she put back into the sheath of her lap. "Murdered. Somebody smashed in the back of his head."

"My God."

She shifted her position again, so that she was showing him her profile. She cradled the glass of whisky in both hands, before tossing down a measure of it which he thought might have floored an elephant. He followed suit and then reached down for the bottle, replenishing both glasses. As he poured her share, she looked him directly in the eyes.

"Who did it?"

He shrugged. "I don't know. And I don't know why. What I do know is that people are dying all around me and I'm not doing a damned thing about it."

"What do you think you can do?"

"Everything. Something. Anything. Just not nothing."

It was the convoluted poem of a drunk, defeated man and she knew it. She watched him flood his system with the whisky and pour himself another. It wasn't going to help him, but nor was she trying to stop him. She knew well enough that when any drinker was in this mood, nobody could get them out of it except themselves. Her father had been the same; except that, in the end, it had killed him.

"Alex, why did you ring me?" she asked.

He looked over at her. "I wanted to ask you for a favour."

"Yes?"

He took a breath, long enough for it to seem as if he had only now remembered how to breathe. "Dorothy Quayle came to see me a couple of days ago. She thought Quayle was being unfaithful. Remember you and your husband said I was crazy for thinking the same thing?"

"Go on," she said, refusing to allow herself to become embroiled in drunk recriminations.

"So, she's a client. Which means I think it should be me who tells her what's happened."

"That's the police's job, surely."

He sniggered maliciously. "The police were only too happy to dump it in my lap, especially when I was stupid enough to offer to do it for them."

She smiled. "Gallant, perhaps, rather than stupid."

"In this world, it's the same thing." He drank slowly. "I wondered if you'd come with me. She may need a friend."

"Of course I'll come with you." She allowed the silence which followed to stretch itself out, like a girl bathing in the sun. "Is that all you wanted me for?"

His mouth moved, but nothing came. Not at first. With each attempt at speech, she moved closer to him. He looked at her and she saw a man who was lost and confused, alone in a world he no longer understood and unable to find any words to express what he wanted to say. He broke her gaze and looked down at the floor, finding the usual false solace of the contents of his glass, which was only too easy to drain.

"Alex..."

"I didn't want to be on my own," he whispered. "Just for once, I didn't want to be alone."

The voice could have belonged to a child. It was barely more than a whisper, so that she had to lean into him to hear it properly. Now, having said it, he said no more. He remained motionless, his eyes fixed on the floor between his feet. She searched them for any traces of tears, but there were none. He was not melting enough for that. Tomorrow, she knew, he would hate himself for saying as much as he had done; tears would be far too much of a personal betrayal of himself.

"How did you get to be so lonely?" she asked.

She had not expected him to answer. She had anticipated either silence or evasion. So, when he did reply, she was momentarily bewildered. What he said, though, brushed away her confusion and left her both compassionate and outraged.

"My mother abandoned me when I was six."

It was said not only without warning, but also without emotion, as if it were merely a statement of fact and feeling anything about it would somehow be dangerous. She watched him closely, realising that he was not expecting any pity or understanding and that either would be unwelcome. He was simply stating a truth, nothing more, even if it was an unbelievable, incomprehensible one. In its wake, Evelyn found that she was unable to say anything in response.

"One day she was at home," he continued, without any prompting, "the next, she was gone. She never wrote, never called, never came back."

"What about your father?"

He shook his head. "If he ever heard from her again, he never told us."

"Us?"

"I have a sister. We don't speak."

"Because of what happened?"

He nodded. "There has been talk of forgiveness. Helen wants to offer it and I don't."

"Your mother is still alive, then?"

There was a blade in his voice. "Somewhere, apparently. My father never spoke about that woman, not after she'd left. Not once. I used to tell myself that something terrible had happened to her, that she hadn't left of her own choice." He smiled bitterly at the memory. "It wasn't true, obviously. If it had been, she wouldn't have taken her dresses, her shoes, or left her wedding ring on the mantel for my old man to find. Which is what that woman did."

She almost winced at his repeated use of the phrase, as if he could never bring himself to refer to her as his mother. "I can't imagine how it has affected you, Alex."

He smiled again, but it was nothing to do with amusement. "Between what she did and the number of broken relationships I'm told about in this office, a happy marriage doesn't seem like something which can ever truly exist."

"That is so sad." And she sounded as if she meant it.

"Is your marriage happy?"

Checkmate. She lowered the lids of her eyes but not as much as she lowered her voice. "Not always, no."

He didn't press the point. To do so would have been cruel, and of all the things he was feeling in that moment, cruelty didn't feature. "I spend my days looking for lost people, missing girls, vanished husbands, as if I'm doing this job just to keep what that woman did fresh in my mind."

She shook her head. "Maybe you're doing it so that nobody else has to feel that pain. Because you must understand it in every one of your clients."

Now, his eyes flashed with bitterness and when he spoke, fleck of spittle exploded from between his gritted teeth. "It's not pain I feel, it's anger. I'm bloody furious about that woman and I have been every day since she went."

"I'm sorry." She had nothing else to offer.

He soothed himself with a mouthful of whisky. His breathing came under control and his head began to shake. "No. I'm sorry. It's just how she makes me feel. And I hate myself for feeling it, probably more than I hate her. Because she's made me how I am. She's dominated my life and she's never been a part of it."

Evelyn let out a long sigh of realisation. "That's why you're how you are around me. Nervous, on your guard, like a caged animal. She's made you hate and mistrust everybody, especially women. You never let anyone get to close to you, in case they run out too."

He didn't reply and perhaps his silence was the only answer she needed. He stood up and walked briskly away from the settee. Evelyn remained seated, knowing that he needed the distance, if only for the moment. Priest turned to face her, a smile on his face which still had nothing to do with humour, and he gave a shrug of his shoulders. "So, that's why I'm alone. You asked and I told you. Too much of this stuff, I suppose." He put the glass down on the desk.

She returned hid smile, but her eyes were filled with sadness. "You poor, broken bastard."

He didn't argue with her. Slowly, he placed his hands in his pockets and stared down at the floor. His hair had fallen over his right eye, the shirt was barely tucked into his trousers any more, and the tie was so far from his throat that it was hardly worthwhile wearing it. He looked like a mass of creases and exhaustion, like someone who has been kicked down too many times, been run over once too often, and who has given up fighting against it. And she had never found him more attractive than she did in that moment.

But there was nothing to be done about that, not after what he had told her. It would be an insult to his frankness, a cheap trick, a slap across his face disguised as a kiss. She couldn't do it, however much she might want to. Instead, she walked over to him and slowly, protectively, put her arms around him, pulling his head towards her shoulder. He misunderstood, and after an initial tensing of his muscles, he succumbed and turned his lips to hers. She held his cheeks firmly, but softly, and put his head on her shoulder.

"No, Alex," she whispered. "Not that."

She felt his body go limp, as if all the anger, the suppressed bitterness, and the emotional wreckage had momentarily been exorcised from him, leaving him exhausted and unable to stand without her aid. She listened for tears and for the shaking of his shoulders which would come with sobbing, but there was no sign of either. Perhaps he was too tired even for tears.

Her hands moved down his back, not to seduce, but to secure the protective hold she had on him. He did not flinch, but her mind did, as a memory stirred from the back of it. She recalled now the brutal scarring to his back, interlaced marks of a past torture, which she had seen both on his back and chest when she had last been in the office. She held him tighter, instinctively, as she realised that his wounds were physical as well as spiritual, as if his suffering was more than someone like her could imagine or understand.

"How do you stand it, Alex?" she said into his hair. "The hurt and the grief you carry with you? Your mother, the scars on your body?"

He did not reply. For the briefest of moments, he was still. Then, gently, he pulled himself out of her embrace, keeping his head lowered, so that he did not have to look her in the eyes or, just perhaps, so that she did not have to see the expression in his.

"You should go," he said.

"Please, Alex, trust me again. You did about your mother, so do it again with the rest. Let me help you."

He smiled at her, with what she thought was genuine affection, and gently, almost tenderly, put his finger on her lips. She looked into his eyes, suddenly aware that her heart was racing.

"Enough secrets for one night," he said.

And now, after a caress of her cheek, he walked back behind the desk and sat down on the leather chair. The armour was back on, the protection reassembled around him. She looked at him over the desk, her hands by her sides, and her expression composed but not offended. Only her heart was out of control.

"You don't have to bottle it all up any more, Alex," she said. "It doesn't have to eat away at you. Because you're not alone any more."

He leaned forward in his chair. "Go home, Mrs Marriott. I'll meet you there first thing in the morning and we can go to see Mrs Quayle."

"All right," she replied.

She did not see it as a dismissal or a snub, so she took no offence. Likewise, there was no point in arguing with him. "Alex, do something for me."

"What's that?"

"Get some sleep. You look half-dead."

For his part, he could take no offence from that either. "Goodnight, Mrs Marriott."

She smiled back at him and pulled open the door. She had almost closed it behind her when he called back to her. She peered back into the office. He had risen from his seat and he stood framed by the window, his hands in his pockets once more, his shoulders square and his weight evenly balanced, as if he was squaring himself for a fight. She could not see his face entirely in the gloom of the office but when he spoke, she knew from his voice what his expression would have been, and she thought later, perhaps those tears had begun to fall after all.

"Thank you, Evelyn."

She did not reply and she closed the door with no sound, so as not to disturb the effect and meaning of the words.

CHAPTER TWENTY-SEVEN

As soon as she had opened the door to them, Dorothy Quayle had known that she should prepare herself for a storm. She had said nothing as she admitted them to the house and nor had they. There had seemed to be nothing to say which was not already explained by their expressions, in which the prospect of disaster was only too clearly defined. The disaster must be connected to her husband, she had thought, because Dorothy had no other connection with Priest other than in terms of Leonard. That Priest had felt the need to bring Evelyn Marriott, as some sort of support, suggested that the news might be the worst it could possibly be. Looking back on it afterwards, when the truth of it all was explained to her, Dorothy thought that this instinct was the only explanation for her inability to cry when the news was broken to her, although when it was all over, she would cry relentlessly.

Priest had done her the courtesy of not skirting around the issue. He had spoken deferentially, but without any explicit or over-rehearsed sympathy. Dorothy was grateful. To her, and perhaps to Priest himself, it would have been embarrassing and perhaps unwittingly insincere. She had known at once that the tears would not come. The news broken, she had sat down slowly on the edge of her settee, her hands clasped in her lap, and had simply stared at Priest without speaking, almost as if she had not understood fully what he had said. He had sat down in an armchair opposite her, his eyes never leaving hers, and she had been conscious of Evelyn Marriott coming to stand behind her, placing her hands on Dorothy's shoulders.

Priest had spoken again. "I asked Mrs Marriott to come with me, in case you needed someone with you. I'm sorry if that was taking a liberty."

Evelyn's grip had tightened on Dorothy's shoulders. "If you want me to go, just say. Perhaps some tea?"

It had been then when Dorothy had found her voice. "There's sherry on the sideboard. Let's have that."

"Good idea," Evelyn had said.

Priest had declined and had waited whilst Evelyn had poured a single glass for Dorothy, stating that she would make tea anyway, as if no English catastrophe could be confronted without some tea being made. Dorothy had drunk the sherry quicker than Priest had expected and she had handed him the glass, in a silent command for a second. He had complied and had sat down again in the same chair and had waited for the tea to be delivered. It was during the wait, before the tea was announced with a rattles and tinkles of metal and china, that Dorothy looked up at him.

"What happened?" she asked.

"There's no easy way to say it," Priest replied. "He was killed."

"An accident?"

"Murder."

And there it was, Dorothy thought. The word, the deed, which had lingered in the back of her mind since their arrival. Hearing it spoken, however anticipated it was, did nothing to dilute its shock. But there were still no tears, only a short gasp of air, which whistled through her teeth.

"Last night?" she asked. Priest nodded. "He didn't come home."

"Did you try to contact him?"

She shook her head. "I wasn't worried. He often worked late. I was only concerned this morning, when I woke and he was not here."

"And we arrived before you could begin to make any enquiries about where he was?" he guessed.

She nodded. "How did it happen?"

He gave her a warning look of caution. "You may not want to know that."

Her eyes were defiant. "You've told me the worst of it, Mr Priest. What can it matter how it came about?"

Whether Priest agreed with that or not was irrelevant. He might think it was a mistake, but it wasn't his to make. "Somebody battered him about the head."

"Do you know who?"

"Not yet."

"Will you find out?"

It seemed to be a plea rather than a request for information. "I intend to."

She did not smile, but there was gratitude behind her eyes. "Thank you."

"The police will need to speak to you. They would be here now, but I wanted to be the one to tell you. I felt I owed you that."

She repeated the thanks, speaking the words with a further, dignified appreciation. "Together, Leonard and I survived all those bombs, all the blackouts, all the fires. And now, just as it has all come to an end, I lose him. All that horror and conflict across the world spares us, only for someone to commit common murder. The irony is the cruellest thing of all."

"I can understand that," said Priest, with no guile or pretence. "I've seen too many women, and men, feel like it. No matter what their marriage had turned into," he added, carefully.

She caught the slight change of tone in his voice. "What do you mean by that, Mr Priest?"

He held her gaze. "You hired me to do a job for you, Mrs Quayle. We need to talk about that."

Evelyn came back into the room. The slight movement of the door and the sudden flash of blue from her jacket and skirt caught Priest's eyes. Without their signals, he doubted Evelyn's reappearance would have been noticed. She was without tea, and for a moment, Priest wondered whether she had intended ever to make any and whether her departure from the room was more a matter of tact than sympathy. She closed the door, equally silently, and stayed standing there against it, her hands behind her back and her ankles crossed.

"What do we need to talk about, Mr Priest?" Dorothy asked.

Priest flexed his fingers, as if to take his mind away from the pain of what he was about to say by giving it another nervous sensation to process. "Your husband was being unfaithful again. I'm afraid you were right about that."

Dorothy seemed strangely relieved. "I knew it."

Priest concentrated on her eyes. "I think Nancy Clayton died, Mrs Quayle. In that house in Southwark where you sent me."

Only now did the eyes flicker with apprehension. "Because of Leonard?"

"Not directly, perhaps. But because of something he was involved in."

Involuntarily, Priest's eyes flashed to Evelyn Marriott and he saw her glaring back down at him, her lips pursed, as though in some deliberate effort to forbid any words from being spoken. He looked back to Dorothy Quayle. "I think your husband was being blackmailed by some dangerous men into doing something against his will."

"What men?" asked Evelyn, now conscious that Priest could have been speaking to either of the women, or perhaps both of them.

But Priest did not look at her. "Mrs Quayle, have you ever heard your husband mention a nightclub, *The Midnight Pearl*?"

"No. Leonard wasn't the type of man to visit nightclubs."

Priest lowered his head, but not his glare. "I'm afraid he was, Mrs Quayle. I have photographs of him in that very one. With Nancy Clayton."

He was not seeking to induce tears, but even if he were, they did not come. "That's a lie."

"I have no reason to lie to you, Mrs Quayle." Priest leaned back in the chair. "Have you ever heard the name Jack Raeburn?"

The small crease above the bridge of her nose suggested familiarity, even if her reply said otherwise. "Never."

Priest could not consider it a lie. She might not know the name, but that did not mean she did not know the man. And Raeburn's appearance, once seen, could hardly be forgotten. "Short, but tough looking, well dressed, with very black hair and eyebrows, neither of which you could ever believe was real. The eyebrows are painted on, when you get close up. Often seen with another small man, but dapper, dresses in black. Walks as if his shoes are a little too tight."

Dorothy Quayle did not move, but the expression on her face altered. Her impassive calm shifted into fearful realisation and her eyes widened in sudden understanding. "Leonard said they were clients."

Priest moved as if he had been confronted by a cobra. The uncrossing of his legs, the removal of his finger from his lips, his shifting in the chair as he leaned forward towards her, all done with such slow precision that his life might have depended on them not being detected. "When did he say that, Mrs Quayle?"

"I came home from shopping one afternoon and they were leaving the house," she replied. "Two men, as you describe. They got into a large black car and drove away. Leonard was standing on the doorstep. I thought he was waiting to help me with the shopping." Dorothy looked across to Priest. "Who were they?"

Priest didn't reply immediately. He was too busy wondering why Raeburn and Wolfe would endanger themselves by visiting Quayle in person. "When was this, Mrs Quayle?"

"About six weeks ago."

Priest froze, his spine suddenly so cold that the familiar spiders of anxiety were forced to stop crawling on his skin. Now he knew why they had been there. Either they had come to find out what had happened to Nancy Clayton in Southwark or they had come to explain it to Quayle.

"You said my husband was being blackmailed," said Dorothy. "About what?"

"Some business."

"What business?"

Priest shook his head defiantly. "I can't say for sure."

"But you think they were using Nancy Clayton as their leverage?"

No, Priest wanted to say, not that. Because Murnaugh's photographs showed that the affair was an open secret in places like *The Midnight Pearl* and Quayle had been forgiven by Dorothy so many times that there was no reason to assume this time would be any different. No, Priest wanted to say, it was something else entirely that they had over him. Instead, what he said in evasive reply was simply, "Possibly."

Evelyn now moved away from the door and came to sit beside Dorothy, placing one hand on the widow's knee. "I'm so sorry, Dorothy. I would never have believed it of Leonard."

Dorothy looked at her with something approaching pity, as if she were sorry that anyone could be so naïve. "I did, Evelyn. I knew exactly what he was capable of."

Priest watched Evelyn try to manage the reply. Her eyes flickered like a moth's wings around a flame and she glanced over at Priest. He reciprocated only for the briefest of moments.

Evelyn took Dorothy's hand in hers. "Listen to me, Dorothy. There's a possibility that what happened to Leonard might happen to Thomas. Isn't that right, Alex?"

The two women looked at him, as if he held all the answers and was under an obligation to them to provide them. Somehow, he felt unable to resist. "It's possible, yes."

If Evelyn had expected more of a response, she did not wait for it. "So, you see, Dorothy, if you know anything about what happened to Leonard, you must tell us."

Dorothy stared, her eyes barely focusing on anything. "What could I know?"

Evelyn shifted in her seat, her grip tightening. "Please, Dorothy. If Thomas is in any trouble, I have to know."

"I don't know anything," said Dorothy, her voice beginning to tremble. She pulled her hand free from Evelyn, not without difficulty.

Priest, watching the exchange with an anxious narrowing of the eyes, rose from his chair and stood over them both, but it was to Dorothy that he spoke. "It might be something you don't realise you know. Something you might have overheard or seen."

Dorothy's eyes were staring ahead, fixed on a point outside of time, looking at nothing in particular and yet seeing everything clearly as her memory stirred, the images forcing themselves out of the swamp of abandoned thoughts. There had been something: a name, perhaps, or a phrase, but one which had meant nothing to her, then or now. But she could recall Leonard's expression at the time, as he gripped the telephone in his hand, so tightly that she had thought him capable of snapping it in two. She could see now his eyes, fierce with terror, so wide that they might have tipped themselves out of his skull. As the memory crystallised, Leonard's voice came echoing through her mind.

"Don't ever mention that to me again. I had nothing to do with it then and I won't have now." There had been a pause, as he had listened. "I'm not going to say anything. What good will it do me to go to the police now? You don't need to worry about me, any more than you need to worry about..."

The memory came to an end as she voiced the last word she could remember of the conversation. "Costello..."

Evelyn frowned in confusion. "What does that mean?"

When she looked at Priest, she had to force herself to swallow her instinct to gasp. His face was carved from marble, the eyes brutal with concentration, and his teeth clamped together so tightly that the muscle in one of his cheeks quivered. What Dorothy had said might have meant nothing to her, but Evelyn could see that it meant something to Priest and it something crucial and terrifying. "Alex..." she began to say.

But he seemed to have forgotten her presence in the room. He was leaning over Dorothy with a terrifying intensity, like an interrogating officer over a suspect, one hand on his knee for balance, the other in her face, the index finger extended in an accusatory point. "Where did you hear that name, Mrs Quayle?"

"Leonard... on the telephone one time."

"When?"

"A few days ago, last week perhaps."

Too recently for Priest's comfort. He bared his teeth, still clamped together, and his hissed the words from between them. "Tell me."

And she did. He listened as she said all she could remember: the grip on the receiver, the look of fear on Quayle's face, the widened eyes, the snippets of conversation. Everything she could recall. Priest's expression did not soften. When Dorothy had finished speaking, only a short speech but one which had seemed to take all her strength to deliver, she sank back into the settee. Evelyn took her hand once more, and this time, there was no resistance.

Priest began to pace the room. Suddenly, it seemed to him to be too small, altogether too much like a cage, and he had the feeling that he was in danger every minute he stayed inside it. It was as if he could feel the snipers' crosshairs between his shoulder blades and was simply waiting for the shot to be fired. A stupid thought, a product of all the conclusions and connections which had bombed his brain in an unprovoked assault.

"Did you ask your husband about any of this?" he asked suddenly.

Dorothy shook her head. "He didn't like me prying."

Priest had the urge to shake the woman out of her subservience. If she had pried, if she had insisted on sharing her husband's secrets, who knew how different things might have been, how many lives might have been saved? Priest doubted that Evelyn Marriott would have been so submissive. She would have asked questions, even if she had received only lies as answers. By contrast, Dorothy Quayle seemed almost complicit in whatever it was which was behind everything. Priest cursed himself. He had no right to think these things. He was being corrupted by a paranoia of something which he didn't fully understand.

"Have you ever heard the name Jimmy Boyd, before?" asked Priest.

Dorothy nodded, cautiously. "A man called a few weeks ago, asking for Leonard. When I said he wasn't at home, the man left a message for him to call. He gave that name."

"Did you ever hear Leonard mention something called the House of Skulls?"

He was conscious of Evelyn looking up at him. Whether she had recognised the phrase or not, or whether she was intrigued or fascinated by it, he could not say.

"Never," replied Dorothy Quayle.

Priest's eyes flicked to Evelyn like a switchblade. "Has your husband ever mentioned anything like that?"

"No." Her voice suggested that the idea was ludicrous, but her eyes suggested something far darker, that she was offended that he had felt the need to ask. "What's all this about, Alex?"

Priest shrugged. "Whatever it is, it's all tied to the House of Skulls."

"Which is what?" Evelyn's voice was strained with tension and frustration. And possibly, fear.

Another shrug of his shoulders. "I don't know. But I think both your husbands were involved in whatever it is, along with Raeburn and Costello."

Evelyn sprang forward towards him. "I've told you, my husband knows nothing about any of this."

Priest shook his head. "Ask him directly. See what he says."

She would have made some further response, but she was prevented from doing so by Dorothy. She had risen from the settee, slowly, as though afraid that her legs might not support her. She clasped her hands together in front of her and looked up into Priest's eyes.

"Did that man with the awful appearance murder my husband, Mr Priest?" she asked.

"Not that I can prove."

Dorothy searched his face for a trace of deceit. He let it happen; he knew she would find none. "I hired you once before to find out if my husband was being unfaithful. You did that. I want to hire you again to find out who killed him."

Priest studied her for a moment. "If I'm going to do that for you, I have to know something first. And you have to give me the truth."

"Of course."

"Did you kill him because of Nancy Clayton?"

The sound of her palm against his cheek was like a pistol shot. From somewhere behind the sudden but bearable pain, he heard Evelyn gasp. Dorothy was trembling, as much from her own shock at her action as from her outrage at his question.

"It's a question I have to ask," Priest said. "The police will certainly ask it and you won't get away with slapping them."

"I did not kill my husband." She spoke with integrity, daring him to contradict her.

He smiled at her, almost insolently, which made her want to slap his other cheek, twice as hard. "I didn't think you did. But I had to ask it."

"Why?"

"Because I couldn't act for anyone I thought was a killer. Asking you directly was a chance to see how you'd react." He rubbed his cheek for the first time. "I'm glad you did what you did."

If she understood his motives, or if she even cared about them, she did not show it. When she spoke, it was barely above a whisper, but it was no less powerful because of it. "Find out who killed Leonard, Mr Priest. No matter what he was, or what he had done, he was still my husband."

She reached down for her handbag. When she opened it, he took hold of her wrist. "Wait until the job is done, Mrs Quayle. If you still want to pay me anything then, we can talk about it. But I won't take any money from you until I am sure you should pay it."

Slowly, she closed the bag. As the clasp fastened, its click was as much a closing of the discussion as it was of anything else.

CHAPTER TWENTY-EIGHT

Priest could see nothing through the windows. Even with the moth holes in the curtains, and the narrow gap where they did not quite meet, he could not see into the room. The grime and filth on the windowpane were too thick to allow it. He had hardly expected it to be any different; the last time he was here, he had been struck by the state of the windows. But then, he had not been so anxious to see inside and he did not have the same sense of dread which was seizing hold of him now with increasing intensity.

It had begun to take control of him when there was no reply to his knocking. Even his voice through the letterbox, promising a supply of whisky, had elicited no response. Priest had banged on the panels of the door with an increasing violence, not strong enough to break the skin of his hands but loud enough to wake a sleeping man, however drunk. But there was nothing in return. The silence of the house, the lack of any movement from within, seemed suddenly to Priest to be more dangerous than any bullet or blade.

He had made his way to the back of the house, in case it told a different story. It did, but the ominous sense of fear remained the same. The back door was ajar, which seemed to Priest to carry its own sense of menace. With the toe of his shoe, he gently pushed it open, its creak sounding like the scream of a terrified woman, and he stepped inside. The same smell of stale drink and sweat slammed him like a fist. Either it had become worse, or his memory had diluted its effect from his previous visit, but it struck him now more forcefully than he remembered. Perhaps, he thought later, it was the almost hallucinogenic power of his own trepidation which had caused the effect, as if it could somehow sharpen his senses. Or, just possibly, it was because time had passed and Priest and his trepidation could go to Hell.

He said nothing as he walked through the hallway. Calling out seemed too futile to consider. It was somehow obvious that nobody would answer.

As he reached the door to the living room, he had a premonition of disaster. He knew that certain animals could smell blood; he could not do that, but he had an instinct that he was surrounded by it. Even as he pushed the door, once again with his foot, he was certain that the lack of response to his knocking was not because Costello had passed out with drink, but that he had stopped breathing altogether, and that his death had not been caused by alcohol, but by something altogether more violent and unnatural.

To Priest, it was all too familiar. The same shattered head, the same mess of grey and crimson, the same lonely room tainted forever by murder. Priest closed his eyes and leaned against the wall. Boyd, Quayle, and now Costello. All battered to death. It was becoming second nature to him now, walking into strangers' houses and finding them with their heads shattered and their bodies cold. He was an expert in it. He was so good at it, he could make a career of finding bodies. New day, new corpse. An ugly smile crept unwittingly across his lips and he might even have let out a coarse laugh, little more than a growl of frustration. To him, it sounded inhuman, like no sound a man in control of himself could make. Only a man surrounded by violent death, a man who spent his time wading through blood and horror, could make a noise anywhere close to it.

The room was familiar but alien at the same time. He had been in there before, reluctantly drinking whisky with a man addicted to it, but who now would never take another shot. Back then, it had been a dirty, stinking place for someone just to exist. It was not a living room, because Costello had nothing of meaning left in his life, and it still wasn't a living room, because nothing in it was alive. It was a death room, just a grim place for a man to have his life beaten out of him. The cheap furnishings, the empty bottles and dirty glasses, the overflowing ashtrays, and the filthy settee and chairs were the same as his last visit, but they were different, too. They were stained with murder. Everything had been corrupted by it, so that its traces were everywhere. The house would never be the same again. People would come and live in it again, perhaps, and they might not know what had happened in it. But that in itself would not rid the room of its sense of violent death. It would always be there, for Priest if for nobody else, and the carpet and the walls would never quite rid themselves of the stains of blood. None of the perfumes of Arabia would ever sweeten their stained and spotted hands. The same snarling laugh escaped from Priest's mouth and he felt, keener than ever, that he was less than human.

The corpse was at his feet and he was looking at it now as if seeing it for the first time. Now, none of the bitterness or frustration took hold of him. He was detached, almost clinical, and his instincts to investigate were what dominated him. The body could tell him nothing, except that it was dead and how it had occurred. That was all it needed to tell him. It was unlikely that Costello had anything of importance in his pockets. It was true that dead men could tell tales, but this one had barely been able to talk when alive. What he could say dead would be of even less value.

Instead, Priest concentrated on the room, occasionally retching at the smells. There was a small writing bureau, the drawers of which had been pulled out and their contents scattered. Costello might have done it in an alcoholic rage, but Priest doubted it. As in Boyd's house, the conclusion that somebody had been searching for something was easily drawn. Oddly enough, Priest thought, Quayle's office had not been ransacked. The killer — and Priest was sure it was only one killer — must not have thought that Quayle possessed anything which might incriminate or betray. Boyd had been in possession of Clem Murnaugh's photographs, but what did the killer think Costello held which might be dangerous?

The bureau was of no help. Nor was a small cabinet, whose doors had been opened, but which contained nothing but glasses and bottles of spirits and whiskies, some still unopened, and a collection of postcards, unwritten, seemingly bought only for the pictures on them. Various coastlines, what Priest knew was European architecture, and what might have been Norwegian fjords. There were other, similar cabinets, and a large, wooden box, not unlike a sea chest, whose lock had been forced and whose contents had been ransacked. There was little of any interest: old journals, photographs of people who might have been family but who were now long dead, and indiscriminate objects collected over the years. Seashells, whittled wooden figures, a compass, and a rusty, useless penknife. Nothing but memories long since forgotten, kept for a reason which even Costello himself would no longer have known. Priest opened every drawer and door he could find, but found nothing which he thought was of any relevance or use. Anything he found was so mundane that it was almost tragic, each item a chapter in a story of a life which had lost its meaning and abandoned any of its purpose. The focus of Costello's life, for whatever reason, had blurred and it wasn't simply a matter of drink.

It was when he knelt by the fire that he saw it. It had been an automatic movement to squat down beside the grate and peer into the dull grey ashes which showed that a decent fire had been lit on the previous night. Poking around in other people's debris, burnt or otherwise, was part of the job and Priest had never complained about it. In his mind, any number of professions had their versions of it: surgeons were covered in blood, farmers in soil and worse, labourers in grime and dust. No reason for a private detective to be exempt.

The fire had not been thorough. There were still remnants of whatever had been tossed onto it. Priest suddenly thought about the missing contents of the empty bureau, of the ransacked sea chest, and of all the things he hadn't found which he might have expected to. Most of it had been eaten by the flames, no doubt, but the hunger of the fire must have been satisfied before everything had been consumed. What was left was almost worthless: charred corners of documents, some legal in nature if the stiffness and texture of the paper was to be believed, burnt remains of letters, the twisted and broken leather covers of several diaries.

Whatever had been written on any of these papers and pages had been taken largely by the fire, but some scraps of meaning were still legible, if not entirely comprehensible. Phrases leapt out at him from the fragments: *...ever the outcome of the war... rewards in Berlin... nnhauser knows what to do... body will miss...* Priest's mind rolled like a schooner in a tempest. Other fragmented words, clearly German, barked out at him from the blackened pages, but none of them made any sense: *zivilarb... itslager... ädelha...* Other parts of the ruins, Priest recognised only too well: the Reichsadler, the Parteiadler, the symbols of Nazi elite.

The implication was clear, but if Priest had any lingering doubt that Costello was somehow connected to the enemy, it was eradicated when he found the unburned segment of a larger photograph. Its edges were curled by the flames, blackened and made brittle by the effects of the heat and the smoke. In its prime, it had been a group shot of at least three men. Two were still visible, although one half of the second man's face had been destroyed. They had their arms around each other and the presence of a third hand on both their shoulders showed that a third man had been present.

How many more, Priest could not tell, but he doubted it was very many more: the dimensions of the remaining picture suggested that it had only been a standard sized print, so there would be no room in it for more than another two men, perhaps.

Such considerations did not matter entirely. What was of greater importance were the faces of the men he could see. The one cut in half by the flames was easily recognisable as Costello himself, but he seemed younger, despite the fact that the photograph could only have been a couple of years old, proof that his alcoholic decline had been all the more dramatic. The smile, with its genuine amusement and happiness, was chilling, not least because there could be no doubt about the man standing next to him in the photograph. He was unknown to Priest, but the uniform said all which needed to be said. Even without colour, the slate grey of the tunic was obvious and the insignia emblazoned on the collar were unmistakable, the medals on the chest suggesting an officer of some importance. The scraps of letters and documents might suggest that Costello had been involved with the Nazis, but the photograph proved that he was not only at ease in the company of high-ranking officers but possibly actively welcomed into it. Priest had the sudden urge to vomit.

From his pocket, he took out an envelope and placed the damaged items inside. They were proof of something, but what it was refused to declare itself. Priest might need help in decoding their secrets, but he had an idea of where that help could be found. For now, he placed the sealed envelope and its sinister contents in his inside pocket. He got to his feet and looked down once more at the remains of Patrick Costello. Somehow, Priest thought nastily, the violence didn't seem as shocking as it had done initially. What a difference a burned photograph and a uniform could make.

He was about to walk back into the hallway when he heard the noise. It was the creak of a hinge, coming from the direction of the kitchen, which told him that someone had entered the house in the same way he had done himself. He remained where he was, his weight balanced and his limbs tensed, in case he was forced to take immediate and effective action. He heard no more sound, other than the rush of blood in his ears, but he could sense the approach of people. Swiftly, he moved behind the door and pushed himself as far against the wall as he could manage, shielding himself from view in the dark shadows of the angel of the door. It was a weak hiding place, but it was better than being caught in the room with a corpse, whether this was the police or not.

It was not the police. Priest didn't know who they were, but he knew what they were and they were not cops. They were an altogether different kind of force. He wondered whether one of them was half of the pair who had attacked him. Only a couple of nights ago and yet it seemed like weeks. One of them could have been involved; the other, he doubted. Altogether too small, too lithe, but no less dangerous for that. Jack Raeburn might not come to the house of a Nazi sympathiser in person, but he was concerned enough to send some of his army. Which meant that he had some reason for needing to check on Costello.

Now was not the time for thought, but action. The two men were at the body now, one of them uttering a curse which would have startled Satan. Their attention was seized by the horror on the floor, and with a careful nerve, Priest took his chance. He prayed for no loose floorboards as he stepped out from behind the door, moving just quickly enough to get the job done but not so swiftly that he sacrificed care. He was a cat on a tin roof, stalking a bird, moving with cool stealth but keenly aware of the need for speed. In a fluid swirl of coat tails, he was out of the room. He waited in the hallway for a moment, to ensure that there had been no detection of his escape, and when neither of the men came out to investigate, he walked down the corridor towards the kitchen, the back door, and the open air.

He reached the first of these when the pain erupted in the back of his head. He felt a sudden surge of nausea and his mouth filled with bile. He heard himself grunt, a dull moan of agony, and the familiar flash of blinding light exploded behind his eyes. Disorientated, he felt his legs crumble and he was conscious of dropping to the floor like a dead man, as the darkness washed over him and left nothing in its wake.

CHAPTER TWENTY-NINE

He woke up unable to move.

At first, he feared paralysis, but there was a dull ache in his arms and legs, which meant that there could be no nerve damage. Where there was feeling, there was hope. But precious little of it, perhaps. His head felt as if it was full of iron and it hurt to keep it upright, so that he allowed it to hang loosely forward, his chin on his breast. The nausea had passed, but he was consumed now with the hangover peculiar to a blow to the back of the head. It was a pain like nothing else. There was a fly somewhere, flitting around his head, but the buzzing was so loud that its wings must have been enormous. It took him a moment to know that there was no fly. The buzz was too deep in tone and nobody else could hear it except for Priest. It was no fly; just his brain settling down.

Slowly, his senses began to return to him. He felt the cold sting of metal on his wrists, and when he tried to move his arms again, he could hear the curiously delicate rattle of metal and chain. Handcuffs. Fastened tightly, too, the small link of chain between the bracelets threaded through the vertical wooden dowels which formed the back of the chair. He could not feel the same metal ice around his ankles, because of his socks and trousers, but the attempt to move his legs suggested that they were shackled too, one to each of the front legs of the chair. There was nothing in his mouth, so whoever had restrained him wanted him free to speak. *Good luck with that.* Then he sniffed insolently at himself. Easy to be tough now, but it might all change later, depending on the agony to come.

He looked around himself. The room was sparse, the walls nothing but exposed bricks, with only two small windows set into one wall. The light came mainly from a naked electric bulb, suspended from the centre of the ceiling. There were old beer barrels and wine boxes stacked in one corner and various stains, brown and red, on the stone floor, which seemed to him to be old wine stains. He didn't want to think what else they could be. There was a faint trace of stale alcohol, straining for dominance over the more overwhelming stench of damp. The ceiling had ominous black squares of mould scattered across it, making it look like a coarse animal hide. The place had evidently been a cellar of a pub at some point, long since disused, except, it seemed, for dark deeds. Priest thought about the buildings Quayle had been buying through Burke & Halliwell. Some of those had been derelict drinking holes. He could well be sitting in one now, which would mean that he could expect Jack Raeburn at any time, either in person or by proxy. The thought did nothing for the pain in Priest's head.

There was the sound of a door opening and a shaft of light appeared somewhere above him. Sounds of shoes against stone, telling him that people were descending the steep, concrete staircase which he could just about make out if he turned his head over his shoulder as far as nature and the aching inside him would allow. Two men appeared in front of him, large and square, like buses in three-piece suits. They stood some distance off, their hands clasped behind their backs. They didn't look at him, they didn't speak to him. To them, Priest was nothing worth their attention, just a fly stuck on adhesive paper. They were followed by Wolfe, who smiled at Priest as he walked past, taking one of the larger crates from the corner of the room and perching himself on it. To him, this was a show which required him to be comfortable.

Finally, almost from nowhere, Raeburn was in Priest's face. There had been no warning of his arrival, no time to adjust to his presence. Suddenly, he had appeared, in all his painted malice. Up close, the wig was twice as obvious and the eyebrows three times as ridiculous, but neither of them distracted from the malevolence in his eyes. If anything, their pretence seemed horrifying in the company of that stare. Raeburn was breathing heavily. He sounded as if he had run up and down the concrete steps a dozen of times, the air snorting through his nostrils like an enraged animal's. His lips were compressed into an inverted smile and his bulbous hands rested on his slightly bent knees. He was crouched just far enough for his eyes to be level with Priest's.

"All right, souse," he said, "let's have it."

Priest looked past him to the bruisers and Wolfe. None of them returned the favour. He looked back into Raeburn's eyes. "Have what? And take these cuffs off. With Fred and Ginger over there, you don't need them."

There was a sharp crack, like a branch breaking. Priest's head was slammed to the side, fire erupting in his cheek. He could taste no blood and his tongue told him no teeth were loosened, but it was a close thing. Raeburn didn't show it, but the force of the blow must have hurt his palm almost as much as it had hurt Priest's face. Priest moved his jaw, in an effort to ease the pain. Really, he wanted to rub his cheek, throw his face into a bucket of ice, but he could do neither.

"You definitely don't need the cuffs," he said, his voice coarsened by the effect of the blow.

"They stay on." Raeburn had stood to his full height now. "I want to know what's going on. How come we found you at that house?"

"I could ask you the same question."

"You're here to answer, not to ask. See? Don't make me feel I have to loosen your tongue, either, or next time I won't just tickle your cheek."

Priest tried to shift his weight in the chair. It would have been easier to drink an ocean or two. He looked up at Raeburn. "You know what I think you're up to, Jack, and you've told me I'm fishing in the desert. All right, maybe I am. If I've got it all wrong, I'll find out soon enough. I'm not going to go through it all again."

Raeburn was barely listening. "What were you doing at Costello's house?"

"Again, I can ask you the same thing."

"What were you doing there?" Raeburn insisted.

"Following a lead. That what you want me to say?"

"What lead?"

Priest shook his head. "I can't tell you that and you know it."

Another branch broke, this time on the other side of his face. Still no blood and no loose teeth. The strike had been carefully calculated by experience. Priest grunted and spat onto the floor.

"You can hit me all you like, Jack," he said, "but it won't change a thing."

Raeburn took Priest's jaw in his hand, almost crushing his cheeks with the pressure. "Am I speaking a foreign language? Do you not understand what I'm saying?"

"I understand," mumbled Priest, "I just don't have to go along with it."

Raeburn snarled and tossed Priest's head backwards. "What makes you so tough, Priest?"

"Maybe it just comes natural."

"I could fucking kill you right now and nobody would notice a damned thing. You're a nobody, a man of no importance, a cheap hack in a cheap suit sniffing other people's dirty underwear."

"I'm important enough for you to feel you have to drive a tank over me." Priest smiled nastily. "I must be doing something right."

"You're not frightened of dying?"

Priest shook his head. "It could happen to any one of us every time we leave the house. A man like me could be killed any day of the week just for asking the wrong question. Anyone else could walk into the street and get hit by a bus. We've just come through six years of dancing with death every minute of every day. War makes you look at death differently, Raeburn. Maybe you wouldn't know that, maybe you would; I don't know and I don't care. But I survived the war and came through the darkness, and I saw and suffered the closest thing to Hell that I can imagine. So, no. I'm not scared of death. Especially not if it comes in the shape of a cheap, painted crook in the cellar of a disused pub. If I wasn't cuffed to this chair, I'd laugh in your face if I wasn't too busy spitting in it."

Raeburn was circling him now, like a shark around a floating wreck. "Brave words from a man in your position."

Priest shrugged as far as he was able. "You'll need brave words when the police come asking about my death. Because they will come. Killing me will give them the final proof they need."

The sound of Raeburn's feet on the stone floor stopped suddenly. "Proof of what?"

"Take off the cuffs and I'll tell you."

For a time, which seemed longer than it must have been, Raeburn only stared at him. He might have been deciding whether to comply or to throw Priest around the room whilst he was still restrained. Priest had the idea that one of the options would give Raeburn far more pleasure than the other. He held the glare, though, conscious that any show of weakness now would decide the matter for Raeburn once and for all. And it would be as final as that.

Raeburn swore colourfully and turned his back on Priest. Jerking his thumb over his shoulder, he barked, "Take them off."

One of the giants moved, swifter than Priest would have expected from the man's size, and there was the rattle of metal against metal. Priest felt his arms and legs burn with relief as he began to move them, to get the blood circulating again. His shoulders felt as if they had been pulled from their sockets and he circled them mercilessly, feeling the joints crack with gratitude. He walked slowly in a circle, just to remind his legs and feet what they were designed for. He stopped when Raeburn was in front of him once more, but he kept rubbing his wrists. They were pulsating now with returning blood and it felt more soothing to him than all the whisky in the Highlands.

"Talk," said Raeburn.

"There's too many coincidences linking you to everything that's happened, Jack," said Priest. "So many, they start to look like proof. Murnaugh was one of yours and he goes missing. A journalist who might have been looking for him is murdered. A girl goes missing and the last place she's proven to be has blood all over the fireplace, suggesting she died there. That girl was known to go to one of your nightclubs and she went there with a solicitor who was buying properties all over London. He's dead too. Murnaugh's girlfriend is a whore, but she goes missing and I learn she's not the only one. I hear girls have been disappearing for months. You run the girls in the East End, Jack, so no way is that happening without your knowledge. Now I find your boys at the house of another dead man. That's three murdered people, Jack, all linked to you. We can make it five if we assume the Clayton girl and Murnaugh are also dead. You don't need me to tell you how that would look to a cop."

If Raeburn was troubled by any of it, he wasn't about to show it. He shrugged his shoulders, but his hands had curled into fists. "Like you said, coincidences. Not proof."

"A cop doesn't need proof if he's clever enough. All he needs is a thread which he can keep pulling until it unravels everything. You're surrounded by loose threads, Jack, and you need to start tying them up."

"No copper in this city would get me on any of it."

Priest shook his head. "You're wrong. When they think there is one coincidence too many, they'll start digging and they'll find something.

Something you've not considered, something you've overlooked or disregarded. Look at Capone, how safe he thought he was. Then, compare it to how safe he actually was."

For the first time, Raeburn's eyes flickered, suddenly not so sure of themselves. The fists uncurled and curled and the animal snorting came back through the nostrils. Priest did not show his satisfaction or his pleasure, but he felt them keenly inside himself. Raeburn on the ropes was a rare thing, made worse for him because a cheap private detective had put him there. It almost made the knocks on the head and the cuffs on the wrists worthwhile.

Priest took a careful step forward. "But here's the thing, Jack. I can help you."

Raeburn's face betrayed disbelief and disgust. "Why would I want your help?"

"Because you're in more trouble than you think and you just might need a friend. And that's me. Because I know that, whatever else you're involved in, you didn't kill any of them." Now, his eyes flashed to Wolfe. "Even by proxy."

Raeburn's eyes narrowed. "Then who did?"

A shake of Priest's head. "What matters right now is that I know it wasn't you."

"What makes you so sure?"

"Everything."

Raeburn waited for more, but there was nothing more to come. He ran his tongue along his lower teeth and then, slowly and meaningfully, nodded his head. "So, what do you want?"

"I need the truth. About Phoenix, about Murnaugh, about all of it. I need to know how involved you are."

Raeburn laughed. "Are you pulling my chain, Priest?"

"I can't put off the police without knowing."

Raeburn placed his hand on Priest's shoulder, squeezing hard. "How about we play it like this? You get whoever you think did these killings and bring them to me?"

"Not happening."

"Take him to the cops, then."

Priest smiled. "If I do that and you're involved, he's going to want to save his own neck. That might mean giving them yours. If I know what's happened, I can make him see that isn't an option."

Now, Raeburn sneered. "I scratch yours, you scratch mine, right?"

Priest shook his head. "Look, Jack, I don't like you or anything you stand for. If I had my way, you'd have been dangling from the rope years ago. I think you're a pimp, an extortionist, a blackmailer, and a killer. I think I've stepped in better things than you. I bet crocodiles stalk tiger cubs with more compassion than you could ever have. But there's such a thing as the law and justice. They might be old-fashioned songs to sing, but they still exist. After the carnage of the last few years, we need to sing them more than ever. So, if you didn't kill anyone this time, or have them killed on your word, I can't let you hang for it."

Raeburn had listened to the speech without any response. What he thought about it was impossible to tell, until he smiled broadly, showing the briefest glimpse of teeth. "You old romantic."

Then, without breaking the smile, he swiped his fist across Priest's face. This time, there was blood and Priest spat it out onto the stone floor. Raeburn held out his hands in a conciliatory manner. "No hard feelings, but nobody can say all that to me and not take home a broken nose as a souvenir."

Priest pulled himself to his full height, wiping the blood from his nose. "I can," was all he said before bringing his foot swiftly and mercilessly up between Raeburn's legs. The knees buckled and the hands instinctively went to comfort the groin. The growl of pain was the same inhuman sound which only an attack like that can produce. But Priest had not finished. While Raeburn staggered in agony, Priest brought his fist down hard on the gangster's cheek, forcing him down onto the floor. There was no blood, but there was a lot of pain and even more gratification.

Wolfe and the heavies stepped forward, but Raeburn barked in pained anger. "Leave it."

Priest was staring them down, his eyes wild with fury, and his shoulders heaving with the effort and the anticipation of further violence. A sound was coming from the floor and those men still standing stared in bewilderment. It took them a moment to realise that Raeburn was laughing. Pulling himself to his feet, wiping down his face with the palm of his hand, he glared at Priest, the smile broader now than before. "Christ, you hit well for a lost cause. Never knew you had it in you."

"I get so tired of people trying to show me how tough they are."

"I could have you killed for it, you know that."

"Do it, then."

The laugh intensified and Raeburn stepped forward, slapping him hard on the shoulder. "Been a long few years since anyone's had enough stuff between his legs to dare kick me in mine. I might hate you, Priest, but I can respect you. You're one cheeky bastard."

Priest was laughing along, but he would make himself pay for it later. Wolfe and the two mountains didn't seem to see the joke. That, Priest decided, was their problem. "Have we got a deal, Jack?"

Raeburn was rubbing his groin and cheek. "Let's go upstairs and have a drink. The place might be an abandoned shithole, but there's still liquor hanging about."

He walked towards the stone staircase. For a moment, Priest remained fixed to his spot, as if unsure how to move. Wolfe was walking in his direction, smiling smoothly, which was more unsettling than comforting. His teeth might have been made of ice, the grin was that cold. The statues in suits followed him. There was no expression on either face. They were carved of stone, like men who had never learned how to smile and who were afraid to frown in case it cracked their faces. In their line of work, Priest thought, the less emotion there was, the better.

Wolfe swung out an arm, like a sinister waiter offering to escort a customer to a table. "After you."

Priest nodded, then began to walk. Raeburn was waiting for him at the base of the stairs, smiling at him as he approached. Priest followed him up the stairs, Wolfe and the bruisers at his back. Priest couldn't help but grin maliciously to himself. They were just a party of friends, going for a drink together. No harm in that, officer; not when you were one of the boys.

CHAPTER THIRTY

The bar was derelict, the smell of damp concrete strong but not overpowering. There were dark patches of mould on the faded white of the walls and ceiling and the varnish on the wooden bar and on any tables or chairs which had survived, was dimmed with age. Beneath the stains and dust, the carpet might have been a paisley pattern, but it looked now like a dull, monochrome purple. The neglect seemed to be temporary only, because there were dustsheets, workbenches, tins of paint, and bags of labouring tools strewn throughout the place, which suggested that renovation was already underway.

The drink on offer was whisky and Priest was glad of it. He accepted the glass from Raeburn and threw the measure down his throat. An instant, soothing comfort. Raeburn did likewise and refilled both glasses. There had been no salutation or toast; their truce was not quite complete enough for that. Taking their drinks, the two of them sat down at a table, Priest having made sure that the old and obviously unstable chair was capable of bearing his weight. Wolfe stood to one side, close enough to hear what was being said but far enough away for him not to be an interference.

Raeburn leaned forward, cradling the glass in his hands. "Talk."

"I've said it all before," complained Priest. "It's your turn."

"Am I using this Phoenix sideshow to smuggle whores into the West End? That's what you want to know, right?"

Priest nodded. "Amongst other things. I want to know how you managed to sabotage Phoenix. What have you got on Thomas Marriott?"

Raeburn smiled. It was a twist of the mouth which made Priest somehow prefer him when he was angry and violent. Some smiles can be more dangerous than fists. "One thing at a time, Priest."

"Fine. I've got all the time in the world." Priest took out a cigarette and lit it.

Raeburn watched the flame of the match as it did its work and the smoke rising to the mildewed ceiling. He watched it carefully, as if it might turn on him in any moment. Finally, his eyes fell slowly back to Priest. "I'm not admitting anything to you. My business is mine and I don't share it with people who sniff at keyholes."

"Comments like that do nothing for you," said Priest. "They're just wasps at a picnic."

Raeburn smiled, but it was a colder amusement than he had shown in the cellar. The effect of Priest's retaliation, its impressive courage, must have been wearing off. "I have some girls under my protection in Whitechapel. Without me, they'd be on the streets, earning a few shillings up against an alley wall or over the bonnet of a car. They'd earn enough for a slice of stale bread, a gin, and a bed for the night. If they were lucky. More often than not, they'd have to choose between two of those things and miss out on the other. I help those girls out, look after them."

"You're a real guardian angel."

"Dead right I am. With me, they get a roof over their head, permanent. They get food, drink, and they only work with people I've given the nod to."

"You're a public service, Jack. You should run for parliament. They'd be glad to have you."

Raeburn ignored the sarcasm. "As a businessman, I see the potential for expansion. I understand my customers. Some of them are shy, I try to see how I can make life easier for them. So, let's say I saw the chance to build a private place where these more timid gents could go to have some fun, forget their troubles for a few hours. Well, I'd be a fool to ignore it. It helps me, it helps the customer. Nobody loses out."

"Except the girls."

Raeburn seemed genuinely confused. "You don't think they'd prefer to be in a comfortable place than a slum on the other side of the river?"

"Silly me." Priest took a mouthful of whisky, but it had never tasted more bitter.

"So, if I had a mind to," Raeburn went on, "and if the opportunity arose, yeah, I would expand across the river."

It was as much as he would say, but it was as good enough. "All right, Jack, so let's agree that Phoenix gave you that opportunity. Marriott still has to allow it to happen. How does he get dragged into it?"

Raeburn spread his hands and shrugged his shoulders. "We can only guess, am I right? Because it ain't real."

Priest was becoming tired of the pretence. "Let's just say it is real, for the purpose of this little chat. Can we do that, Jack, to save a bit of time? You might not think mine is worth much, but I'm damned sure you think your own is."

Raeburn drank silently for several moments. Priest smoked and drank only occasionally during the brief hiatus. Wolfe was so silent, he could have been almost anywhere except in the same room as them.

"Ever heard that thing about the sins of fathers?" asked Raeburn finally.

"Don't tell me you're a Bible scholar, Jack, because I won't believe it."

The painted eyebrows rose. "Is that where it comes from? I thought my old man read it on the back of a match book once. You live and learn."

"Some people learn and die," said Priest. *Like Jimmy Boyd and Clem Murnaugh.*

Raeburn either didn't hear it or thought it was unworthy of comment. "Well, it isn't always the sins of fathers which come back and kick the son in the face. Sometimes, it's the sins of the mother's brother."

Priest felt as if somebody had clamped his whole body in a vice. "You knew Marriott's uncle?"

Raeburn nodded. "Everyone knew him. And almost everyone wished they didn't."

"A villain." Priest did not need to phrase it as a question, but Raeburn nodded anyway.

"Old school. There was no messing with him, Priest. You knew exactly where you stood. He'd leave you in no doubt. Either you were with him or you weren't. That was how he saw things."

Priest sneered. "Isn't that how people like you always see things?"

Raeburn raised his glass and knocked it gently against Priest's in a perfunctory, almost mocking toast. "If it was, we wouldn't be having this nice, quiet drink."

Priest drank some of the whisky, but only to get rid of it. Somehow, he doubted they would let him leave until the drink was gone. It would be seen as bad manners. Raeburn could rip your head off without blinking, but be offended if his offer of a drink was refused. Priest could only shake his head at the morals. They made less sense to him than Pythagoras.

"Marriott told me his uncle was dead," said Priest.

Raeburn nodded. "He is now. Shame. A great man in his day."

Priest doubted he would be able to agree. "You going to tell me his name?"

A shake of the head. "I've told you what you wanted to know. Nothing else matters."

"You know I could find out without breaking a sweat."

"The man's dead, so what do you care?"

"I might even already know it."

"Then you don't need me to tell you."

Priest shrugged. "No skin off my nose either way, Jack. Even if I don't know, I can make guesses as well as the next man. And some of them can be educated ones."

Raeburn drained his glass and leaned back in his chair. "You've got what you wanted, souse. Time to go. Like you said, time is precious for some of us."

Priest leaned forward and curled his lip into a snarl. "You're telling me that you blackmailed Marriott into letting you into his Phoenix scheme by using his dead uncle's past as a crook against him?"

Raeburn laughed. "Good to see these little knocks to your head have cleared out your ears."

"Why wouldn't he just tell you to go to Hell?" Priest insisted. "It's not as if Marriott himself was one of you. He could just distance himself from his uncle and be no worse off. There would be some damage to his reputation, maybe, but he'd survive that. He's charming enough."

"For the public, maybe," said Raeburn. "But privately speaking, things might not be so easily dealt with."

"Meaning what?"

"Would Marriott risk losing that lovely wife of his?"

Evelyn. Raeburn's reference to her was like a blow to Priest's stomach. It almost winded him, buckling him over in a gasping heap. He remembered

Marriott in his office, accusing Priest of trying to steal her away, and his confession that, when it came to her, he could be jealous. Priest had not believed him then; now, perhaps, it seemed easier to accept. Especially if, as Raeburn was suggesting, Marriott was willing to sacrifice his dream to protect Evelyn from his past.

Priest shook his head. "I know Mrs Marriott. She wouldn't hold anything like that against her husband for long. She isn't that easily swayed."

Raeburn shrugged. "Marriott must see her differently to you. Maybe he idolises her. Maybe you do."

Priest was not about to reply to that. "There has to be something else."

Raeburn stood up from the table and walked around to Priest. He leaned forward and said, "Just because you want something to be true, Priest, doesn't mean it is."

Priest looked up at him and smiled. "And just because you say something is true, Jack, doesn't mean it is."

He got up from his seat, so that he was facing Raeburn directly. Wolfe had moved, almost simultaneously, as if he could predict every one of Priest's moves and decisions. Perhaps he could. To Priest, the man was barely human, so who knew what he was capable of? Priest did not acknowledge him, keeping his attention fixed on Raeburn.

"A few days ago, you referred to Marriott as Tommy," he said. "I'd say that made you good friends."

"Associates in business," was Raeburn's reply.

Priest leaned forward. "Marriott's mother. What was her maiden name?"

Raeburn's expression of friendly disinterest remained in place, but it was impossible for Priest to know what was going on behind the eyes. "Never knew his mother. Or his father, come to that."

Priest sighed silently. "You're not telling me everything, Jack. I can't help you if you don't trust me."

"I've said all you need to know to do what you have to." The hands suddenly on Priest's shoulders suggested that it was the only answer he was likely to get.

"Time to go," whispered Wolfe, so close to Priest's ear that it made his flesh goosebump.

Priest shrugged himself free of Wolfe's grip. No way he was being escorted out of the place. He had been thrown out of pubs before now, but only after he had enjoyed himself. He wasn't going to tossed into the street after a nightmare like this. Not again. He stood his ground long enough to show Raeburn that he was not afraid. Or, at least, that he was leaving on his own terms. He walked across the naked floorboards and pulled open the door, letting it swing back and close of its own accord.

CHAPTER THIRTY-ONE

Billy was behind the bar at *The Runners' Retreat*, casually polishing a glass and listening to the tales of an old regular. The expression on Billy's face said that the stories were either of no interest or had been told so often that any interest they might once have held had been killed. Priest looked around the pub but could see no sign of Hoffmanstahl. He checked his watch. If the old historian was running to schedule, Priest would not have to wait long. In the meantime, he felt obliged to rescue Billy.

"You been in a tussle, Mr Priest?" asked the barman, reaching for a pint glass.

Priest watched him pull the beer. It was cool and dark and it would do fine. It was no substitute for whisky, but it seemed like a safer option. The bitter taste of Raeburn's drinks still lingered at the back of his throat. "Just a minor disagreement, Billy. Looks worse than it is."

Billy nodded, allowing the lie to pass. He had suffered some beatings himself in his time and he recognised the aftermath of a good one. The black, blue, and yellows of the healing bruises told their simple but unmistakable story. And Billy didn't dare think about the raw circle of red around both of Priest's wrists.

"Are you expecting Herr Hoffmanstahl today?" asked Priest.

Billy looked at the clock above the bar. "Any time now, sir."

The old regular, glaring furiously at Priest for interrupting his fascinating flow, made a strident whine of agreement. "Once old Gustav's pulled his nose out of his books, he gets a good thirst."

He meant it to be humorous, a mild and inoffensive gibe at an old friend, but somehow, the sneer on the man's face and the tone of his voice made it seem petty and disparaging. Priest looked across at him, unsmiling, and wondered what the rivalry was between the two men, beyond the obvious one of nationality, of course. And was Priest not guilty of that particular prejudice himself? Yes, but Hoffmanstahl had not seemed unduly troubled by it. Perhaps he had grown accustomed to it or perhaps he just didn't care about it any more. Priest couldn't imagine, from what he had seen of him, that Hoffmanstahl was intimidated by anybody. He was one of those men who were so comfortable in their own intelligence that it didn't matter what other people thought or said. Priest could envy him that.

"I'll be sitting by the window, Billy," he said. "Tell Hoffmanstahl I'd like a word when he comes in."

"Right you are, Mr Priest."

"And I'll have another of these." He indicated the half-drunk pint of ale.

"You've not finished that one," said Billy.

"It's getting lonely," replied Priest.

The old man watched the second pint be pulled. "Everything in moderation, lad."

Priest looked over at him. "Including your unwanted advice."

He sat down at a lonely table and looked out onto Bow Street without seeing anything. He reached into his inside jacket pocket and pulled out the envelope which contained the burnt fragments he had taken from Costello's grate. Quietly, he raised a toast to good fortune. She seldom seemed to smile on him, but she had done when she had not permitted Raeburn or Wolfe to find the envelope. If he had been searched whilst he was unconscious, it must have been rudimentary, aimed primarily at locating any form of weapon, so that something as slim and discreet as an envelope at the bottom of a pocket would have been missed. Either that or they had thought it little more than a meaningless, old, unaddressed envelope. Or maybe they had not searched him at all. There was no way of knowing, and he supposed, it didn't matter. What mattered was that he still had the evidence.

"You wanted to speak to me, I think."

The voice came from lips whose movements were impossible to see under the mass of the white beard, so long that it made him look like a sorcerer from tales of fantasy. He wore a black fedora, perched on the back of his head like a growth, and the matching coat hung around his thin frame like the plumage of a strange, gothic bird. The usual traces of chalk, the familiar smell of old books and academia, and the effect of study in the rounded shoulders were all in place. Priest wondered whether Hoffmanstahl was aware of the untidiness of his appearance, or of the distinctive smell of his clothes and person; if he were, Priest did not need to wonder if Hoffmanstahl cared about them. There was no doubt about that. And Priest wondered further, what impression did he himself give to people: unkempt, exhausted, bruised, and too often surely reeking of whisky. Some people had no right to judge.

"Can I get you a drink?" Priest asked.

"Are you not afraid of being seen drinking with a German?"

Priest deserved the sarcasm and he knew it. "Let's say I've learned to look out for the same old spokes coming up."

"A pint of what you are having, then." Hoffmanstahl nodded his gratitude and removed the battered hat, as if he feared the movement of his head would displace it with less dignity. He sat down as Priest rose from the table and made his way to the bar. He ordered one pint only. There was no need to incur the indignation or disapproval of the old bird at the end of the bar for a second time.

Gustav Hoffmanstahl was sitting with his hands in his lap and staring out of the window. It was an oddly prim, almost prudish, attitude to adopt and it seemed to Priest that sitting at a table with a drink was less favourable to Hoffmanstahl than sitting at the bar, where he was usually found.

"Would you prefer to sit in your usual spot?" Priest asked.

Hoffmanstahl smiled, showing his appreciation of the offer, but he shook his head. "I tend not to sit there if old Jacob Kendall is in here before me. What he says is seldom of interest and too often inaccurate. I try not to patronise or argue with anybody, certainly not in public, but Jacob makes it difficult."

Priest looked over at the old man at the corner of the bar. "I've never had the pleasure."

"Do your best to keep it that way." Hoffmanstahl took his drink and toasted Priest. He sipped at it slowly, almost lovingly, and let out a low murmur of appreciation as he lowered his glass. "At my age, there are few pleasures left open to a man. Books and beer are two of the finest."

"I agree on one," said Priest. "I can't say I'm an expert in the other."

Hoffmanstahl considered him carefully. "You are a private detective, I understand."

"That's right."

"A dangerous occupation, judging by the look of you."

Instinctively, Priest's hand went to his damaged eye. "It can be. If it isn't a thug's fist, it's a woman's nails."

A twist of the beard made Priest think he was smiling under it all. "Such treacherous work."

Priest allowed them both a long moment of silence whilst they drank the beers. Then, reaching into his pocket, he took out the envelope which contained the charred fragments of evidence. "I thought you might be able to help me. Would you mind?"

"Help you with a case?" Hoffmanstahl had struggled to find the word.

"Is that all right?"

Hoffmanstahl spread his hand and raised his bushy eyebrows, as if to give silent approval of the request. Priest opened the envelope and carefully tipped the contents onto the table. He glanced around, making sure there were no peering eyes or straining ears. Even now, he thought, loose lips sank ships, just as burnt letters and photographs put men in graves. Hoffmanstahl had brought out a pair of steel-rimmed spectacles, which he now placed on the tip of his nose, forcing the fragile arms through his hair and around his ears.

"Can you tell me what any of this means?"

Hoffmanstahl was flicking the fragments of paper and photography gently, using the tip of his finger to do so. The grooves on the bridge of his nose had deepened, not only in concentration but also, it seemed to Priest, in fear. He looked over the rims of his spectacles. "Where did you find all this?"

Priest shrugged. "I can't say for now. Do you know what it means?"

Hoffmanstahl did not reply. His eyes dropped again to the jumble of information scattered on the table in front of him. He was shaking his head, but the movement was so delicate that Priest doubted the academic knew he was doing it.

"*Gott vergib uns*," the old man muttered.

Priest did not need a translation of that. He pointed to some of the burnt papers which had clearly been letters and correspondence before the flames had taken hold. "The symbols speak for themselves, the Reichsadler, the Parteiadler. And I can guess at some of these words. *Zivil*, I suppose must mean civil, yes? I'd guess *nnhauser* is part of a name. But what about the rest?"

Hoffmanstahl leaned back in his chair and sipped some of the beer. "Whoever destroyed these letters was correct to do so."

"Not if they were trying to hide a crime."

"Some crimes should be forgotten." Hoffmanstahl stared into Priest's eyes, willing him to agree. Suddenly, into Priest's mind came Costello's ranting voice: *Leave it alone, you bastard. Leave it alone.*

"I can't leave it alone," said Priest. "I have to know."

Hoffmanstahl removed his spectacles and rubbed his eyes, gently to begin with but then with increasing vigour, as if trying to erase the images of what Priest had shown him from his retinas. Slowly, he opened his eyes and contemplated Priest, as he might if he were seeing him clearly for the first time.

"The word is *Zivilarbeiter*," whispered Hoffmanstahl, so gently that Priest had to lean forward to hear him. The academic pointed to the burnt fragments of paper. "This word here — *itslager* — is part, I think, of the term *Arbeitslager*."

"Which was what?"

Hoffmanstahl almost choked on his own words. "It means a labour camp."

"Concentration camps?" Priest felt his stomach contract. He had asked Costello the same thing and the old bastard had rejected the idea. Even drunk, he'd been in control of himself enough to lie about it.

But Hoffmanstahl was shaking his head. "Not concentration camps. People remember only that phrase and think it applies to all camps. A common misunderstanding. The Nazis had all types of such places: concentration camps, extermination camps, forced labour camps. They were not identical in purpose. Concentration camps held prisoners, political and otherwise, in one place. Without trial, you understand. Extermination camps had a more specific purpose."

"You don't need to say it."

Hoffmanstahl nodded. "The depths of human depravity are without measure. These extermination camps were not politically motivated, but racially so. Anyone of a race deemed to be degenerate or inferior would be placed in such a camp."

"And forced labour camps?"

"Places where people were forcibly put to work for the Nazi cause. Many from the east. They were not run by the SS, as the other camps were, but they were no less terrible for that."

"And the prisoners were forced to do what?"

Hoffmanstahl sighed. "During war, a country's finances suffer, just as this country's has. The poor souls in these camps were forced to produce supplies for the continually strained economy. Repairs to bombed railroads and bridges, construction work, farming. Anything which could help sustain Germany through the war, they were forced to undertake."

Priest went for a drink, but saw that his glass was empty. He didn't remember drinking any of the beer. "How many people were in these camps?"

Hoffmanstahl snorted with derision. "How can a man know such things? They will still be counting the numbers. Tens of millions, Herr Priest. Some were prisoners already, but many were taken from their homes, off the streets, kidnapped, pressganged."

"Women and children?"

"Of course. The Nazis did not discriminate in that regard. I need not tell you how the women were treated. When men in power feel they are at liberty to control any woman under their command, they will generally use her in the same fashion."

"You don't have to draw a picture, Hoffmanstahl," snarled Priest.

The old academic bowed his head. "The people condemned to these places were temporary measures, easily replaced. There was no concern at all for their health or the conditions in which they were forced to work. Food was scarce, their clothing and the equipment they were given to use were barely adequate, little or no time for rest or breaks." Hoffmanstahl leaned forward. "The Nazis did not call these places extermination camps, but that is exactly what they were. Death was common. Not from gas or bullets, but from starvation, thirst, exhaustion."

Priest pointed to the scattered debris on the table. "Some of these letters are in English, talking about rewards in Berlin. Were we in any way complicit in this?"

Hoffmanstahl shook his head violently. "The Allies fought to liberate these places, not to swell their numbers."

"But if someone from Britain did a deal with the Nazis to do exactly that…?"

Hoffmanstahl laughed, coarsely and cruelly, but without any humour. "To have British forced labour would have been a particular pleasure to the monsters in command of such places."

Priest stood up violently and walked to the bar. He ordered two more pints of the dark, bitter beer, having no thoughts about how it matched his mood. He watched Billy pour them and ignored the quizzical glances from the old man at the end of the bar. Billy took Priest's money but paused as he counted it.

"Too much here, Mr Priest."

"The rest is for however many whiskies it will buy."

"A large one only."

"A fair trade, Billy."

He carried the drinks back to the table and placed them down. Hoffmanstahl glanced at the whisky in some surprise, but Priest made no apology for it. Hoffmanstahl sipped the fresh pint, and slowly sifted through the papers once more. With a long finger, stained with ink and frosted with chalk, he carefully slid across the damaged photograph of Costello and the German officer.

"Erich Stannhäuser," he said. "The other man I do not know, but Stannhäuser was one of the officers in charge of Zwangsarbeit, forced labour, throughout Poland and Germany. A man of extreme cruelty, entirely without compassion or empathy. When Stannhäuser saw that the defeat of the Third Reich was inevitable, he shot himself in the mouth with his own Luger. Clearly, he did not relish the idea of spending his life in prison, working on meaningless tasks as a punishment for being what he was. Is that irony or hypocrisy?"

"It's cowardice," said Priest, without hesitation.

Hoffmanstahl inclined his head in silent appreciation of the response. Then, his eyes looking meaningfully at Priest from under their heavy, white brows, he slid another of the charred remains across to him. "This word here — *ädelha*. This, also, is part of a name, I think. Not the official name, you understand, but the name by which a particularly horrific camp in Poland came to be known."

"What name?" Priest's voice was dead, without emotion, like Stannhäuser's conscience must have been, but only because he already knew the answer.

"The word is *Schädelhaus*. In English, it means…"

Priest finished the sentence in a low growl. "The House of Skulls."

Hoffmanstahl, if he felt any, showed no surprise. He simply nodded his head. "So called because of the emaciated faces of the prisoners, staring out from behind the barbed wire fences, their souls and their hope starved and beaten out of them."

Priest was nodding. He had seen those same abandoned souls, the skull faces, and the empty stares. He had seen them in the photographs taken by Clem Murnaugh. Which meant Murnaugh had been to the House of Skulls personally, and he wouldn't have gone there alone, of his own accord. He'd have been following orders. Maybe, at the time, the photographs had been designed originally for proud posterity, like any other images of a moment demanding remembrance; but somewhere along the line, they had become dangerous. And Priest could only think of one event which would mean that images like that were suddenly treacherous for British men: the end of the war itself, when the scales had tipped against the Nazis, when causing and praising death with a smile would be deservedly punished. The moment Germany had surrendered, Murnaugh's photographs changed from souvenirs to indictments.

"What happened to the House of Skulls?" he asked.

"As with the other camps of its kind, it was liberated. Some of the prisoners were still too emaciated and weak to survive even their freedom. The deaths did not stop simply because the gates were opened."

"But some people did survive?"

"Handfuls," said Hoffmanstahl. "The Allies liberated the camps, but the damage was done. Fewer people left those places than were dragged into them."

"We never learn, do we?" said Priest. "No matter how often that same spoke comes up?"

Hoffmanstahl shrugged. "We have the capacity to do so. We must place our trust in that."

"How can you be an optimist after all this?"

The old academic smiled. "Because we must have faith in people as well as in God."

Priest scoffed. "I've found both have let me down more often than not."

"Perhaps that is more a failure of yours than anyone else's."

Priest had no answer for that. He began to bring the scattered fragments of evidence together and carefully placed them back in the envelope. Hoffmanstahl made no effort to assist, sitting instead with his hands in his lap and his head sunk onto his breast, weighed down by the memories of the recent past. Priest wondered if the academic felt a special type of guilt, a particular responsibility peculiar only to those people who shared the Nazis' nationality but abhorred their politics and actions as much as the rest of the world. Perhaps those Germans who had privately reviled Hitler and his regime, but kept their disgust secret for the sake of their lives, detested it all more than anybody else could fathom. The soiled pride of a nation, besmirched by blood, fire, and hatred. And Priest had brought it all up again, picking at a still open wound until it oozed with fresh blood and stung with a fresh pain, which no amount of beer and books could soothe.

Hoffmanstahl looked up at him. "This case of yours. What has it to do with Stannhäuser and his atrocities?"

Priest shook his head. "I can't tell you that, I'm sorry."

"But it concerns Schädelhaus?"

"Absolutely." And more, thought Priest. So much more.

Hoffmanstahl frowned, the heavy brows colliding over the bridge of his nose. "Do the shadows of Zwangsarbeit still linger?"

"Yes," said Priest. He rose from his chair and threw the whisky down his throat. It seemed a callous, primitive, almost inhuman gesture. "But not for much longer."

He offered no word of thanks before he left, but he placed his hand on Hoffmanstahl's shoulder and let it rest there for a prominent moment. It seemed to say more than any speech and to say it louder.

CHAPTER THIRTY-TWO

It was dark by the time Priest arrived at the house. He had spent what was left of the afternoon and much of the early evening in his office, sitting in silence, letting his mind drift over the whole business. He stayed away from the bottles on the filing cabinet, choosing instead to sit staring out of the window across the ravaged skyline of London after the war. It would still be rebuilt, he felt sure of that, but there was no way the Phoenix project could proceed, not now Priest knew what he did. The bombed buildings and half-destroyed panorama of the city seemed now to cry out to him, to plead with him for silence, so that they could mend, heal, and grow once more. But Priest could not be silent, however much he wanted to be. It was too late for that. And like flowers in the winter frost, the city would have to find another way to regenerate.

It was Marriott who opened the door. He was dressed casually, but no less elegantly, holding a large whisky in one hand and resting the other on the frame of the door. He was smiling as he answered the door, the ingratiating good humour of a polite and affable businessman, but the smile faded and the head inclined in confusion when he saw Priest standing on the step.

"What are you doing here?" he asked. "Evelyn's asleep."

If there was an innuendo in that, Priest refused to look for it. "I've come to see you."

Marriott stepped aside. "You'd better come in."

Priest stepped into the hallway, removing his hat and running a hand through his hair, brushing it back into place away from his forehead. He followed Marriott into the living room and accepted the offer of a drink. Hell, he would need it and he felt as if he deserved it. Any hesitation at drinking with a killer had vanished. Hadn't he shared enough booze with Jack Raeburn, after all?

Marriott sat in the armchair he had used when Priest first came to the house. It must have been his favourite place to sit. Priest remained standing, saving any seat for the moment when his knees gave way, if it ever came.

"What can I do for you?" asked Marriott.

Priest's eyes bored into him. "I want to talk about your uncle."

"I've told you before that I won't discuss him with you."

Priest took a step forward, so that he was leaning over him. "I'm afraid you're going to have to."

"I have nothing to say, Mr Priest," said Marriott calmly.

Priest nodded, a smile forming on his lips almost involuntarily. "I have plenty to say."

"Then say it and get out of here."

Priest turned away and moved to stand by the fireplace. He could feel the heat on the back of his legs, but they did not seem to him to be the comforting flames of a warm fire in the cold, but those of the entrance to Hell itself.

"Your uncle was a man called Patrick Costello," Priest said. "He was your mother's brother, estranged from the family, but not because of a simple falling out. It was because he was a villain, one so notorious that even Jack Raeburn was in awe of him. Evelyn said he was obsessed with money and power. Was that why he did business with the Nazis, just in case they won the war? Hedging his bets, so that he came out in favour either way?"

Marriott's eyes could have melted steel. "Have you come here only to insult my family, or do you have a point to make?"

Priest spat out a laugh of contempt. "Don't act like a cliché, Marriott. You're too good for that."

"Good at what?"

"Murder." Priest said the word casually, as if it had no meaning in the world any more. "But let's not get carried away. I have to tell you this in order, or else my brain will fall over itself in its confusion."

"And where do you suppose the beginning is?"

Priest had begun to pace the room. "It all started whilst the war was still on, with prostitutes disappearing from the East End. Your uncle, Costello, was friends with a leading Nazi officer, Erich Stannhäuser, who was one of the principals in the German Zwangsarbeit initiative — forced labour camps, Marriott. The worst of these camps was known as Schädelhaus, the House of Skulls. I think your uncle and Raeburn were selling the missing prostitutes to Stannhäuser as Zivilarbeiter, civilian workers. To the Nazis, having prisoners from the Allies' side would have been an added triumph."

Marriott sniffed. "This is ridiculous."

"There's evidence, Marriott." Priest watched the indifferent expression darken slightly. "Raeburn and Costello were keeping in with the enemy, just in case. But when the war was over, Stannhäuser killed himself and the labour camps were liberated, although Raeburn and your uncle carried on as normal, as if nothing had happened. They won their war, no matter which side came out on top.

"Then, you began the Phoenix scheme. Maybe, initially, it did have good intentions. I could almost give you the benefit of the doubt about that, but I think you were brought up well enough by Patrick Costello that you don't have any benevolent thoughts like those. I think you saw an opportunity for glory, money, and power, all disguised as philanthropy. Like Snow White's apple; rosy, shiny, and beautiful on the outside, but rotten and malevolent inside. I know Raeburn was using the project to move his girls into the West End without anybody suspecting. What I couldn't understand was why you were letting him do it. Then, I realised. You weren't being forced into anything. You were letting Raeburn in."

"Why would I do that?" Marriott's voice was suitably incredulous.

"He was friends with your uncle, the man who brought you up. But Raeburn is close to you, too, perhaps in some sort of mark of respect to your uncle. Whatever the reason, he calls you Tommy. Not something you do with a stranger."

Marriott rose and walked aimlessly over to the drinks' cabinet, pouring himself another large drink. There was no offer of a second for Priest. "You talk about Snow White. Very apt, since this is a complete fairy tale."

"I told you," said Priest, suddenly at Marriott's elbow, "stop acting like a cliché. I don't think it took too long for things to start to go wrong. Firstly, Raeburn found out Clem Murnaugh had been taking illicit photographs of all his operations. Pictures of girls, doped up and raped; images of the new properties being bought up; photographs of parties at places like *The Midnight Pearl*. I think Murnaugh was planning a flit with his girl, Jenny, and the photographs were his insurance. Raeburn couldn't have that, so he dealt with Murnaugh. I think he's already farmed out Jenny to one of these new brothels, too. Either way, they've both vanished. The police think Raeburn murdered Nancy Clayton and Jimmy Boyd, too. I don't."

"And why is that?"

"Because, like Murnaugh and Jenny, when Raeburn deals with a problem, there is seldom any trace left. Whoever killed Nancy and Boyd left evidence of the fact. Jack Raeburn would never have done that."

Marriott smiled. "Suppose I take your point on that."

Priest, his glass empty and with no offer to refill it, helped himself to the whisky. "What Raeburn didn't know was what happened to the photographs Murnaugh took. Murnaugh must have known he was in danger, because he sent them to Jimmy Boyd. That was when the real trouble began. Boyd started digging. He found out that the properties being bought by Leonard Quayle on behalf of Phoenix were all sourced from Burke & Halliwell estate agents. Slowly, he began to uncover the truth, just as I did. He'd been watching Quayle's offices and I think Quayle got spooked. I think Boyd had called him, or gone to see him, and started provoking him. And Nancy Clayton overheard.

"She and Quayle were having an affair. One of their meeting places was an abandoned apartment tenement in Southwark, bought by Quayle through Burke & Halliwell, on behalf of the Phoenix Development. I have evidence that she died there." He waited for some reaction from Marriott, but none came. "One threat was eliminated, but there was still Boyd. He was still sniffing around, so he had to be dealt with."

Marriott drank in silence for a long moment. "And Leonard Quayle? You think he knew about whatever it is you think was happening?"

Another, more forceful nod. "I think you were all in it. You, Raeburn, and Quayle. His affair with Nancy wasn't much of a blackmail threat, because his wife's own insecurities forced her to turn a blind eye to his infidelities, but consorting with gangsters in nightclubs definitely was. He'd have been struck off because of it. I don't say he went along willingly, but he did go along with it."

"But if he knew everything, he would be in a position to blackmail me as well," challenged Marriott.

Priest conceded the point with a shrug of the shoulders. "True, and maybe he did. I don't know. If he did try to blackmail you, too, all the more reason to kill him."

"I did not kill him, let me remind you," cautioned Marriott. "I did not kill anybody."

Priest smiled wickedly. "Yes, you did. You killed them all: Nancy, Boyd, Quayle, and Costello."

Marriott laughed. "Hardly consistent, are you, Priest? You say Raeburn couldn't have killed any of them because he would leave no traces. What about Nancy Clayton? Has her body been found?"

Priest shook his head. "No."

"Then that doesn't make sense. Either Raeburn isn't the killer because he wouldn't leave a body or I am because I am careless enough to do exactly that. Nancy is a fly in your ointment."

"Not necessarily." Priest began to walk slowly towards him. "She was the first person you had actually killed. You might have seen death before, but you'd never committed murder. Nancy was your first victim. Scary enough for anyone, no matter how tough. You panicked, called Raeburn for help. He disposed of Nancy's body, but he didn't kill her. That was you. After her, you didn't mind killing so much. They say it gets easier after the first."

"Do they?" Marriott's voice was low, almost a whisper, but it was no less menacing for it, although Priest's eyes would have stopped a predator in its tracks. "You'd better have proof of all this, Priest."

"You'd kill me before you sued me, Marriott. It's second nature to you by now. You've done it so often that you hardly notice the blood any more. You don't see the fear in the person's eyes now. You just see a solution to your own problems. You don't even see their faces when you close your eyes these days."

Marriott had no reply to give. Either Priest's words had struck him harder than either of them could have imagined, or they had been so irrelevant to him that he had dismissed them without hearing them. It was impossible to tell.

"Be that as it may," he said, "let's see what proof you do have."

Priest drained his glass. "Another drink first."

Marriott obliged. Priest watched him pull the stopper out of the decanter and pour the drinks, watching for any trace of disturbance in a shaking hand or a rattle of glass against glass. There was nothing. Priest accepted the drink and watched Marriott toast him. There was no way of looking at the gesture which did not appear mocking.

Marriott smiled, the cool politeness of the deranged. "Please, go on."

"Quayle told you that Nancy Clayton had become too demanding. You assured him you'd deal with it and you did. You arranged to meet her at the flat in Southwark. There, you killed her. You cleaned up fairly well afterwards, but you missed some blood on the grate and her necklace had come off and been kicked under the bed in the struggle. When I told Quayle I thought she was dead, he had no idea about it. Maybe he thought you had farmed her out to one of Raeburn's brothels; maybe he thought you had killed her, but wasn't sure until I confirmed it. Either way, Quayle had no idea she was dead — but he put things together after he spoke to me. So, he confronted you. And we know how that argument ended."

"And this journalist and my uncle?" So easily said, so effortlessly mocking.

"You killed them, too. Whatever Raeburn did to Murnaugh before he killed him was enough for him to confess about the photographs. And he probably told you and Raeburn that he'd sent them to a journalist. I daren't think what horror Murnaugh suffered for that information and I don't want to know. My imagination is enough."

"So, Boyd was killed because of these photographs?"

Priest nodded. "And to keep him quiet. You searched his house for them, but you only found an empty camera. You destroyed that in frustration. You still didn't know where the photographs were and I still don't think you do."

It was a risky thing to say and Priest immediately regretted it. Marriott did not react. To have done so would have given away an advantage. He simply sipped at his drink and watched Priest over the rim of a glass, his eyes like pools of black sin.

"But if Boyd thought I was a killer, he wouldn't let me into his house, would he? That makes even less sense than you're making right now."

Priest smiled. "He thought you were me. Frank Darrow said it himself, that I must have missed the killer by minutes. It was sheer coincidence, but a fatal one for Boyd. He'd arranged to meet me and when he heard a knock on the door, he opened it without any fear. He couldn't know that you'd chosen to get him at the same time he was expecting me. He must have been badly frightened when he saw you. The back door was still open, which makes me wonder whether he ran as soon as he recognised you and you followed. The business done, you left the same way."

"This is preposterous."

"Change your act, Marriot, the old one's getting tiresome," snarled Priest. "Before you left, you searched Boyd's house and I think you found evidence that Boyd had identified Costello. Over the years, your uncle's drinking had got worse and I think his tongue had loosened — or you were frightened it had. Raeburn or you, maybe both, decided to get him away, put him in exile by the sea, where he could do no harm. As long as he had a supply of whisky, he'd be no trouble. But you couldn't be sure what he had said to Boyd, could you? And you couldn't know what he had said to me either." Priest leaned into Marriott's face. "And you know I went to see him. I saw your car following me when I was walking away from his house."

Marriott shrugged. "If you say so."

"The real tragedy is that Costello probably wouldn't have said anything coherent, let alone useful."

"Get on with it," snapped Marriott. "You're beginning to bore me."

It was the first indication that the cool exterior of impassive arrogance was beginning to crumble. "Getting scared, Marriott? People like you think you can walk in between the raindrops, don't you? That the dirt you walk in will never stick to your shoes? But I'm here to show you that you're soaking wet in the rain, you bastard, and your shoes are covered in filth."

Marriott's eyes flashed with violence. "You're a nothing, Priest. Do you think anybody is going to believe this delirious paranoia of yours? You're just some drunk who has designs on my wife, so you make up these lies to discredit me. That's how you'll appear to the public and that's how you'll appear to Evelyn. It is certainly how you appear to me."

Priest was unmoved. "I don't have designs on your wife."

"That won't matter in the scandal sheets or the courts, Priest. Without proof of anything you are accusing me of, you will just be another spiteful, jealous waste of life."

"You're making a huge assumption."

"What is that?"

Priest sipped his whisky. "That I have no proof."

Marriott snorted. It might have been a laugh of derision, but his eyes were still flickering with uncertainty. "And what proof do you have?"

The voice came from behind them. "Yes, Alex. What proof do you have?"

Both men turned to the door, although neither of them had heard it open. She was wearing a silk nightgown, her feet bare. Her eyes were like glass, almost devoid of emotion, with only the merest trace of fear discernible in them. They were like the eyes of a child who had woken from a nightmare. Priest had to force himself to look away from them. His concentration was demanded elsewhere. Because, in her outstretched hand, Evelyn Marriott held a revolver.

CHAPTER THIRTY-THREE

Her eyes were on Marriott, but the gun was turned unquestionably on Priest. He found himself glaring at the small, merciless black eye of the barrel of the weapon. It was a dark hole of nothing now, but in a quick, uncertain, fearful moment, it could erupt in a deadly mixture of sound and vision, as the sharp crack and the blinding white light of a shot rang out. Priest had looked down the business end of many guns, but this was the worst and saddest of them all.

Slowly, Priest's eyes moved from the gun to Marriott. He was motionless, his limbs frozen in anticipation, but he seemed somehow unafraid. His eyes were cautious, fixed on his wife, but in them Priest could see hope rather than despair. By contrast, he suspected his own eyes were like the wheels of a bus screeching to a disastrous halt. Marriott's lips were not quite smiling, but there was a calculated twist around them which Priest did not like. He knew he had to speak first. Marriott's thoughts were so obvious that they might have been lit up in neon across his face. The gun was on Priest and the woman holding it was Marriott's own wife. In terms of danger, Marriott thought he was far away from the edge of the cliff. It was Priest who was hanging over the precipice, his fingers losing their grip.

He looked back to Evelyn. "Put the gun down, Mrs Marriott. You don't need it and it won't do anybody any good."

She made no movement. "I heard what you said, Alex."

"All of it?"

"Enough." She was still looking at Marriott, but her words were only meant for Priest. "Is it true?"

Priest had no time to answer before Marriott had barked his own reply. "How can you possibly ask that?"

She still didn't move, but the voice, when it came, was harsher. "Is it true, Alex?"

Priest, in a position he found almost impossible to manage, tried to reply as calmly as he could muster. "It's true."

"Prove it." Only now, with this curt demand, did her eyes shift to him. They were like diamonds: cold, hard, their facets glittering with tears.

Priest was suddenly aware that his arms were stretched out in front of him. It had been an instinctive reaction to the appearance of the gun, a defensive gesture as much as a placatory one. Slowly, he lowered them, as if by doing so he could diffuse some of the tension and make it seem like three people having a normal conversation in a living room. But it was not that and it never could be, not while the gun was raised.

"It's easy enough to prove that Patrick Costello is your husband's uncle," he said. "It wasn't too much of a leap of the imagination to make the connection and all it will take is a trip to Somerset House for a copy of his parents' marriage certificate. His mother's maiden name will be on it. And it will say she was a Costello." This last spoken directly to Marriott.

"I don't deny he was my uncle." Marriott spoke calmly, still recognising no danger to him from Priest or Evelyn.

Priest spoke again, just so that Evelyn's attention was kept off the gun. She was glaring into his eyes and he felt as if he wanted nothing more than to hold her, maybe for one last time. "When I spoke to Jack Raeburn about your husband's uncle, Raeburn said he was dead now. He said it almost immediately after his men and I had found the body. The word 'now' was a joke, not very funny."

"So what if this man was Thomas' uncle?" Evelyn asked.

Priest shrugged. "I'm just trying to explain things as I saw them, Mrs Marriott."

She blinked away unwitting tears. "Go on."

Priest looked back at Marriott. "When you set fire to Costello's papers, they didn't all burn. There were scraps of letters referring to the camps, to rewards in Berlin. And there was part of a photograph. It shows Costello with Stannhäuser, smiling, old friends, arms around each other's shoulders. There were obviously more men there, but their images were burnt away."

"And you think I was one of them?" asked Marriott.

Priest nodded. "You and Raeburn. Visiting the camps you were helping to fill, a personal, guided tour from Stannhäuser himself."

"But there is no photograph to show me there? Only my uncle?"

"That's right." Priest thought swiftly. "But what will your passport say? How many trips to Poland will it show you made?"

Priest's eyes fluctuated from one Marriott to the other. In both, he saw disquiet. In Marriott, there was the first indication that he could sense a trap; his eye began to twitch, almost imperceptibly, and his lips slowly parted. For Evelyn, there were subtle signs of betrayal, as if she had resigned herself already to the fact that Marriott would not be able to answer the point.

"That would prove nothing," Marriott whispered.

"Not on its own, perhaps." Priest was watching Evelyn closely now. He doubted she had realised that the gun was now slowly moving towards her husband. "But with everything else it might."

Marriott's glare fluctuated from his wife to Priest. "Everything else like what?"

"Things which didn't make sense at the time, but do now," said Priest. "Like why you came to see me in my office that day."

Evelyn threw a glance to Priest with the speed of a circus act throwing a knife. "He went to find out what we had been saying to each other."

Priest shook his head. "No, Mrs Marriott. That was what he told us. What he really came for was to see how much I knew. Without knowing it, I gave him as little as I would have done if I'd suspected him at that time. That was good luck. I don't have it often, but I do sometimes. And because I told him nothing, he went to see Raeburn. Next thing I know, I'm getting kicked around an alleyway like a football. When that didn't work, old Jack tried plying me with a cocktail as strong as tank fuel in an effort to get me to talk. That didn't work either."

Evelyn's eyes, now soaked with tears which glistened down her cheeks, flickered to Marriott once more. He was shaking his head. He had regained something of his composure and he demonstrated it by taking a step closer to her. The gun, which she had lowered, either out of indecision or out of an aching in her arm, hung listlessly by her side. It would never look so harmless again.

"Everything he's saying is lies, Evie," Marriott said, his voice not quite as assured as his expression. Close, thought Priest, but not quite. "Yes, my uncle was a villain, but I had nothing to do with him. I'm trying to help the city, for God's sake, not run it into the ground. Phoenix is about rebuilding, about healing."

She was breathing heavily, her mouth hanging loosely open and the bottom lip pulsating with the deep intakes and exhalation of her breath. Marriott was close enough to take her in his arms, but he didn't. Priest felt his breath freeze in his throat. He was losing the battle, hanging bleeding on the ropes, and he knew that he had to say something, anything, and that he had to say it quickly.

"Murnaugh's photographs," he said. "I've got them. They were in my office all the time. You were close by them when you came to see me, Marriott, and you had no idea."

Marriott kept his attention on Evelyn. "No idea then, and no interest now, Priest."

"Shut up," hissed Evelyn and the world seemed to tilt on its axis. "I want to hear."

Priest took advantage. "Boyd sent me the photos and he'd only have done that to get them out of his possession. Just like Clem Murnaugh had done. He passed them to Boyd, who passed them to me. He was fond of tailing people and he was certainly watching Quayle. Maybe he saw him with you and Raeburn on one occasion. That seems most likely to me. So, he sent the pictures to me for safekeeping, just in case he was caught off guard at any point. He could always pick them up afterwards. Except you killed him, Marriott, before he could do it."

"I've killed nobody," cried Marriott. The lie was for Evelyn's benefit rather than for Priest's. "And these photographs mean nothing to me."

"How long before I find one with you in it?" insisted Priest. "I haven't looked through them all, just enough to get a flavour. And I was distracted by the ones showing Nancy Clayton, because she was all I was concerned with at the time. If I go through them, one by one, am I really not going to find you in there?"

It was working on Evelyn more than her husband. The hand holding the gun was twitching, as if the weapon were stirring back into wakefulness of its own accord. Priest tried to swallow but his mouth was desert sands. Marriott began to shake his head, assuring, comforting, and only slightly reptilian.

"Give me the gun, Evie," he whispered. "You don't need it, not with me."

She could barely summon her voice. "Everything Alex has said…"

"Lies. Give me the gun and I'll get rid of him."

She lowered her head. "He seems so sure."

Marriott's voice unsheathed a blade. "He's a liar, Evie. A dirty little man, peering over windowsills and through keyholes. He's a piece of filth which just needs to be thrown out with the rest of the rubbish."

Priest had no time to register the insults. His attention was still fixed on Evelyn and the gun, his mind still searching for the means to make her see the truth. "How long before we trace some of the survivors? And are you absolutely sure none of them will recognise you, Marriott?"

Now, the teeth were bared as Marriott inclined his head away from his wife towards Priest. "That's enough. More than enough."

Priest walked towards him, his face darkened by determination. "Nowhere near enough yet. There's still the small point about what Mrs Marriott said to me."

The silence which descended was the same as that which follows a grenade. The air was still charged with explosives, but the quiet was so intense that it seemed more oppressive than the noise. Both Marriotts, husband and wife, stared at him now, but he kept his attention reserved for her.

"I called you after I was told that Leonard Quayle had been murdered," he said. "I apologised for it being late and you said it didn't matter. You told me your husband wasn't at home, that he was at his club. At least, you supposed so. Your words. Let's phone the club now and see if he was really there. How does that sound?"

Marriott was quick to reply. "She doesn't have to. They will confirm it if anybody asks."

Priest was glaring at Evelyn. "Do you think so, Mrs Marriott?"

Marriott snarled. "If she doesn't, it doesn't matter. Even if you do prove I wasn't there, it's no proof I murdered Quayle. I could have been anywhere."

"Maybe, but if I put it alongside everything else, it would be more than enough for the police to look into you," said Priest. "I know you're guilty, but I'm just a lone private detective, with nothing to rely on but his guts and his instincts. Know what that means, Marriott? It means that I don't have to prove a damned thing. That's for the police. And all I have to do is give them a start, a nudge in the right direction."

"And what about Raeburn?" Marriott's eyes were wild now.

Priest frowned. "What about him?"

"If the police come looking for me, I can make them go looking for him."

Priest smiled. "That's almost a confession, Marriott, but it's a lousy idea. What do you think Raeburn would do?"

"He'd have more difficult questions to answer than me, that's for sure."

"Horse shit, Marriott, and you know it. People like Raeburn and your uncle aren't who they are without being next to untouchable. They have power you can't buy and a perverse kind of respect which you can only earn. You think that if you say he was involved in any of this, he's not going to be able to provide himself with a dozen people to say he was anywhere other than where you say he was and doing anything except what you say he was doing? He's got a network, all too loyal or too scared to betray him, and all ready and willing to say whatever he tells them to say. Who've you got, Marriott, apart from a wife who is seriously doubting your innocence right now?"

Marriott looked over at her. "Evie, I..."

Priest interrupted. "And Raeburn isn't going to help you. It's not how it works, Marriott. Even if you hadn't killed anybody and Raeburn had, he wouldn't swing for it. He'd make sure of that. Someone else would hang in his place, and in some cases, they'd do it willingly. You don't have that sort of power or influence. And let me tell you, if Jack Raeburn isn't prepared to swing for his own crimes, he sure as shit wont swing for yours. You're on your own and the walls are closing in."

Marriott gritted his teeth. "Do you believe any of this, Evie?"

Evelyn's eyes were glazed momentarily, but slowly, they shifted in focus, replacing the emptiness with a sudden flare of realisation. "Blood," she said.

The word seemed incongruous, almost meaningless. Priest watched her closely, not sure what she was thinking, but knowing that something had clicked in her brain.

"You came home with blood on your shirt." Evelyn's mouth had moved uselessly for a few second, before any sound came out of it. "You said it was an accident. A woman. Run over in the street."

Marriott had held up a finger. "Now, Evie, listen…"

"Blood," she continued, her voice like that of a hypnotised subject, the monotone of an automaton. "So much blood. You said… tried to help her. The car… drove… didn't stop. Held her, you said. Waiting for the ambulance. You told me."

Priest spoke in the softest voice he could manage. It sounded nothing like him to his own ears. "Leonard Quayle. It was his blood."

Marriott raged. "Shut up, you bastard."

Evelyn's expression was betrayed confusion. "I comforted you. Held you. And all the time… After such a tragedy, I…"

"You comforted him after he'd killed a man," said Priest. He stepped closer to Evelyn. "We just need to call the club, to make sure."

Evelyn had no idea Priest was in the room. Only her husband existed for her now. "A killer… you…"

Marriott, his upper lip and temples now beading with sweat, shook his head and held out his hands. "No, Evie. I promise you…"

"He's lying, Mrs Marriott," cautioned Priest. "You know he is."

"Shut up!" hissed Marriott.

"Look at his eyes." Priest was glaring at Marriott. "Just confess it all, Marriott. Put an end to it."

"Evie, please," said Marriott, "just think about things. About Phoenix and all the good it can do. Think about the future, Evie. You can see how I'll be helping thousands of people get their lives back. Doesn't that atone for any wrong I may have done in the past? Isn't that redemption? You can see I'm putting things right, can't you?"

Evelyn had been staring at him as if she had no idea who he was. Now, her eyes narrowed and her lips curled back from her teeth. "Putting it right? Selling people to those German bastards, exploiting young girls, killing men. How's that putting it right?"

"Phoenix can be a positive thing, Evie," he insisted.

Priest watched her shake her head as she replied. "No, Thomas. It is corrupt, wicked, and dangerous. Like you."

Marriott prepared himself for a harder line of defence. "Evie, listen to me. What I may have done in the past doesn't matter as much as what I am doing now and what I will be doing in the future. Please, you have to let me explain…"

But there was no explanation to be made. Evelyn seemed to have stopped hearing any of it. To Priest, she was a woman who existed elsewhere completely, now. Detached, uninvolved, none of it any of her business. Her silence, her stillness was so acute that Priest thought time had stood still. Only the deep thumping of his heart, reverberating in his mind, told him that the world was still turning and that life was still being lived.

But not entirely. Into the void, there came the violent intrusion of death, a small explosion of fatality. To Priest, it all occurred in slow motion, each sound amplified in the peculiar distortion of time which occurred in his brain. There was the roar of the gun, loud enough that it might have been capable of splitting eardrums, followed immediately by the familiar, sudden flash of fire from the newly raised barrel. A shower of blood erupted and spat itself across Priest's face. There was no scream, no crying out, just the terrifying roar of the gun and then that same deep, impenetrable silence.

CHAPTER THIRTY-FOUR

Priest wiped the blood from his face. His ears had a million bells inside them, but they weren't chiming in tune. For a moment, he could not understand what had happened and he remained fixed where he stood. He stared down at the blood on the palm of his hand, as if unsure what it was and what it meant. He pulled his handkerchief from his pocket and wiped it over his hands and face as vigorously as he could, like Lady Macbeth, but with more hysteria.

Marriott lay on his back on the hearth rug, his arms by his sides and his legs twisted unpleasantly. His shirt and cardigan were stained with his blood but there was no trace of any wound in his chest. As Priest's eyes drifted up the dead man's body, he saw where the blood was coming from. There was almost nothing left of the lower part of Marriott's face. What had been his jaw, mouth, and teeth was now just a jumble of flesh, cartilage, and bone, all soaked in the darkest red. Above the wreckage, his eyes were wide open in a sickening blend of surprise and shock. His cheeks were stained with thin tramlines of red, which had flown up from the wound and hit his face at such an angle that it looked as if he was crying blood. Priest recalled the injuries he had seen on various battlefields. They were not dissimilar, but the domestic setting of this example of human horror made it seem all the more intrusive, and by extension, all the more terrible. Priest lowered his head, bending his spine, and resting his hands on his knees.

"Damn. Damn. Damn." The words were little more than a whisper.

He looked across at Evelyn Marriott. Only seconds before, she had seemed to Priest to be detached from the situation. Now, it was as if the sound and flash of the shot had brought her crashing back to reality, like a bombed Spitfire falling out of the sky. She was glaring down at the body of the man she had shared her life with, transfixed by the mangled ruins of his face. She was crying, the tears falling with furious intent, but there was no sound coming from her, only the violent shaking of her shoulders, racked by the sobs. The gun now dangled uselessly from her shaking fingers and Priest made a slow movement to take it from her hands. She did not resist, her fingers relinquishing their fragile hold on the weapon. Once it was in his hands, Priest stepped back away from her and ran his fingers through his hair. The gun felt like a lead weight of guilt in his other hand.

"Got to think," he said, to himself as much as to Evelyn. Then, in a moment of weakness, he cursed savagely. "What the hell did you shoot him for?"

Evelyn did not reply, other than to give a hollow gasp, almost a wail of agony, and to sink to her knees. She began to rock, her hands clasped in front of her, as if in some sort of mockery of prayer. Priest shook his head. She was beyond prayers now; perhaps they both were.

He pulled out his handkerchief and wrapped the gun in it, dropping it in his coat pocket. He strode over to the drinks and poured two large measures of whisky. One, he threw down his throat mercilessly; the other, he took over to Evelyn and offered it to her. She ignored it, lowering her head, the sobbing intensifying. Priest knelt beside her, and with a snarl, grabbed her hair and pulled her head back. He pushed the glass to her lips, forcing them open, and poured the whisky down her throat. She coughed, spluttering, but the whisky soon took hold. She pulled her head away from the glass, breathing hard, and took it from him.

"Give it me, you bastard," she said. The tears glistened on her cheeks still, and the voice was twisted by the sobs, but her eyes showed that some of the fire had returned to her, fuelled by the drink.

Priest helped her to her feet and let her finish the drink. "We have to get you away from here."

She looked at him wildly. "What?"

He wasn't looking at her. "You can't hang for this."

"What are you saying?"

He gestured to the thing that had once been Thomas Marriott. "He's the one who should have hanged. Not you. He's the one who should be known as a killer. All you've done is save Pierrepoint a job, but the law won't see it like that, even if it's true. So, we have to get you away."

She was by his side now, her head shaking with doubt and confusion. "Alex, we can't. I mean, how would we do it? It's madness."

He spread his arms, a look of wild bewilderment on his face. "The whole thing is madness, Mrs Marriott, but letting you hang for killing that bastard is beyond insane."

She put her hands to her head. "I can't think. I'm so confused."

He grabbed her by the shoulders. "You don't have to think. You just have to do what I say. Go upstairs and clean yourself up, but not too much. You must still look as if you've been crying. Then get dressed and go and sit in another room. Doesn't matter which, as long as you stay there."

"Why?"

"Because here's what happened." His voice was urgent now. "You were having an argument with Marriott. He was going mad, frightening you, talking about the killings and Phoenix, saying things you didn't understand, but which you thought suggested he was responsible. He had a gun in his hands. You didn't know what to do, so you came to get me. It was all you could think to do. You left Marriott alive. I came back here with you and we found him dead. Shot himself. That's the story and that's what happened. Understand?" He watched her nod. "Repeat it."

She did. Her voice was unsteady and she fell over some of the words, but it was enough. He told her to keep repeating it to herself and he pushed her out of the room. He watched her mount the stairs, mumbling to herself, and he waited until she had disappeared from view. Then, with a deep intake of breath, he went back into the room.

He took the gun out of his pocket and used the handkerchief to wipe it down. He did it thoroughly, several times over and once more again to be sure. Then, still holding it in the handkerchief, he pressed it against the savage wound, in the area where Marriott's chin might have been, so that the barrel was covered in blood. He placed the gun in Marriott's hand and closed the fingers around the butt and the trigger. Too many times he had seen situations like this where a suicide had apparently shot himself, but had not left any prints on the trigger. A simple, but stupid mistake. Priest supposed you learned by experience.

He looked at himself in the mirror above the fireplace. His face was spotted with blood and his hands were still stained red. He went through to the kitchen and ran some water from the tap. Wetting his handkerchief thoroughly and rubbing it with soap, he attacked his hands and face. After several long minutes, he went back into the living room and checked again.

His face was flushed from the scrubbing, but it would subside and the blood had gone. Same with the hands. He looked around the room. Anything else to be done?

Three whisky glasses. Marriott's, his own, and Evelyn's. One too many.

With a sigh, which turned into a curse, he took the glass he had used and ran back to the kitchen. He washed it thoroughly, dried it on an old tea towel which hung by the sink, and held it up to the light. The cut glass of the tumbler sparkled and glittered back at him. It couldn't have looked cleaner if he had asked the staff at the Savoy to do it. He took the glass back to the living room and placed it on the tray. He took another look around the room, trying to think like an outside cop, and finally, nodded in satisfaction. Only the twist in his gut reminded him of the crime he was committing, but it was meaningless to him. He felt sick enough already; one more lurch of his insides was nothing.

Evelyn came back into the room. She had changed out of the silk nightgown and into a black, woollen utility dress. Whether the choice had been conscious or not in the wake of death, Priest could not say, but it was suitably neutral that nobody could read anything into it. She looked at the corpse only once, and briefly, and then stared up at the ceiling. She had not applied any make up, so that the eyes were still raw with emotion and fear, the cheeks still pale with shock, and the lips continued to tremble, albeit not as frantically as earlier. Priest said nothing, but her courage was impressing him. If it could be called courage.

"Go into the kitchen or the parlour," he said. "Anywhere but in here."

She lowered her gaze and looked at him. She might have been a lost child, so far from home that she might never make her way back. Her life would now never be the same again. Comfort and normality would return, but they would be different. Her memories of this night would fade, but they would never disappear. The house, her home, would be the same but altered. Like soldiers returning from war, the same men but changed completely.

"Tell me everything will be all right, Alex," she said. Her voice sounded as if she had been running for hours.

He stepped towards her. Without planning to, and without any regret later, he took her by the shoulders and leaned her towards him, kissing her softly on the head. "Just trust me."

It was all he could give her, and in the flicker of her eyes and the small spasm of a smile, it seemed to be enough. She turned away from him and walked into the parlour. She looked around to see if he had followed her, but he hadn't. She remained still, conscious only of the dull ticking of a carriage clock on a small table beside one of the armchairs. She listened more intently, desperate for a trace of any sound from Priest. Then, in the stillness, she heard the vague ping of the telephone bell. A second or two later, she heard his voice, unmistakable, serious, and yet somehow protective.

"Police," he barked, "and quickly."

Evelyn Marriott began, slowly and silently, to weep once more.

CHAPTER THIRTY-FIVE

A few weeks later, the inquest into Marriott's death brought in a verdict of suicide. The inquests into the four murders had also returned predictable verdicts: murder by person or persons unknown. It was all that could be said, but to Priest, there was no person or persons unknown. The person was very definitely known and he was now dead himself.

Frank Darrow had attended the inquest, his eyes never seeming to leave Priest's. Both men knew that there was nothing Darrow could say now that the verdict had been given. Whether he had believed Marriott's death was suicide or not, Darrow could do nothing. If he suspected Priest and Evelyn had played him for a fool, he was going to have to live with it. Any lies Darrow might have assumed he had been told were now the official truth.

Jack Raeburn had been at the Marriott inquest, too. Priest had ignored him throughout the proceedings and it wasn't until they were concluded that Raeburn had cornered him. The painted eyebrows and the wig seemed to glisten in the fading afternoon sun. Wolfe was leaning against the parked car across the street. Somewhere, although Priest couldn't see them, two or more of the muscle would be close by. Some planets never tilted on their axis.

"Suicide," Raeburn had said. "And you were there when it happened?"

"No." Priest had looked into the dark eyes. "I was there afterwards."

Raeburn had shrugged his shoulders, as if there was no difference in the distinction. "You kept your mouth shut about certain things, Priest. That's good. I respect it."

"Shove your respect," Priest had said, leaning forward. "Next time you pass by the side of the Thames, Raeburn, jump in it. And make sure you're wearing concrete trousers."

He had turned away, clenching his teeth and desperately trying to ignore the laughter coming from behind him.

One afternoon, Frank Darrow came to the office. He had gone through Murnaugh's photographs, which Priest had surrendered as ordered, but there was no trace of Marriott in them. It came as no surprise. Before handing them over, Priest had examined every inch of each frame and hadn't found Marriott either. But it wasn't all bad news. It had been proved that Patrick Costello was Marriott's uncle and Darrow could not only place Marriott in Germany and Poland during the war, but he could put him in towns known to have housed forced labour camps. Including the House of Skulls. To Priest, it was some sort of vindication, but not absolute.

"Still no definite proof Marriott was involved, though," he had said. Darrow had not replied. Instead, he had slapped Priest on the shoulder and promised him a drink one night soon. After almost a month, Priest was still waiting but he wasn't bitter.

Days later, he was sitting in the office, watching a spider spin a web around the window frame, when the telephone rang. The girl's voice was familiar and he smiled instantly at hearing it. "I just wanted to let you know I'm going home."

"Good for you." It struck him that he had never asked Mary Latimer why she was on the streets at all. It hadn't been any of his business, but now he found that he was curious.

"I phoned my ma," Mary said. "She told me my step-father died a couple of years ago. Maybe that means it's safe to go back." Suddenly, Priest wasn't curious any more.

He filed his final report to Margaret Clayton, maintaining the official cause of Marriott's death. He didn't send her any final invoice. To him, that was an end of the matter, but not for her. When she telephoned the office, he realised that she had unfinished business.

"You haven't asked me for any money," she said. "For your services."

"You hired me to find your daughter, Mrs Clayton, and I haven't."

"You've given me something more than I had before, though, Mr Priest. I can learn to live with that."

"That still doesn't entitle me to take any money from you, Mrs Clayton." She began to protest, but he said goodbye and terminated the call.

That evening, he sat with Gustav Hoffmanstahl and drank a couple of pints of beer. Priest kept to the official version of events, the academic listening in silence, only nodding at certain points to show that he was following it. Priest ended with a word of thanks. "I wouldn't have got as far as I did without you."

Hoffmanstahl bowed his head. "What those men did was despicable."

"Don't they say all's fair in love and war?"

"They do, but they are wrong."

"How can you bear it, always living in the past the way you do?"

The academic smiled. "A student of history doesn't live in the past, Herr Priest. He looks at it over the distance of time. He can be detached from it. And the past is immoveable; it has happened and it cannot be changed. The present and the future, we have no control over. In that respect, the past is a far safer place to live and it can teach us many things."

"What about?"

"Ourselves," Hoffmanstahl said.

Priest had no answer to that. That night, he slept in the office, his breath and brain drowned in alcohol. He woke on the following morning feeling as if he had been minced through a rusty meat grinder. His head was too big for his neck, his legs too heavy to move, and his brain was clamped in irons. He promised himself that he would lay off the booze today; in the same breath, he laughed maliciously at himself.

CHAPTER THIRTY-SIX

A month passed without incident for Priest. Business had been slow and the phone had been silent for too long, so that its bell seemed deafening when it finally rang out, filling the office with its noise. Priest snatched up the receiver swiftly, cursing harshly to himself.

"Thought you'd want to know," Frank Darrow said. "We've found a body, washed up on the embankment. Dead some time, several months. A girl. Difficult to tell the age, because the body's been in water for all that time, but she must have been in her twenties. Best guess."

Priest held the telephone so tightly that he felt close to shattering it. "Nancy?"

"We don't know for sure," cautioned Darrow. "Could well be."

Priest closed his eyes. So, Nancy had never gone far away, after all. "Murdered?"

Darrow's voice lowered, so that Priest had to strain to hear him. "There's a wound to the side of the head."

Priest nodded. "Marriott hit her, she fell and struck her head on the grate of the fireplace in that apartment in Southwark. Raeburn disposed of her, but you'll never prove it."

"Still no word on Clem Murnaugh or Jenny Barlow, though." Darrow sighed. "I suppose some of them never do come home."

Priest had shaken his head. "Murnaugh's in the Thames too, I'm sure of it. Jenny, no idea. Alive somewhere, but better off dead, maybe."

If Darrow disagreed, he didn't say so. "At least Margaret Clayton can bury her daughter."

"Yeah," Priest said, forcing a smile to his lips. "Thanks, Frank. Let's have that drink any day now."

He expected the line to go dead, but Darrow lingered. Priest could hear him breathing and a curious sense of dread took hold of his spine. At last, Darrow spoke. "Do you ever hear from her?"

"Who?"

Another, shorter silence. "Evelyn Marriott."

Priest closed his eyes. "No, Frank. Never."

This time, the line did go dead, as dead as Priest felt inside. He had tried not to think about Evelyn since he had last seen her and the time which had passed had allowed him to do it. Almost. What had prompted Darrow to ask about her, Priest couldn't say, but he knew why he had lied in his answer. No secret about that. The truth just wasn't worth telling. But he had heard from her, a brief message on the back of a postcard from a southern area of France which Priest had never known existed. He couldn't remember much of what she had written, only the last few words: *I won't see you again. Goodbye, Alex.*

Before she had left England, never to return, they had met by the sea, a wind blowing, refreshing rather than cold, bringing with it the taste and scent of shingle and seawater. In the cloud-dimmed sunlight, she had looked more radiant than she had ever done under the electric bulbs of her house or his office, her hair more golden, her eyes brighter, and the red of her lips all the more vibrant. She had seemed rejuvenated, resurrected from the violence and tragedy by the prospect of this new start away from the past. By contrast, Priest had thought he had never felt more ruined.

"I'm heading for the continent," she had said. "I don't think I'll ever come back. I want to put it all behind me forever."

"For the best." He had tried to keep the disappointment out of his voice.

"Do you think so?"

He shrugged. "If I didn't, would it change your mind?"

"No." The word should have hurt, but he had expected it. "We would remind ourselves of it constantly. Of what we did."

"Right," was all he had been able to say.

"I wish things had been different, Alex," she had said.

He had turned to look at her, staring deeply into her eyes, before looking around her face, as if committing it to memory because he knew he would never see it again. Both of them must have known that the kiss, urgent and passionate, was now inevitable, no matter how destructive or mistaken it was. Once ended, their foreheads had remained locked together, their breath entwining from their successive gasps. Her hand had remained on his cheek for a moment, as if she couldn't bear to let him go.

At last, the time had come. They had risen to their feet and she had leaned into him, embracing him. No kiss now, as if another touch of the lips would be a signature to a contract neither of them would be able to honour.

"Goodbye, Alex." Her voice had been held together with little more than fraying cotton. "Be happy. Don't ever let that woman stop you from being happy."

That woman...

He had watched her walk along the grass knoll of the seafront, hoping she would turn back to look at him. But she hadn't and perhaps he was glad. If she had looked at him one more time, it might have meant too much for either of them. Some looks can be as deadly as knife blades. He had heard nothing more from her until the postcard and its final farewell. He had torn it in half and tossed it into the wastebin. Out of sight and all that. And it had worked, until Frank Darrow had brought her up without reason or warning.

"Damn her," Priest said. "And damn you, Frank."

On the following morning, he received a letter from Margaret Clayton. It explained that she had identified her daughter's body formally, that it was all over, and Nancy was at peace. So, because she now felt able to do so, Margaret was sending Priest a cheque for his fee, ending the letter with a word of thanks, brief but sincere, and a hope that he was keeping well.

Priest felt ashamed. Of the letter, of the cheque, and of himself. He spent most of the morning sitting at his desk, watching the walls, knowing that he would return the cheque to her. There was no doubt about it in his mind, no argument or debate. He would send it back, thank you, and he would do it that afternoon. Not immediately, because his attention was diverted now by a knock on the office door. Priest locked the cheque in the drawer of the desk and looked at the silhouette of a man outlined behind the glass panel where his own name was etched: *Alexander Priest, Private Investigations.*

"Come in." He watched as the handle of the door turned and the stranger stepped into the room. Priest pointed to one of two chairs which were set on the opposite side of the desk to him. "Sit down."

Here was a new client, with a new set of troubles.

THE END